HERE IS DANGER

Here Is Danger

A Patrick Dawlish Mystery

**John Creasey *writing as*
Gordon Ashe**

OPEN ROAD
INTEGRATED MEDIA
NEW YORK

This edition published in 2025 by Open Road Integrated Media, Inc.
180 Maiden Lane
New York, NY 10038
www.openroadmedia.com

HERE IS DANGER

CHAPTER I

SNOW-BOUND

"I shall be surprised if we get to Hurn to-night," said Patrick Dawlish to Felicity, his wife. "We'll be lucky if we get as far as Salisbury."

Felicity Dawlish, huddled in mink and with an attractive woollen scarf wound turban-wise about her head and pulled over her ears—her tiny hat was in the back of the car—said, "I suppose so," and looked out of the window. A tiny patch had been rubbed clear of steam, but was rapidly clouding over. All she could see was the heavily-falling snow and glimpses of the white countryside. Now and again a telegraph pole, dark on one side, interrupted the general whiteness. Occasionally a gust of wind created the illusion that the snow had stopped for a moment; when the wind dropped, the snow seemed to be falling thicker than ever.

It was bitterly cold.

At Bagshot the electric heater for the car had ceased to function. They had stopped at two garages to try to get it repaired, but had got so cold waiting for mechanics to discover that they had not the necessary spare part that they had decided to dispense with it. Felicity had fur-lined ankle boots, but the cold was so intense that they retained no warmth. Her nose was red and her eyes were watering. Dawlish wore a heavy Harris tweed coat and two woollen scarves, but felt as if he were dressed for the tropics and had strayed into the arctic regions. When they spoke their breath froze into white clouds which hung about the Talbot.

The cold was the least of Dawlish's anxieties.

The windscreen wipers worked reluctantly, snow piled on to them and, when they slowed down, coated the screen. Now and again a plug missed. There were chains on the back wheels, but the snow was nearly a foot deep everywhere, and at corners so much deeper that he was afraid they would be stranded. They had strayed off the main Andover-Salisbury road half an hour before, and had passed no traffic since. They knew that they were heading in the right direction now, but the risk of being forced to stop miles from the nearest inn or habitation was becoming an obsession.

"Cigarette?" asked Felicity, shivering.

"No, thanks. That wiper—" Dawlish broke off, for the windscreen wiper, more heavily laden, quivered to a half immediately in his line of vision. Slowly it made its way up again, came down more speedily, but collected so much snow that it did not begin its next journey. He banged the windscreen. Snow cascaded down, and the wiper started again, but only for a few seconds.

"We can't stay *here*," said Felicity.

Dawlish did not speak. The offside window was clearer of snow than any of the others, and he had to rely on looking through that. A sign-post loomed up at a cross-roads. It was so laden with snow that there was no hope of reading it from the car.

"I'll go," volunteered Felicity, heroically.

"I'll manage," said Dawlish.

As he opened the door a flurry of wind and white flakes filled the car. He jumped out, slammed the door and hurried as best he could to the sign-post. Snow spilled over his shoes and his socks became wet. By stretching to his full height he was able to rub the snow away, but had to tackle three indicators before he saw: *Salisbury, 1 miles.* The bleak, empty countryside seemed to grow a little more friendly, and he bundled himself into the car, finding it comparatively warm; his eyes were brighter.

"A mile and a half to go," he said. "I think this is the main road."

A few hundred yards along they came upon a small car axle deep in a drift. A man was waving frantically from it. Dawlish stopped the Talbot in the middle of the road, and the man came out and stumbled towards them. Felicity opened her door.

"Could you *possibly* take me into Salisbury?

"Of course, jump in," said Dawlish.

"Thank you *so* much. I must catch a train," said the stranger. "I'll have to call at a garage and get them to send for my bus." He collapsed on to a back seat. "By George, it's warm in here!"

"Warm!" exclaimed Felicity.

"Well, comparatively." The stranger sat on the edge of the seat. "Once you're over the top of the hill you'll be all right," he said, "they usually keep the road clear as far as this. It's the city boundary," he added informatively.

"That's a relief," said Dawlish.

"I've never known a blizzard like it," said the stranger. "I was afraid I'd be there all night! It's about half an hour to dusk, isn't it? Yes—it's after five." He chatted on as they plugged slowly to the brow of the hill. When they reached it they could see the snowcapped roofs of the houses and, once or twice, imagined they could see the tall spire of the cathedral against the leaden sky. "It's a bit clearer, I *think*," added the stranger, "but I wish

I hadn't got to catch a train. I'm going to Exeter," he added. "I expect I'll be hours late. You're stopping in Salisbury, I suppose?"

"We hoped to get to a village near Shaftesbury," said Dawlish.

"Shaftesbury! You won't have a ghost of a chance in the North Dorset hills, I'm afraid. They catch the snow worse than anywhere around here. Still, you can try."

"Not to-night," said Felicity, firmly.

Soon they were travelling more freely. Some attempt had been made to sweep the roads, and there was a little traffic. A few people were on the pavements, and lights gleamed from shop windows as they drove along the wide road. 'Buses were running, and their passenger said hurriedly:

"If you'll put me down here, I can catch that 'bus—it's going to the station. Thank you *so* much." He opened the door, letting in the icy air, slammed it quickly and hurried off.

"We'd better make for the White Hart, I suppose," said Dawlish. "I hate disappointing Barney, but—"

"He won't expect us now," said Felicity, "and you can telephone him."

"If the wires aren't down," said Dawlish.

They knew the White Hart, and pulled the car into the courtyard before hurrying into the large lounge, where two fires blazed and half a dozen couples sat about, comfortable and warm. They had no trouble in getting a room, and were promised tea in the lounge immediately. Soon they were sitting in front of one of the blazing fires, warmed by that and the hot tea, but still showing signs of their exposure. Felicity was conscious of a shiny nose and a ladder in one stocking, each enough to spoil the effect of her lime-green wool frock trimmed with rich brown velvet. Dawlish wished he had changed his socks and shoes. Before going upstairs to do so, however, he went to the telephone and put in a call to Barney Day at his cottage in Hurn.

"There will be a delay of half an hour," the operator said, "some of the lines are down."

"I suppose I will get through," said Dawlish.

"Yes, unless we have more trouble," the girl said crisply.

Dawlish went upstairs, changed, and was down again in a quarter of an hour. Felicity, now looking thoroughly warm, made room on a settee for two.

"I suppose I ought to be thankful that we got here," said Dawlish, "but on an occasion like this—"

"It's no use worrying about it," Felicity said. "Probably everyone else will be held up, and the house-warming will have to be postponed for a day or two. It would be worse if he were opening the shop to-morrow."

"Gallery," corrected Dawlish with a grin. "The Day Gallery!" He took out his pipe and filled it slowly. "Of all unexpected developments, Barney opening a shop in the wilds of Dorset is the limit! I wonder what Trivett thinks? And whether he has warned the local police".

"*Shhh!*" hushed Felicity, glancing at the nearest people.

Dawlish lowered his voice.

"That they have a man suspected of being the cleverest fence in London among them. I hope he hasn't," he added thoughtfully. "Barney's trying to make a complete break from the past. If he thinks that the local police are watching him closely he may lapse from sheer devilment. If the policeman concerned were anyone else but Trivett I wouldn't give much for Barney's chance of remaining unmolested, but I think our William believes in the rehabilitation of even the most hard-ened crooks!"

"If it rests with Trivett, Barney will have a chance," said Felicity. "I wonder what made him do it?"

"Item: weariness. While he's in London, anyone with a rope

of pearls or a scintillating tiara hot enough to burn their fingers would gravitate towards Barney; if he is out of London, they'll have to look elsewhere. Item: he has a liking for the country; I think he would have left London years ago but for the raids and a general dislike of running away. The more I think about it," went on Dawlish, drawing at his pipe, "the more I'm convinced he'll have most trouble with his own crowd. The police will give him a chance, but people with whom he's dealt for the last twenty years might not take it kindly."

"He wouldn't have left London without feeling fairly sure of himself," said Felicity.

She broke off as a porter came from the telephone booth and announced that a call had come through from Shaftesbury. Dawlish hurried to take it. Felicity lit a cigarette and sat looking into the fire.

She was thinking of Pat and his whims and fancies and odd friendships. Barney was, perhaps, the oddest of all the people whom he knew and liked. It was some years since he had met the man, who was nearly sixty—Dawlish was in the middle thir-ties—and discovered what the police had suspected for a long time. Barney Day was a fence. That is, he bought stolen goods knowing they were stolen. He did it with a genial friendliness which was captivating. Even the police liked him, despite their suspicions.

Some men might have lodged the necessary information with the police; others, feeling that it was none of their business, would have cut Barney Day and let the police get on with their own work.

Dawlish had done neither.

There were extenuating circumstances. Felicity smiled as she thought of them, and the firelight danced in her green-grey eyes.

Dawlish and Barney had met on the night of one of London's

biggest raids. Dawlish had been busy. He could be busy in several different ways, but generally the term meant that he was engaged on an errand of some importance which would, undoubtedly, lead to violence. At the time he had been working for a branch of the Intelligence, chafing under the fact that he was not sent to one of the fighting fronts. During that time his only relief from what he called the dread monotony of life at Whitehall, was when some chance thing happened to make Whitehall realize that there were bad men, even Nazi bad men, active in the country. True, even Whitehall's oldest inhabitants knew that there *were* such things as spies, but usually those spies worked furtively and hid themselves and refused to come out into the open. Now and again, however, something was wanted urgently enough for Berlin to send men who would not shrink from open violence—and it was one of Felicity's complaints that Dawlish always found himself engaged against them. As a matter of fact there were many other men working on the same tasks, his share was neither less nor greater than theirs; but to Felicity, who loved the massive, fair-haired, broken-nosed Dawlish to distraction, although she rarely admitted it even to him, all the really difficult and dangerous jobs were reserved for her Patrick.

The chase that particular night had led Dawlish to Fulham during a vicious air-raid, when Fulham suffered badly. The house in which his quarry had taken shelter had disappeared, and no one survived. Several other houses had gone the same way, and one nearby, badly damaged, belonged to Barney Day. Dawlish had told Felicity one story, Barney Day another. Barney's version was the one she preferred, because it seemed more in character. Dawlish had gone beneath the rubble of a damaged house to find survivors—Dawlish's version said he went to take shelter—and a wall had collapsed, fire had started. It was one of those nights when so many things happened near the same place that the Civil Defence organization worked under an intolerable strain. No one else being near, Barney, with his own house damaged, had gone to Dawlish's rescue.

A great many people were heroic, like that. The thing which lifted Barney Day out of the common was that the H.E.'s had broken open his safe, and in his house, visible in the front room for all to see, were jewels, stolen jewels. Yet Barney, seeing Dawlish in trouble—in fact in grave danger—in the red glow of the nearby fires, had risked the police discovering his hoard, and helped Dawlish out, scratched but not seriously hurt. Barney had offered a drink. Going to what remained of his front door, they had met a terrified little man who had seen the jewels. He knew Barney's occupation and started to talk in a frenzy—talk which was dangerous for Barney.

Policemen were coming to help the work of rescue. Nothing would stop the little man. Then Dawlish had punched him on the jaw, and knocked him out. Just like that. Dawlish afterwards distracted the attention of the police and Barney quickly covered up the traces of his nefarious activities.

"One turns a blind eye," Dawlish had said, "when a man has pulled one out of a mess of rubble which, a few minutes later, was a roaring furnace."

Barney was a tall, well-dressed, suave, even mellow man; in fact, his neighbours considered him a cut above themselves. He was unmarried, and had a faithful, youngish housekeeper, named Jane, who knew what he did and, Dawlish thought, was in love with him.

Barney was a denizen of that queer criminal world, then, hardly a man likely to be a friend of Dawlish's. Yet he became one. He had a jeweller's shop in Chelsea and gravely assured Felicity, on one occasion, that not all he handled was stolen. Felicity, as gravely, said she believed it.

Superintendent William Trivett of New Scotland Yard, a close friend of Dawlish's for many years, had come to know of the odd association, and warned Dawlish—knowing, as he said, that he was wasting his time. Mellowed when off duty, Trivett admitted that in some ways he would be sorry if anyone ever brought Barney Day to court. During the war Barney had been a tower of strength to his neighbours, a leading Civil Defence worker, and he did much good by stealth. Moreover, he did not touch looted gems. Trivett had himself been present when Barney had stopped a man from looting a jeweller's shop—a man who, had he possessed the courage, could have betrayed Barney for what he was.

"He's a curious mixture," Trivett said, "and he won't let you down over anything, Pat, but—well, when you mix with thieves, some people dub you thief. I'm putting it bluntly."

"Yes," said Dawlish, beaming. "Bad men, thieves. Not my cup of tea at all. I must talk severely to Barney."

Of course, their ways of life did not take them together very often, but they met occasionally and had a drink. From time to time, Barney admitted that he had been a fence too long. He wanted to retire. The trouble was that he could not decide what to do. That had gone on for a long time. Now Dawlish was out of the Army and Intelligence work, and Barney Day was opening a gallery in Shaftesbury; naturally, he had written, he wanted Dawlish to be there—and, if possible, Mrs. Dawlish.

It was a pity that it was snowing so hard.

Dawlish began with a hearty 'Hallo, Barney' into the telephone, and was immediately disappointed, for the voice of a woman answered him—Jane, Barney's housekeeper and general servant. Jane, he imagined, disliked the idea of being dragged from her native London, but would follow Barney wherever he led her.

"Mr. Day isn't in, sir. Who is that, please?"

"Dawlish," said Dawlish. "I—"

"Oh, *good!*" cried Jane, surprising him with her fervour. "What time will you be here, Mr. Dawlish?"

"That's why I've telephoned," said Dawlish. "I don't think I can make it. The roads are shocking, and—"

"Oh, but you *must*," cried Jane, and there was deep distress in her voice. "It doesn't matter about the others, but you must come, Mr. Dawlish; he telephoned only twenty minutes ago, and said if you was to ring up, I was to ask you to come through *somehow*. I—I don't know what," went on Jane, schooling herself to speak calmly, "but something's wrong, Mr. Dawlish. Mr. Day wants—no, he *needs* some help, Mr. Dawlish." She was growing breathless. "Isn't there *any* chance of you getting through?"

"I'm at Salisbury," said Dawlish. "The Shaftesbury road is probably impassable."

"You could come by train to Gillingham," said Jane, quickly, "it isn't very far from there to Shaftesbury, and the village is only a mile from the town. Mr. Day would have a car waiting for you at Gillingham, I know—just a minute, I'll look up the times of the trains." She put the receiver down, leaving Dawlish to stand and contemplate the walls of the telephone booth. She was gone for some minutes, and was breathless when she got back. "I had to hunt for the timetable, Mr. Dawlish. There's a train reaches Gillingham at 9.30. You should be able to catch that, and have some dinner before you come. You will, won't you?"

"I'll try," said Dawlish, wondering what Felicity would say.

"You *must*," cried Jane; "he wouldn't have telephoned and said what he did if it wasn't important."

"I'll do all I can," said Dawlish. "Tell him I'll ring through again if I'm unlucky."

"All right," said Jane. "Good-bye."

When Dawlish stepped into the lounge from the booth Felicity was lying back with her eyes closed. He went to the side door through the dining-room. The snow was coming down more heavily, and a car which had just come in was thickly covered. He went up to his bedroom and looked out. The traffic in the streets was almost at a standstill. A little farther along a double decker 'bus was in difficulties, and half a dozen men were trying to clear the clogged wheels. Shivering passengers were sitting inside. He went down again and telephoned the station. The inquiry clerk was not optimistic. The nearby lines were clear so far, but there was some trouble west of Gillingham, and there was no guarantee that trains would get through; the blizzard was worse to the west and south. There was some delay with the London trains, too—the 2.30 had left London late.

He telephoned a garage; would it be possible to hire a car to go as far as Shaftesbury?

"I'm afraid not, sir," said the man who answered. "We're not letting our cars go outside the city limits to-night—too much risk. Shaftesbury's the worst road, too, there wouldn't be a chance of getting through. In fact, some cars have already been stranded near Tisbury. Take my tip, sir, and don't try anyone else. If the snow stops soon it will be all right in the morning, but if it lasts all night I don't know how long it will be before that road's clear."

"A gloomy prospect," said Dawlish. "Thanks—good-bye!"

Any thought of risking the journey by road must be given up. Few people would have enticed him into travelling by train that night, but as he rejoined Felicity he was deciding to go on alone, and leave her at the hotel. She opened her eyes as he sat down.

"Did you speak to Barney?"

"No." He told her what had happened, and added before she

13

could comment: "I'll have a shot at it by rail. You keep warm for both of us here."

"Oh, *very* warm," said Felicity, and glanced at the clock over the reception desk. "We ought to have dinner early, if we're going to catch the train—what time did you say?"

"There's no sense in us both getting frozen to the bone," argued Dawlish. "Barney loves your green-grey eyes, but I don't think he'll be heartbroken if I turn up alone this time."

"You've finished your lonely adventures, darling," said Felicity, getting up. "I'll find out what time we can have dinner."

CHAPTER II

THE COTTAGE

Except for a wait of over an hour for the train, the journey as far as Gillingham was bearable. The carriage was full and the heat on, and with the doors and windows tightly shut the temperature kept up fairly well. The train should have been a non-stop to Gillingham, but instead stopped at every little station; a slow train, due to follow, was not likely to come out that night. At Gillingham they stumbled out into the icy blast of the blizzard, which showed no signs of abating. People loomed like ghosts out of the white blanket, lights were dimmed, snow had even blown into the waiting hut. Crossing the bridge over the lines was an ordeal; breathless and almost frozen, they reached the booking-hall, and Dawlish went out to look for the car which Jane had promised. There were three cars, but all were there to meet other passengers.

"Shaftesbury?" a man said. "You won't get up there to-night, that hill's impossible."

"It's only a few miles, isn't it?"

"Five, but it might as well be fifty," said the man. "Not a chance, sir; don't waste your time trying."

"What about Hurn village?" asked Dawlish.

"Hurn! That's ten times worse, right in the valley, that is. Hurn! It'll be three days before anyone gets into Hurn, *or* out of it."

Glumly Dawlish rejoined Felicity. There was a fire in the waiting-room, and she was sharing it with half-a-dozen other people. She had mentioned Shaftesbury, and been warned what to expect. A portly man suggested that they went to the hotel at once, there were other passengers stranded and there wasn't much spare room in Gillingham.

"I think I'll ring Barney," Dawlish said.

When he unbuttoned his coat to get some coppers, his legs seemed to freeze. It was some time before the operator answered, and she put the finishing touch to his gloom. The lines to Shaftesbury had been down for the last half-hour.

"And that appears to be that," said Dawlish. "We'd better get over to the hotel and beg a bed in the bathroom. I suppose it's too much to hope for a porter."

It was. Dawlish picked up the two large cases and Felicity the smaller one and some oddments, and they went out into the teeth of the blizzard. A man directed them to the hotel, and as they bent their heads and turned towards it the headlamps of a car gleamed on the falling flakes. There were drifts several feet high on either side and against some of the station buildings. The car crunched through the beaten track made by other traffic, and Dawlish straightened up and raised an arm.

The car pulled up.

"Are you from Mr. Day of Hurn, by any chance?" asked Dawlish.

"That's right, sir." The driver sounded bright. "Bit o' trouble getting about to-night, isn't there? Can't get you right to the door, but—"

"Let's talk inside," said Dawlish.

"That's a good idea." The man did not get out of his seat but waited until they were sitting behind him and then slowly reversed out of the station yard, talking all the time. He wouldn't have come out on a night like this for many people, but Mr. Day said it was really urgent, so he had decided to have a cut at it. No use going through Shaftesbury—hopeless, that hill! There was a way round to Hurn, and it would depend on what the road was like up and down a nasty little hill, but one that wasn't so bad as that up to Shaftesbury. He *certainly* couldn't get them right up to Mr. Day's house, but he could probably get them within two hundred yards of it. And then, he declared triumphantly, they would have to *walk*.

Dawlish sat back resignedly.

A dozen times on the journey he doubted whether they would get through. Three times the wheels locked and began to spin, but the driver managed to get free and drove on, rarely travelling more than five miles an hour. One window was broken, and he insisted on keeping the driving window down. They sat stiff and frozen, and the ordeal seemed never ending.

Still cheerful, the driver turned round in his seat.

"Soon see what's what now, mister. Beginning of the 'ill, this is. Ironic, ain't it? Only 'arf a mile from Mr. Day's house, that's all we are. 'Arf a mile." He put the car into low gear and went slowly down the hill. "I don't mind admitting I wouldn't 'ave chanced it if I 'ad to come *up* again," he said. "My garritch is at the bottom of the 'ill. Oo! Thought I'd gone inter the ditch *that* time!"

"*Is* it worth it?" asked Felicity helplessly.

"We'll make it now," said Dawlish. "I wish I knew why Barney was so determined about it."

"'*Ere* we are," said the driver triumphantly. "Bottom o' the 'ill. I'll get up as far's I can, but it won't be far."

"We can't carry our cases," said Dawlish.

"Oo, I forgot," said the driver. "Mr. Day said 'e'd got everything you wanted, an' I was to take the cases 'ome with me ter be collected in the morning. Satisfactory to *you*, I 'ope."

"We've got enough for one night in the small case," said Felicity, alarmed. "Can't we manage that?"

"We'll try," said Dawlish.

The car came suddenly to a standstill. The friendly glow of a lighted window close to the road helped them to see the white hedge and the steep road in front of them.

"I'll leave the bus 'ere, and lead yer to the gate," said the driver. "S'all right, I'm wet through as it is, I can't get no worse." He helped them out, and Felicity stepped knee deep into snow. "Bad luck," he said, and chuckled. "'Ere, lemme 'ave the case." He took the small case, shone a torch, and led the way up the hill, keeping to the middle of the road. Dawlish started off by trying to help Felicity, but they slid and stumbled so badly that she went on her own, and they made better progress. Dawlish reckoned that they had gone uphill for a hundred yards when the driver stopped.

"S'funny thing," he said. "'Ere's the gate, an' Mr. Day said 'e'd leave the front room lights full on, wivvout drawing the curtains. No light there, is there?" He sniffed. "Maybe the wire's down— over'ead cable they 'as for electricity 'ere, that's the trouble. 'Ope we don't step on the broken part by accident, don't you?" He laughed; his cheerfulness was astonishing. "I'll lead the way, mister, I gotta torch."

The drive was as steep as the road had been, and the snow hid everything from sight, even the trees on either side. They were floundering and gasping when at last the torch-light picked out the front porch. No light, not even from a candle, shone from the windows. The only sound was their breathing and the howling of the wind. The driver put the case down on the porch and shone the light on the front door. "Coo!" he said. "Piled up three foot wiv' snow, it is." He thundered on the knocker.

No one came; the wind seemed louder and the darkness more intense.

He knocked again and then turned; they could imagine the frown on his face.

"Well, 'ere's a go," he said. "I coulda sworn 'e'd wait up for yer. It ain't much past eleven, yer can't call *that* late." He stepped back into the drive and raised his voice: "*A-hoy, there! Anyone about?*"

The wind picked up the words and carried them away, and then silence fell. Dawlish stepped forward and, while the driver held the torch steady, examined the lock of the door. It was an old-fashioned one, and he would have no trouble in forcing it.

"I think I can get in," he said. "Mr. Day is an old friend of mine, he won't object."

"Don't see 'ow 'e could," said the driver. As he watched Dawlish manipulate a pen-knife in the lock, he grew loud-voiced in wonderment. "*Strewth*, you've done that before, I bet. Well, would yer believe it! Proper cracksman, you are! I'd better tell my old woman to keep 'er jewels locked up!" He laughed again as the door swung open. "Well, you're in, anyway."

"Thanks to you," said Dawlish. "Will you be able to get back all right?"

"Oh, yes. Run the 'bus down 'ill, if it comes ter that, it won't do any 'arm. I wish I knew where Mr. Day was," the driver added, "it ain't like 'im, this ain't. 'Ere, you'd better borrer me torch, mister. I got anuvver one back 'ome. I'd better get moving," he added, "my missus will get the wind up proper if I'm out much longer. Good night! See yer to-morrer!" He turned and made his way off into the darkness, showing no hesitancy in spite of the snow, and soon disappeared from the light of the torch.

Dawlish turned and pushed the door wider open. Felicity's teeth were chattering, which worried him, but there was a deeper anxiety on his mind. It was incredible that Barney would knowingly leave them in the lurch like this.

"I-I-I-h-hope there's a f-f-fire!" stammered Felicity.

"If there isn't we'll soon light one," said Dawlish. He saw the electric light switch in the narrow, low-ceilinged hall, and pressed it.

Light came on, bright enough to dazzle them!

"It's farcical!" exclaimed Felicity.

"I don't like it," said Dawlish, frowning. "But perhaps he went out to try to find us at the station. He might not have trusted the driver. That would probably mean he won't be back to-night."

He stepped into a room on the right and switched on the light. There were red embers of a fire in the grate, and by it was a hod of coal and a box of logs, so full that the lid was pushed up. Dawlish put on some small logs and a few small pieces of coal, and straightened up. "It isn't too cold in here," he said. "You'd better get into some dry slippers." He put the wet case on a stool, opened it, and beamed at her. "I'll explore the kitchen for tea or coffee," he said, and left her taking off her shoes and stockings. Thanks to the mackintosh, her coat was wet only at the edges and sleeves.

The house was silent.

A small, crooked staircase led up from the middle of the hall. The oak beams were so low that Dawlish had to lower his head; he was over six feet tall, and vast in proportion, and seemed too large for the little hall. A dining-room was opposite the lounge, and an electric fire was on in there. He stood at the foot of the stairs and called up, but there was no answer.

He found his way to the kitchen, cheered up by the sight of an electric stove and kettle. He filled the kettle—to his surprise the water ran hot—and switched the kettle-plug on. A tray was laid, and on a dinner-wagon were sandwiches, biscuits and cheese. He lifted the lid of a saucepan on the electric stove and found it full of soup; an appetising smell rose from it.

"We were expected all right," he murmured, and turned away after switching on the hot plate beneath the soup. "Food in plenty!" he called out to Felicity. "I'm going upstairs."

"Wait for me!" she called.

"You stay and keep warm," said Dawlish. "Them's orders."

Felicity appeared in the hall, her bare feet poked into fur-lined slippers. That, together with the mink coat, made him grin. She obviously meant to come with him, so he led the way up the stairs to a small landing with five doors leading from it. There was also a narrow passage with two more doors.

He stood on the landing, undecided.

He had no real desire to go into any of the rooms, for he was almost afraid of what he would find. That was absurd, but a true reflection of his feelings. Everything about this business was mysterious and full of menace, and he wished Felicity had stayed at Salisbury. There was at least a chance that Barney had been attacked and robbed; in fact, now that he was approaching the rooms where he expected to find Barney and Jane, he felt sure that violence had been committed in the cottage.

The light of the landing was dim, as if intended to add to the sense of brooding mystery.

"We can't stand *here*," protested Felicity.

"True, light o' my life." Dawlish stepped to the first door, which was ajar; it was an empty bathroom. Two empty bedrooms and an airing cupboard were examined next. Felicity kept close to him. The wind howled eerily down the large brick fireplaces, and rattled the windows. Now and again there was a hush, when the wind stopped and all noise seemed suspended.

In it, their breathing sounded loud and clear. The sight of the empty rooms, the knowledge that the house had been occupied not long before they had arrived, made them hesitate as they approached the remaining doors.

One was that of a small well-appointed study. In one corner stood a small Genoese silver table, with superb inlay work; it was Barney's most prized possession. Books lined the walls on three sides, heavy curtains were drawn across the window. The lighting was subdued; the effect was of charm and cosiness. The swivel chair behind a small desk of inlaid mahogany was turned towards the wall, as if Barney had got up in a hurry and left it standing like that.

There were two more rooms.

It was useless for Dawlish to tell himself that his fit of jitters was unjustified and unmanly. His fear that they would find Barney and Jane dead or badly injured was very real. He conquered his reluctance and went into another room. It was Jane's bedroom, small, neat, with austere-looking modern furniture; a soiled cap and apron lay on the bed.

"One more hurdle to jump," said Dawlish. Felicity gripped his arm as they went into the last room.

At first he thought that too was empty. It was larger than any of the other bedrooms. A huge four-poster bed was against one wall. Heavy tapestry curtains were drawn, and a log fire was burning low in a large fireplace. There was a smell of tobacco smoke, and a faint haze, as if the room had been occupied until a short time ago. Opposite the bed stood a large wardrobe; in one corner, incongruous in this old place, was a fitted wash-basin. The brown carpet was thick, with a rich fur-like pile.

One bedside lamp burned; there was no ceiling light.

"You knew where to come for warmth," said Dawlish, stepping forward.

He went far enough into the room to see beyond the bed, and stopped dead. A man was lying there, face downwards.

Felicity stifled an exclamation. Dawlish went nearer; the stillness of the man was ominous; he thought that he was looking at a dead body, yet he felt more relieved than distressed, for it was not Barney Day.

It was bad enough, however. The man wore police uniform. His thick-soled boots, covered with hobnails, were damp, and he wore cycle clips round his ankles. He had no cape, and his helmet was missing.

Dawlish went to his side and knelt down.

CHAPTER III

THE MURDERED POLICEMAN

The policeman had been shot through the chest. The body was still warm, but he was dead. Dawlish let his hand fall, after testing the pulse, and straightened up. Felicity was by his side. After the first shock, she had steeled herself to face the situation. Her first golden rule was never to worry Patrick. Yet his cool appraisal of the situation was almost too much for her.

"Shot in the chest and presumably he fell forward where he was standing," said Dawlish in a far-away voice. "He was standing—" he glanced at the policeman's feet and the wall— "eight or nine feet from a wood-panelled wall."

"What does the panelling matter?" asked Felicity, impatiently.

"Probably everything," said Dawlish. "Of course, the man who shot him might have been standing with his back to the wall; he would have been six or seven feet away. There is no sign of burning about the wound, it's a clean hole—a shot fired from nearer at hand would have made a greater mess. Sorry, darling, but there is deep, dark mystery in those wooden panels. Secret doors and hidden cavities!" He gave her a cigarette and lit it. "It's a pity the telephone lines are down. Isolation isn't to-night's cure for all ills."

Felicity said: "And we can't go out again."

"We might have a try," said Dawlish. He stepped to the wall and tapped; it sounded dull, and gave no indication of hollowness. He ran his hands along the carved lines and grooves, his long, strong fingers missing nothing. He got no result. He stretched up and ran his fingers along the top of the panelling, while Felicity watched, half hoping and half fearing that the panel would move. It did not.

Dawlish turned away, and rubbed his broken nose. His fine blue eyes were smiling, as if he were not at all distressed by the situation; he was being cheerful, Felicity knew, for her benefit. She watched him closely. Emergencies such as this always made him look different; they gave a touch of extra vitality to a lean, tanned face which often looked dull. His looks were spoiled by his broken nose, but as he looked then, that was forgotten. Then:

"Not so good," he said, inanely. "We won't sleep in this room!"

"What *are* you going to do?" asked Felicity. Her voice was steady enough, but the cigarette was already half-smoked and her hands shook a little.

"Have something hot to eat and drink, and then invoke the little grey cells," said Dawlish. "You were right, we can't go out to get help, so the only chance of sharing our burden to-night is an unexpected visitor, which isn't exactly likely. Of course, Barney might turn up." He tucked his arm under hers. "Let's get downstairs."

"Aren't you going to move him?" Felicity asked.

"Certainly not," said Dawlish. "First principle for all finders of dead bodies: leave severely alone until the police have an opportunity to take photographs." He stopped suddenly. "There is something we can do—the grey cells are working already." He led the way into Jane's room, with an air of some excitement, and espied a small box of face powder on the dressing-table. "Ah, that's the very stuff we want!"

He took it and turned back to the main bedroom.

"What are you going to do with it?" demanded Felicity.

"Sprinkle it round the wall," said Dawlish. "If anyone comes out again, they'll tread on it and leave a trail. We'll then know what part of the panelling can be used for fancy tricks."

"Well, don't use her face powder," said Felicity practically. "There'll probably be some talcum powder in the bathroom."

"Oh," said Dawlish, abashed. "Your economics are sound."

There was a large box of talcum powder with a filter top in the bathroom; it was easy to sprinkle it about the sides of the room, and Dawlish did so with zest. The carpet was not flush to the walls, and the powder showed in a clear white line when he had finished. It gave off a pleasant scent. He took the box back to the bathroom, then returned to the big room. The key was on the inside of the door. He took it out, locked the door on the outside, and then hurried downstairs with Felicity.

As they reached the hall a loud hissing sound made them stop quite still.

"*What is it?*" whispered Felicity.

"I don't know," said Dawlish, *sotto voce.* "It's coming from the kitchen. Hide behind my massive figure." He led the way on tiptoe. The hissing continued, but there was no other sound. It grew louder as he reached the kitchen door. A whitish vapour which looked like smoke was curling lazily from the room.

"Steam!" exclaimed Dawlish. "The kettle's boiling!"

The incident brought them back to earth. They busied themselves making tea, and while they drank it and ate biscuits, the soup was heated. They put it in a tureen and wheeled the dinner-wagon into the sitting-room. In there it was now snug and warm; the fire was blazing cheerfully and the logs crackling.

The howling outside the windows seemed to recede. It was easy to imagine that they were alone in the house, and to forget that a dead man was upstairs. The soup was delicious; Jane had always been a specialist in that essentially English art. The sandwiches were fresh—fresh enough for Felicity to comment that they had been cut quite recently.

"Oh, the place hasn't been empty for much more than an hour," said Dawlish. "However, I haven't been able to think up any bright notions about what to do. The fact that Jane and Barney are missing gives me a nasty feeling in the pit of my stomach. Same as yours! I don't think they're far away."

"You're sure there are secret passages, aren't you?" demanded Felicity, unhappily.

"Quite sure," said Dawlish; "and in a place like this that isn't surprising. Barney was delighted with his sixteenth-century cottage, you remember." He stood up, snapping his fingers. "There's one thing we ought to do—try the telephone! We might be able to speak to someone in the village."

The telephone was in the hall. Felicity stood with him in the bright light as he lifted the receiver. There was a long spell of silence, broken suddenly by a whirring sound which made them both jump round. It came from behind them. Suddenly a grandfather clock struck a harsh, booming note.

"The witching hour of midnight," Dawlish said with a one-sided smile. "Darling, our nerves are not what they might be. I—*hallo!*" He turned round to the mouthpiece, in pleased surprise. "Hallo. . . . Yes, I am calling! . . . Is that the Shaftesbury exchange . . . oh, *Hurn*," he exclaimed. "Put me through to the village constable, please."

A woman who sounded sleepy told him to hold on, and he looked at Felicity, his eyes hopeful. "We should have thought of this at first," he added, *sotto voce*. "Not that I expect we'll have a reply from the local Robert—he's with us." He jerked his head towards the stairs. "Hallo," he said again. "Is that—"

"I'm sorry, there's no reply," the operator said.

"Oh. Is he usually out at this time of night?"

"His wife is stranded in Shaftesbury," said the operator, "and I did hear that he was going to try to bring her back, sir. That isn't Mr. Day, is it?"

"No, I'm a friend of his," said Dawlish, quickly. "Who else is likely to be about in the village?"

"Not many people, at *this* time of night," said the operator. "Bert Willing might be—he's at the garage."

"Put me through to him, will you?" asked Dawlish.

A moment later a bright, familiar voice answered him. Willing's cheerfulness in the car had not been assumed.

"I'm speaking from Mr. Day's house," said Dawlish, "you brought me here a little while ago."

"Very glad yer got on okay, mister," said Bert Willing. "Perishin', ain't it? Would yer believe it—I 'ad ter take me car out again to-night. Marvel 'ow she takes it, ain't it?"

"Where—" began Dawlish.

"Only just outside the villich," said Willing. "Friend o' the missus in the fambly way, little perisher *would* start 'is tricks when yer can't git a doctor out 'ere, wouldn't 'e? Midwife, the missus 'is, couldn't very well not go out, could she?"

"True," said Dawlish. "So you're alone to-night?"

"S'right. Say, mister!" exclaimed Willing, anxiously, "yer don't want me ter come out *again*, do yer? I don't mind in a real emergency, but it's getting worse, it's inches thicker than when I took you up to Mr. Day's. I 'aven't 'ardly got me clothes orf, either."

"I don't want you to take the car out," said Dawlish, "but something has gone wrong here, Willing. There's no trace of Mr.

Day or his maid, and I think there's been trouble. A policeman is here, badly hurt—"

"Wot, ole *Bob!*" exclaimed Willing in alarm.

"I'm not sure he's from this village," said Dawlish, "but that seems likely. Where is the next policeman's house?"

"Shaftesbury," said Willing, in a subdued voice. "Can't get in touch wiv' Shaftesbury ter-night. Okay, mister, I'll come. Take me 'arf-a'nour, I specks." He paused. "Hurt bad, did yer say?"

"I'm afraid so," said Dawlish.

"It *would* 'appen on a night like this," said Willing. "Can't git a doctor—I say, I know who yer *could* try. Colonel 'Amblin. Depooty Chief Constable, 'e is, lives just outside the villich. Hurn 20, that's 'is number. 'Ot stuff at first aid in the 'Ome Guard, 'e was. Try 'im, mister."

"I will," said Dawlish.

"I'm on me way," said Willing, and rang off.

"That man is worth his weight in gold," said Dawlish, and immediately called Hurn 20. This time the operator was prompt in replying, and there was no delay at the other end. A pleasant, cultured voice said:

"Colonel Hamblin speaking."

Dawlish said: "You won't know me, sir, but . . ." he explained at some length, breaking off only when Hamblin put an occasional question. He got the impression that Hamblin was not greatly surprised, although that might have been nothing more than his habitually calm manner.

"I will try to get there," said Hamblin. "Yes, I know the cottage well, although I haven't met Mr. Day. I don't quite know how I shall make the journey to-night—" he broke off. "Yes I do, you can rely on me getting there, Mr. Dawlish." There was another pause before he added: "You're sure that the policeman is dead?"

"Yes," said Dawlish, firmly.

"All right. I'll see you later."

"A very workmanlike gentleman," said Dawlish, replacing the receiver. "We're in luck." He led the way back to the sitting-room, and looked into Felicity's eyes. "You're tired out," he said. "Pile some cushions on that couch, and get a nap while the going's good. I'll bring some blankets from upstairs," he added, and was gone before Felicity could protest.

The silence inside the house was unnerving. The dimly-lit hall was full of shadows. Dawlish walked quickly up the stairs and into a small bedroom, dragged the blankets and an eider-down off the bed, and hurried downstairs. Felicity was already lying on the settee, wriggling her bare toes in front of the fire. Dawlish tucked the blankets round her and then went into the kitchen. He found a large enamel kettle, filled it, and brought it into the sitting-room, where he put it on the hob. When Willing and Hamblin arrived they would be glad of a hot drink. He felt disinclined for further exploration; the less he did on his own the better it would be. He knew the police well enough not to usurp their duties except in dire emergency.

Felicity said sleepily:

"Things won't let you lie, will they?"

"No, thanks," said Dawlish.

"Fool! I mean—"

"I know quite well what you mean," said Dawlish. "Go to sleep!"

She closed her eyes and was soon dozing.

Dawlish lit a cigarette. He would have preferred a pipe but he had not brought much tobacco with him, and there was no certainty that he would be able to get more next day. The house was very quiet, and he sat brooding. He knew only too well what

Felicity had meant. Before the war he had become involved in a number of remarkable cases, and his reputation had then stood high with the Press and low with the police. That, in fact, explained his eagerness not to do anything about which the police could reasonably complain.

There were times when he resented his reputation. He did not, he said, go out to look for trouble; it came to look for him. That was only half true, however. The truth was that he never liked the prospect of taking part in any case, but that when one was upon him, he delighted in it. It was not unnatural that the police had often suspected that he took a deeper interest in unusual people than he should have done. Barney Day was a case in point. There were other cases. Little Sol Gordon, for instance, whom he had met through Barney. Sol was another fence, still on the active list, a bright-eyed, humorous little man, but certainly not a man to 'know'.

Against these facts there was his relationship with the Assistant Commissioner, Sir Archibald Morely. They were second cousins. There was, too, his friendship with Superintendent William Trivett, who respected his unusual ability. Dawlish had a habit of setting aside all irrelevancies and getting to the heart of an affair. If only he would curb his habit of acting on his own sometimes, without consulting the police, Trivett would have consulted him frequently. As it was, they sometimes worked together, but the official police attitude was one of guarded suspicion. No one at Scotland Yard suspected him of criminal activities, of course, but they knew that he was not above condoning crime in certain circumstances. It was, he often said, the difference between the spirit and the letter of the law; he was all for the spirit.

Dawlish saw heavy breakers ahead.

The police would have to come here, and the truth about Barney Day might be brought out. That would be a great pity, in more ways than one, for Barney deserved a break. The question was how far Dawlish ought to go to give him that break? Had he been wise to summon Hamblin? Or would it have been wiser to wait until morning?

He decided that he had been right. There was a chance that Barney Day had been taken away by force, and while that possibility remained it was necessary to summon all possible help. The trouble was that if when the police came they found evidence of Barney's past activities, they might put a sinister construction on the discovery. The policeman upstairs might have learned the truth; to save himself Barney might have committed murder.

Dawlish did not think that was even remotely possible; but the police probably would.

Dawlish tried to reason as they would, having in mind all the circumstances as he knew them. If Barney had attacked and killed the policeman upstairs, would he have fled the house and left the body there? Would he have gone away, of his own free will, even for a short time? Some policemen might think so, but Dawlish doubted whether Trivett would think it likely. If Hamblin were worth his salt, he would also have grave doubts.

The habit of doing a thing and thinking it out afterwards was so deeply ingrained in Dawlish's character that he did not find it strange. He was, however, gratified that reflection confirmed his immediate reaction to the discovery.

He felt restless. Had he been on his own, he might have been tempted to look round outside, but he did not fancy leaving Felicity here alone. Mysterious people coming from movable panels in the wall might take advantage of such lack of caution and materialize. In any case it was pleasantly warm in here, and Felicity, he thought, was asleep.

He pondered on Barney's hopes and plans.

The Gallery where he was to sell antiques and pictures

and *objets d'art* deserved success, but this murder might bring about its failure. It was not easy to start afresh after a life of crime, and there was more than a touch of bitterness in the situation.

It was, too, a wretched ending to another bright idea. Barney had invited the Dawlish's and other friends for this house-warming. All of them should have arrived to-night, but apparently none of the others had. Unless, of course, a guest had come, committed murder, and flown.

No, that did not make sense.

Yet he was uneasy about it. Barney's friends were likely to be members of the same fraternity as his, cracksmen and fences on the retired list. Barney might have misjudged the character of one of them.

One thing was certain: he had realized that trouble was impending, otherwise Jane would not have been so insistent on the telephone.

"Pat," said Felicity, unexpectedly.

"You stay with Morpheus," said Dawlish.

"I wasn't asleep. I've been thinking."

"Haven't we enough to worry about to-night?" asked Dawlish.

"What a wonderful wit you have," said Felicity, witheringly, and opened her eyes. Dawlish grimaced at her. "I have been thinking," she went on with dignity, "that one of the people invited might have done this."

"Barney would choose well," said Dawlish.

"He might be misled," said Felicity. "And it's no use telling me that you've thought of all this before, you must think about it now. I'm not a bit sure that we ought to have come."

"Very helpful," murmured Dawlish.

Felicity would not be put off. "If the others *are* men like Barney—or men who've done the kind of things he—I mean—"

"If they're crooks," said Dawlish, helpfully.

"All right," said Felicity, "let's suppose they *are* crooks. Barney doubtless had a lot of valuables here. He might even have been planning to do a last deal—"

"With us on the premises?" asked Dawlish. "I don't think it's likely. Nor do you."

"I suppose not," said Felicity, but she sounded reluctant to admit it. "Have you thought of what's going to happen when the names of the other guests are known?"

"I haven't given it any thought," said Dawlish, untruthfully.

"I was afraid not. All of them will be known or suspected criminals. Some will have served prison sentences, and others will still be wanted. The local people are bound to learn that, and—"

Dawlish raised his eyebrows: "They'll wonder what we're doing in such company!"

"Yes," said Felicity. "Nice to think about, isn't it?" She looked too snug and comfortable to be really troubled, but there was an underlying note of seriousness in her voice. "We ought to be far more worried than we are. Of course, Barney's probably alive or they wouldn't have taken him away, but even assuming that, we ought to be more on edge. I suppose it's the relaxation after the cold." She was silent for a moment. "We might even be wrong about Barney. He might be dead outside. I—"

"We're not going to make anxiety for the sake of it," said Dawlish, firmly. "We've done all we can, and now we've just got to sit back and wait for the others. There'll probably be no contact with London for two or three days, and the whole thing might be settled by then."

"I suppose so," said Felicity, doubtfully. "I—*oh!*"

"That's the front-door bell," said Dawlish, jumping up as a hearty clanging sounded from the hall. "It's Willing or Hamblin. Faster work than I expected."

He left the room as Felicity sat up and ran her fingers through her hair. He opened the front door, prepared to see the taxi-driver or a stranger, but instead he saw a little man, a ball of a man whose face was glistening with melted snow and blue with cold, who carried a single suit-case, whose Homburg hat was pulled low over his forehead and whose teddy-bear coat was wrapped tightly about him. In spite of his odd appearance and the fact that he was obviously exhausted, Dawlish recognized him, and stood aghast on the threshold.

"Let me in, sir, let me in!" The squeaking voice sounded thin with fatigue. "I have had a terrible journey, terrible! I am frozen! I—"

He entered the hall, and for the first time looked up at Dawlish's face and recognized him. He was Sol Gordon!

"Dawlish!" he gasped. "Daw—why, has Barney taken leave of his senses? Why are *you* here?"

CHAPTER IV

SOL GORDON

"I like to think that Barney invited me as a friend," said Dawlish, closing the door. "It isn't a 'business only' conference, is it?"

"I had no idea—" Gordon began, and then broke off. He shivered violently, his eyes were watering now that he had entered the warmer atmosphere, and yet there was the suspicion of a twinkle in them. To Dawlish this little Jew, who had taken a Scottish name by deed-poll and for business purposes, was the epitome of incorrigible youth. He knew of no one, a few fanatical anti-semitics apart, who would not like Sol Gordon. It was less the man than his astonishment and the inference in his remark which worried Dawlish.

"Well, well, well, my boy!" said Gordon, recovering. He rubbed his hands. "Lead me to the warm fire, Mr. Dawlish, I beg you! Inform Jane that a very hungry man has arrived after a most terrible journey, oh, terrible! It is a miracle how I got here!" He strutted into the sitting-room, taking off his coat from which the melting snow was dripping. "Put this away for me, my boy, I do not wish to spoil the beautiful carpet. I—why! Mrs. Dawlish." He gaped at Felicity, and Dawlish sensed his deeper astonishment. "Well, well, well! I come to the wilderness, and what do I find? The most beautiful woman in England!" He advanced with outstretched hands and gripped Felicity's, who exclaimed when he touched her. "Yes, I am cold," he declared. "Dawlish, be a good boy. Send for Jane at once. Look at me!" He peered down over his round stomach, and saw the pools of dirty water which his boots were making. "My, my, what a fool I am, what a fool! The carpet!" He sped towards the door and stood in the polished hall.

"I'll warm the soup," Felicity said, faintly.

"I'll take Mr. Gordon upstairs," said Dawlish, heavily. He put a hand on Gordon's arm and led the man unprotesting up the stairs. At the bend in them, Gordon was almost jammed. He now seemed speechless. Dawlish led him into a bedroom, and put his case on the luggage stool. "Have you got a change of clothes, Sol?" he asked.

"Underclothes only, my friend," said Gordon in a low voice. "I have a big warm dressing gown, that will do—your wife will not mind?"

"It ought to amuse her," said Dawlish, gravely.

"Ah-ha!" said Sol. "A joke, yes? You were always a man with a great sense of humour. Oh, my, my! What are you doing here with your lovely wife? What has Barney been thinking of, I ask you, what—Dawlish!"

"Yes," said Dawlish.

Gordon was taking off his clothes. He wore three sweaters, two scarves and two pairs of long pants; the pants were wet from the knees downwards, so he had to change completely. He looked at Dawlish owlishly, rejoicing in the warmth of the electric fire, but not recovered from his surprise.

"You must forgive me if I am impertinent, my boy. But am I making a big mistake, or *is* this Barney Day's house?"

"It is," said Dawlish, "and—"

"Excuse me," said Gordon, raising a hand and holding thick woollen pants about his middle with the other, "permit me to go about this my own way. It is a new experience to visit Barney and not to be admitted by Jane. A most efficient young woman, most efficient. Are they unwell?"

"They're missing," said Dawlish.

"Oh," said Gordon. He looked at Dawlish with his wise old eyes, the lids drooping. "Missing. So there is mystery. I smelt it. I travel from London in these appalling, yes, appalling conditions, and I step into mystery. A great pity, a *great* pity. Tell me, are they hurt?"

"I don't know," said Dawlish, "but—"

"Please! My own way. I have the kind of mind which will only work one way," pleaded Gordon. "Forgive me. Why did he invite you here? Let me be frank. You are Patrick Dawlish, a collector of trifles, a gentleman of some leisure—are you not in the Army?"

"I was," said Dawlish.

"Ah! You have a very fine reputation, very fine indeed, one to be proud of. And a charming and gifted wife. I have always thought that Mrs. Dawlish was the most charming of women, and so understanding. She permits you to amuse yourself in so many unusual ways. Do not misunderstand me," pleaded Gordon, "I am not being rude. But we are sometimes, my friend, on opposite sides of the fence. We must be frank, this is a time for frankness. You do not approve of me—"

"Nonsense!" said Dawlish.

Gordon's eyes glowed.

"Then you *should* not approve of me. But I know you are an unusual man, you help the police sometimes and anger them at others—or you did, before the war. I know your reputation.

I know you have worked for the Intelligence Department, even the newspapers have mentioned that. You are brave, you are kind, you are—perhaps—wealthy?" He shot the question out unexpectedly.

"Not what you'd call wealthy," said Dawlish, slowly.

"Ah! You see now what I mean? Barney and I have been known to cause the police some anxiety. What are you doing in such company? Should you be in it, here and now?"

"Barney has retired," said Dawlish, "and he and I have known each other for some years. Scotland Yard is aware of it."

"Yes, yes. A good answer, but no answer. I read between the lines. If there is a risk of being misunderstood, you agree to take it. So! Now I ask you another question, Dawlish. You arrived to find Barney and Jane missing. It is a wild night. No one would leave a warm house willingly. Do you know where they have gone?"

"No" said Dawlish. "I came here and found the body of a policeman in one of the bedrooms, and the house otherwise deserted."

"Body!" ejaculated Gordon. "Policeman!"

"The only other policeman with whom I could get in touch was the Deputy Chief Constable," said Dawlish, "and he should be here very soon."

Gordon flung up his hands.

"My boy, I give up! I do really give up!" He strutted to the door, but stopped with his hand on the handle. "Dawlish, *why* did Barney ask you here?"

"To the house-warming," said Dawlish.

"No, no. Frankness, please. *Why?*"

"I know of no other reason."

"It is incredible," said Gordon. "Such a man on such an occasion. Did he not tell you that he wished to discuss with me and with others the disposal of certain precious stones which have been troubling him? Did he not tell you that he proposed in this house to hold an auction of these gems and of other valuables, believing that he would best be rid of them now that he had stepped from one life to another?"

"He certainly didn't tell me," said Dawlish, and the information seemed incredible. He remembered Felicity's suggestion, which had been so near the truth.

Gordon rubbed his hands.

"Well, well! Perhaps he thought that you would not come if you knew the real reason for this house-warming, as he calls it, and he wished you to have the opportunity of seeing how such things are done. Yes, yes. Dawlish—"

"Go on," said Dawlish grimly.

"Barney is missing. Jane is missing. There is a dead policeman. There *should* be a collection of valuables, not all of which could safely be shown to the police. I do not know all of Barney's guests to-night. I do not, my boy, believe that he would invite an active *thief.* Those who buy and sell, like myself, yes—because such men as I never *steal.* However, you are in some danger of being gravely misunderstood. So! I shall, of course, not mention jewels. No one must mention jewels—if they can be stopped. The police must not know why Barney brought us here. Have you searched the house, my boy?"

"Only for Barney and Janet," said Dawlish.

"Very commendable, but—somewhere there might be a list of to-night's guests. Or a record of those jewels—Barney was always a meticulous man with his records. The police will, of course, search thoroughly. Shall I go and entertain your wife?"

Dawlish found no papers which gave an indication of the list of jewels or the identity of the other guests; five were not yet here, if Barney had said rightly that eight were due. As he searched the study and the other rooms, Dawlish felt restive and on edge. Gordon was reliable, but the others if they arrived, might not be. Why had he been invited? Certainly not as a prospective buyer of stolen jewels. There was another mystery; how had Gordon managed to get here? Obviously he had walked part of the way, but he had not explained how he had got as far as the village. It was possible that he had been here before, and had seen Barney; he might have been a party to the mystery. Dawlish could not dismiss the notion as entirely untenable; in any case he knew that the police would want a full explanation from Gordon.

He finished all the rooms except the large bedroom.

He had not intended to go in there again until the police arrived, but Gordon was right; the search must be thorough. He took the key from his pocket and opened the door. The light was on as he had left it. The policeman was still on the floor by the bed. Dawlish looked at the white powder, conscious of the heavy perfume in the air.

None of the powder had been disturbed.

The search took him ten minutes, and when he had finished he was ruefully aware that any piece of furniture might have a hidden drawer. In such a house hiding-places would abound. The police might stumble on one by accident, but all he could say for certain was that none of the obvious or likely places had been used.

Gordon was talking gaily to Felicity; their voices came from the sitting-room. Dawlish went into the dining-room and then a smaller one, filled with books, at the end of the passage. Ten minutes later, still unrewarded, he went into the sitting-room where Felicity was sitting with her legs tucked under her on the couch, and Gordon was leaning over the blazing fire, red and perspiring, like a fluffy brown ball. His grizzled hair was thin at the temples but thick at the back, and cut in Lloyd George fashion.

"Ah, my friend, come in, come in!" he cried. "Your wife has

been entertaining me beautifully, and I am content like a cat after that wonderful soup. Hear me—I *purr!*" He pursed his lips and made a purring sound, his eyes beaming. "Your friend the Chief Constable is late, Dawlish!"

"The Deputy C.C. and not my friend," smiled Dawlish. Felicity's eyes were on him questioningly. "I've made a thorough search and found nothing."

"Good!" cried Gordon. "Excellent! I—"

He broke off, and looked startled as the clang of the front-door bell came to their ears. Something that might have been alarm showed in his eyes, and he jumped up. Dawlish told him to stay where he was, and went to the door, expecting to see Willing. Instead, a man muffled up in a belted coat and several scarves, with a tweed cap pulled low over his eyes, was standing on the porch with one foot raised; on it was a snowshoe!

"Just a moment," he said. "Ah!" The shoe dropped to the snow-filled porch. He picked up its fellow, put them together in a corner, and stepped into the hall. "You're Mr. Dawlish, I suppose? I'm Hamblin. Happy thought, those snowshoes—first time I have used them in England!" He took off his coat, then sat on a settle and let Dawlish help him off with his knee-length waders. He was the first visitor to the cottage that night who did not look perished with cold.

He was neary as tall as Dawlish, a well-built man dressed in brown plus-fours, ruddy complexioned, with short, white hair. The set of his shoulders and his carriage dubbed him 'military', but Dawlish was relieved to see the smile in his fine grey eyes; he was no stiff-neck.

"Has Day turned up?" Hamblin asked.

"No, but another guest has."

"Faithful friends," said Hamblin, raising his eyebrows. "Not many people would have made the journey to-night."

"Once started, it was as easy to come here as go back," said Dawlish.

"Yes, I suppose so." Hamblin took out a slim gold cigarette case, and they lit up. "Before I meet anyone else I'd better see the body," he said, and as they walked up the stairs, both bending their heads to avoid the beams, he went on: "This is hardly my kettle of fish, you know. I don't remember having been first on the scene of a crime before—you're sure it was murder?"

"Quite sure," said Dawlish.

"Hurn. From what I can see of the weather, it will be the day after to-morrow before we can get anyone from outside the village," went on Hamblin. "I've been trying to remember where I've heard of you before—are you Patrick Dawlish?"

"That's right," said Dawlish. He hoped that Hamblin was a friend of a friend, but his hopes were dashed.

"Aren't you acquainted with Trivett of Scotland Yard?"

"Well acquainted," Dawlish said.

"I hoped you were that Dawlish," said Hamblin with apparent sincerity. "We had Trivett down here a few months ago, and the talk led to amateurs in detection!" He smiled. "Trivett has a high opinion of your powers, and I shall be very glad of your help."

"Nice of you both," murmured Dawlish.

"Nonsense! Well, let's see the man." Hamblin stood back as Dawlish opened the door. He let Dawlish go in first. Dawlish shot a swift glance about the room and was relieved to see that nothing had been disturbed; he could not persuade himself that he was wrong about a secret entrance into the room. His relief was the greater when he saw the policeman still there; for a moment a wild thought, that the body might have been moved, had entered his head.

"I'm afraid it will be Dawes, the Hurn man," Hamblin said.

"He looks about his build. Just a moment!" He spoke sharply as Dawlish was about to turn the policeman over on his back, and when Dawlish glanced up he saw a small camera in the other's hands. "I wonder if you'll switch on all the lights," Hamblin said.

Dawlish did so. Hamblin took three photographs, and appeared satisfied. Dawlish was impressed by the thoughtfulness which had made Hamblin bring that camera; he certainly had his wits about him.

"I hope it isn't Dawes," Hamblin went on. "Useful man, and I liked him." He watched Dawlish turn the policeman on his side, and exclaimed: "It *isn't*!"

Dawlish did not ask him whether he were sure; the face of the policeman, a heavily-built, large-featured man, pale in the glaring light, was not one likely to be mistaken for anyone else.

"And it isn't a Shaftesbury man," said Hamblin in a sharper voice. "Nor Gillingham—I know them all. It might be a man from Salisbury, that's outside my area, but—"

Dawlish interrupted: "Come and look at this."

He was fingering the letters and numbers on the collar of the dead man's tunic. Hamblin joined him, and as soon as he felt them he exclaimed:

"They're tin! They should be chromium. I—"

"He isn't a policeman," said Dawlish, as he stood up slowly, "he's wearing stage uniform. The material's thin—not a police serge." He stood looking down at the dead man, conscious of Hamblin's startled gaze.

Then a faint sound from the wall attracted him, and he glanced towards it. He saw that a panel opposite the dead man was open—there was a gap of at least an inch between it and the rest of the wall.

CHAPTER V

ALARM!

Dawlish looked away quickly.

Hamblin was still staring at the body and did not appear to have noticed anything else. Dawlish looked about him; he wanted something which he could insert quickly into the narrow gap. The great fireplace was fitted with brass fire-irons, and a poker was glistening on the curb. He stepped away, out of sight of anyone behind the wall, and took out cigarettes.

"So it's not a pukka policeman. That's a shock," he said, and when Hamblin looked at him he put a finger to his lips. Hamblin stared, but then grasped his meaning quickly, and bent down over the dead man, fingering the uniform. Dawlish picked up the poker. He could not get it into the gap from where he was standing, he would have to get nearer the bed. Holding the poker in front of him, he stepped between the body and the wall. There was no sound but heavy breathing. He did not risk looking over his shoulder again, but took a firm grip on the poker and swung round, lunging forward with it.

He heard a sharp exclamation of alarm as he thrust the end of the poker into the gap. Wood closed on it, and then the *panel swung further open.* Dawlish levered at it with the poker, keeping to one side, out of the direct line of the gap. There was a sound of splintering wood; whoever was behind the wall was trying to close the panel. Suddenly a hand appeared and gripped the poker a few inches from the handle. A quick twist loosened it in Dawlish's grasp, but he held on and then flung his full weight against the panel. There was a cry, the thud of a falling body, and then, from further away, a sharp voice:

"Mario, what—"

There was the thump of heavy footsteps. Hamblin went forward towards the foot-wide gap, but as he reached it Dawlish called a warning. Hamblin backed away, and the sharp crack of a shot sounded loud and echoed in the wall passage. A bullet struck the wall behind Hamblin and Dawlish, who dropped down on his face but retained his hold on the poker. The panel closed on it, leaving the gap less than half an inch wide. There were more footsteps. The pressure on the panel seemed to lessen, and after a few seconds of silence, Dawlish stood up.

"I think we're all right now," he said.

"Thanks to you," said Hamblin. "Do you think they've gone?"

"For the time being, yes," said Dawlish. "Have you a torch?" Hamblin handed him one, and he stepped forward cautiously. The panel moved back on a hinge. He shone the torch into the passage beyond. It was nearly two feet wide; the floor was of wood and the wall of stone. The torchlight shone bright and eerie into the void. Dawlish stepped into the passage and looked towards the right, whence the shot had come. Ten feet along there appeared to be a blank wall. He approached it cautiously. It was faced with stone, cemented in. There was no handle, and the joins against the inner and outer walls were so good that the whole thing looked solid.

"It locks from the other side," said Dawlish. "We can stop them from using this door for a bit, anyhow."

"How?" asked Hamblin.

"By blocking it—we can use a piece of furniture," said Dawlish. He turned and looked along the passage in the other direction. There seemed to be a solid wall there too. This might also be a dummy, but Dawlish thought it more likely that it was actually the outside wall of the house. It would be easy enough to check that when daylight came.

In the bedroom was a heavy blanket-box. They carried it through the panel and towards the stone-faced wall, and lodged it so that no one would be able to open the door from the other side. A small chest served the same purpose at the far end. Not until then did Dawlish examine the wall which ran parallel to that of the bedroom. It was cement-faced, and there was no crack or join; satisfied about that, he went back into the bedroom, where Hamblin, apparently recovered from his bewilderment, was lighting a cigarette.

"We've shut 'em out of here," Dawlish said, "but there's no telling what other doors there might be. The passage probably runs the whole length of the upper floor, and may be on the ground floor, too."

"That's a cheerful thought," said Hamblin.

"It's no use shutting one's eyes to probabilities," said Dawlish. He examined the broken panel and pointed to the lock on the passage side. "I doubt if it could ever be opened from inside," he said. "Barney Day probably knew nothing about it."

"No," said Hamblin. He frowned as he peered along towards the blanket-box. "I'm not a bit happy about blocking that up, Dawlish. Day and his staff might be along there, and if they are—"

"We can only open the wall up with a charge of dynamite, an electric drill or a pick-axe," said Dawlish, "and even the pick-axe isn't available. We may as well make sure that they can't do more damage from that quarter. Taken by and large," he added with a faint smile, "we're stymied. We can't get out of the house, but we can't be sure that no one can get in; we've one murdered man on our hands and a pretty mystery." He stood looking down at the pseudo-policeman. "It would be worth a bit if he could return to life for five minutes, wouldn't it?"

"Let's keep sane," said Hamblin rather sharply.

"Oh, by all means! This room being reasonably safe, we'd better keep the body in it. Did you bring any finger-print equipment?"

"I'd none to bring," said Hamblin.

"Then we've done all the formal work we can," said Dawlish with forced brightness. "It's odd that nothing was heard downstairs," he added, "I expected them to be up full of anxious inquiries. I—" His body stiffened.

"*Now* what's the matter?" demanded Hamblin.

"There might be trouble downstairs!" snapped Dawlish.

He was in the hall before Hamblin had reached the head of the stairs. He was thoroughly alarmed—until the sitting-room door opened and Gordon appeared, his arms touching the door-posts on either side. He was smoking a large cigar, and there was an inquiring look on his red face.

"My dear boy, there's no cause for alarm, I trust!"

"Not now," said Dawlish, somewhat sheepishly.

Hamblin came up and was introduced. Hamblin looked hard at the fat man, without returning Gordon's extravagant greeting. They went into the room, and Hamblin's manner thawed when he saw Felicity flushed from the fire.

She was obviously tired out. Her hair, between colours, was untidy but attractive, and her eyebrows were drawn in a straight line, a sure indication that she was puzzled. She was not beautiful, but men found her attractive, and her ready smile was charming. Her chin had a cleft and her lips were full. There was character in Felicity Dawlish.

"We're doing fine," said Dawlish, and he explained, speaking lightly without making light of the situation. Gordon's heavy-lidded eyes stared at him all the time; Felicity sat back on the settee, her eyes narrowed; Hamblin fidgeted, with his back to the fire.

"And there we are," finished Dawlish. "We can't do much until the morning, except try to find out which rooms are connected with the passage. Probably only one wall is affected, and when we've got the lay-out clear in our minds we shall have a good idea which are the danger spots. Two places we haven't looked at yet," he added, "are the cellar and the loft."

"There isn't a cellar here," said Hamblin. "The loft was turned into an extra room by the previous owner—I knew him and the house well."

"That's a help," said Dawlish. "Was there much work done here at the time?"

"It was an old cottage, almost tumbling down," said Hamblin, "but Jeffries, the owner, who loved old wood, saw the possibilities. He spent a small fortune on thoroughly modernizing it, as you've seen. If you're thinking that he put in the secret passage, I think you can forget it," he added, with a smile. "I am quite sure that this is not what you might term a hang-over crime."

"Oh," said Dawlish. "Day is the victim, you mean?"

"Undoubtedly."

"Isn't it a bit early to feel sure of anything?" asked Dawlish lightly. "Let's have a look at the attic room."

"I'm coming," said Felicity quickly.

"I think I would like to join you," said Gordon, with dignity.

Hamblin put his head on one side.

"It's approached by a narrow spiral staircase, Mr. Gordon."

"My, my!" said Gordon. "And I am too fat for it! Very well then, I will come to the foot of the staircase and there stand guard!" He bounded from his chair and pattered out into the hall.

They were half-way up the stairs when Dawlish remembered Willing. He paused, and told Hamblin about the man.

"He'll get here if he promised to come," said Hamblin, "he's a most reliable fellow. You needn't fear missing him when he rings the bell, it sounds right through the house."

"It's a good thing you know it so well," said Dawlish.

He was annoyed with himself when they reached a door in the wall between the bathroom and Jane's bedroom. Like the rest of the house, it was wood-panelled and dark with age, and he had passed it as a part of the wall, yet there was a small handle, carved out of the wood. It was not locked. The dark void beyond was illuminated by the light from Hamblin's torch. The staircase, well-shaped, was of wood, and the steps were very narrow at one end. Gordon put his head into the doorway, squinted up, and withdrew.

"You were quite right, Colonel Hamblin," he said sadly.

"I'll lead the way," said Dawlish.

"My privilege," said Hamblin.

There was no point in objecting. Dawlish admired the man's courage as he led the way, the stairs creaking at every step. He followed, and Felicity brought up the rear. Gordon spoke to her, as if trying to persuade her to keep him company. The loud creaking had the odd effect of making the quiet in the rest of the house seem more profound.

"Just a moment," called Hamblin. "Hold the torch, will you?"

Dawlish obliged. The light shone on a heavy wooden hatch, like the cover of a loft-hole. It was bolted on the inside, Dawlish saw with relief. Hamblin pushed the bolt back and then opened the hatch. It moved silently on well-oiled hinges. It fell slowly, leaving a gaping hole. Hamblin proved the extent of his knowledge of the cottage by groping along the floor; a moment later light flooded the well-staircase from a switch let in the boards.

"Nothing to fear here," he said.

He hoisted himself up. Dawlish let Felicity squeeze past him and helped her from below while Hamblin raised her from above. Soon they were standing in the largest room in the house. It was low at the sides because of the sloping roof, but in the centre it was seven or eight feet high. It was furnished as a bedroom, with a touch of luxury which characterized the whole place. Two-poster twin beds were against one wall, and there was cleverly concealed wall lighting.

"All safe and sound," said Dawlish. He looked at the panelled walls, and thought a little uneasily that they, too, might conceal a passage. There was a faintly fusty smell, as if the room had not been aired for some time. Two windows were in one wall, partly in the ceiling. Blinds covered them. When they pulled the blinds aside they could see the snow falling through a little pane of glass which was not already covered.

"They're dormer windows, well protected on one side," said Hamblin, trying them. "They probably haven't been opened for weeks. The room is exactly the same as when Mr. Day took over the house—I heard that he had bought some of the furniture." He stood aimlessly in the middle of the room, and added: "It's surprisingly warm."

"Good central heating," said Dawlish. "I think you and I might use this for an hour's sleep, darling."

"Not I," said Felicity, decidedly. "I'm going to sleep in the sitting-room!"

Hamblin laughed. "I think you're wise." He lit a cigarette from the stub of another. "I would be happier if we had *any* course of action open to us, but as far as I can see all we can do is to wait until morning. I can't believe that anyone else will get here to-night."

Dawlish said: "At least two people are here, besides ourselves. I got here, so did you—and you haven't the only pair of snow-shoes in Dorset, remember. We'll have to arrange a watch-and-watch system for the night. One thing we keep pushing to the backs of our minds, and I'm not sure that we should, is that Day and his maid are missing."

"What can we do?" asked Hamblin, helplessly.

"Is there a garage to the house?"

"Yes, but—"

"And other outbuildings?"

"Several, but they're all in the garden behind the house, up a steep drive. I expect the drive is three feet deep in snow."

"We must try to reach them," said Dawlish.

When they got downstairs, Gordon was nodding by the wall. He sat up with a jerk and apologized profusely. He had been travelling all night, he was really tired out, but it was unforgivable—to sleep while on duty!

"It only proves you've a healthy conscience," said Dawlish with gentle sarcasm. "Supposing you have a chair in the sitting-room, and Felicity takes the settee, and you both try to sleep for a few hours? We'll wake you in time to get a nap ourselves."

Gordon looked sleepily at Felicity.

"If Mrs. Dawlish has no objection—"

"I can always scream for help," said Felicity.

Gordon stared at her, astonished. "Scream for—my dear, my *dear* Mrs. Dawlish, that was most uncalled for! I am hurt, I really am hurt!" His eyes twinkled. "The truth is, if I can believe my wife, that I snore. However—I *must* sleep! Even an hour will make a lot of difference, and then, I assure you, I will do my duty in every way, Colonel Hamblin, every way! You will find me eager to be in the forefront of the fray!"

"I hope there won't be any fray," said Hamblin.

Either he was tired and his sense of humour dulled, or else Dawlish had been mistaken in his first estimate of the man. Dawlish spent some time thinking about that, and then pulled himself up with a jerk. It was a ridiculous waste of time. His mind would not work as he wanted it to, something about the place seemed to stifle his power of thought. Perhaps it was simply fatigue. He arranged pillows for Felicity, and brought more blankets down from one of the bedrooms. He put one over Gordon, who looked up with one eye closed.

"How thoughtful, my dear boy! I shall not forget your kindness, I really shall not. Good night!"

"Where are you and the Colonel going?" asked Felicity.

"For a glimpse of the garage," said Dawlish.

Hamblin was sitting in the hall. The radiator was hot and the atmosphere pleasantly warm. The wind appeared to have dropped, for there was no sound at the windows.

Dawlish was on edge, now, for Willing. After half an hour of desultory conversation, all of it aimless, he said:

"Well, we'd better go outside."

"I tell you it's useless," said Hamblin.

"All right, I'll go alone," said Dawlish.

"There's no need for that," said Hamblin, stiffly.

Yet his reluctance to venture out to the outbuildings was peculiar. Dawlish pondered over that as they put on their outdoor clothes. A pair of Wellingtons in the kitchen was just large enough for him, and he also found a useful oil-skin cape. Hamblin was already prepared. They opened the kitchen door, and the light shone on snow which was falling less heavily.

"I think it's stopping," Hamblin said.

"We'll still be cut off to-morrow, I suppose?"

"Quite definitely," said Hamblin.

The wind had certainly dropped, but outside the kitchen porch there was a drift of snow several feet deep. Using the kitchen shovel Dawlish cleared away enough for them to get into the garden. He went into snow almost knee deep with every step. Hamblin followed, shining the torch on the crystal whiteness.

"We mustn't go too far from the house," Hamblin said in a muffled whisper. "You're taking a risk with your wife's safety, Mr. Dawlish. We don't know what rooms these people might be able to enter, and with the house otherwise empty—"

"I think we've scared them off," Dawlish said.

"Yet they wanted to find out what we were doing there."

"They wanted to know who had arrived," said Dawlish.

"Yes. Natural enough."

Hamblin fell silent.

He had been right about the difficulty of reaching the garage, the door of which was visible in the light of the torch. Two or three feet of snow was piled against it. Dawlish still held the kitchen shovel, and began to shovel enough away to get the doors open. It was icy cold; all the beneficial effect of the warm fires had gone, and he was beginning to think that Hamblin was right when he heard the man exclaim.

"Now what?" he asked.

"Be quiet!" muttered Hamblin softly.

He had let the torch move away from the door. Its beam shone part of the way down the drive, and Dawlish saw what had attracted his attention. There was something dark in the snow by the side of the drive. He could discern the figure of a man who seemed to be kneeling. That was absurd; probably it was someone standing knee-deep in the snow. There was a curious stillness about the man. Dawlish felt a queer sensation along his spine as Hamblin stepped forward and the torchlight drew nearer to the stranger.

Suddenly Hamblin exclaimed: "That's Willing!"

The man's eyes were closed. He was quite motionless, and when they forced their way nearer to him they saw that he was kneeling. The piled snow supported him. He was wearing no hat, and the snow was thick on his head, face and shoulders. Hamblin reached him and shook him, and he fell forward as if frozen stiff.

"This is dreadful!" exclaimed Hamblin.

"Dreadful's the word," said Dawlish. "We may save him yet." He put his hands beneath Willing's armpits. They were warm. He hoisted him up, and with a great effort lifted him clear of the snow. Hamblin led the way through the path they had already made, and at last they reached the kitchen door. The warmth of the room began to melt the snow, but did not lessen Willing's stiffness. Dawlish put him on a long kitchen table and began to unfasten his clothes.

"Look at that!' exclaimed Hamblin, and pointed to his head.

Dawlish leaned forward. Where the thawing snow fell from Willing's hair to the floor he saw the ugly wound in the man's head, glistening red with blood.

CHAPTER VI

WILLING TALKS

"Is he—is he dead?" asked Hamblin, in a low voice.

"Not yet, by a long way," said Dawlish.

They stripped the man's clothes off, opened the boiler-grate so that the room grew hotter, and covered Willing with a blanket. Then Dawlish began artificial respiration. Willing was breathing, and within five minutes his limbs began to twitch. Dawlish was perspiring with the effort of massaging him, and he was nearly all-in when Hamblin volunteered to take over. He stood close by, watching the taxi-driver's face.

The wound was not as severe as they had first thought; it was a simple contusion, and the skin had broken, but the cold of the snow had helped to staunch the blood. It had obviously been enough to knock him out, however. Probably he had been unaware of the presence of his assailant; but if that were so, why had he walked up the drive to the garage instead of going to the front door?

"Will he do?" Hamblin asked with a gasp.

"I'll give him another five minutes," said Dawlish. "Put the kettle on, will you?"

In half an hour Willing was tucked up in Jane's bed, smothered in blankets and hot-water bottles. He had not regained consciousness, but there was a healthy colour in his cheeks and it was unlikely that he would suffer any serious ill-effects. Hamblin had justified his reputation as an expert in first-aid: in a box in the bathroom he had found what he needed to cleanse and pad the wound, and had cut the hair away, so as to affix sticking-plaster.

Suddenly Willing grunted.

Hamblin straightened up. "He's coming round!"

"That was never more than a matter of time," said Dawlish.

Willing grunted and groaned for several minutes, and his eyelids began to flicker. Dawlish switched off the main light, and in the subdued light of a bedside lamp Willing opened his eyes. He blinked, stared dazedly at Dawlish without recognition, and then his gaze fell on Hamblin.

He started to struggle up.

"Colonel—"

"Take it easy, Willing," said Hamblin authoritatively. "You'll be all right if you rest."

"Take it *easy!*" gasped Willing, but he dropped to the pillows again, and winced. "Strewth, my 'ead ain't 'arf buzzing!"

"Who hit you?" asked Hamblin.

"Perished if I know," said Willing. "Strewth, it wasn't 'arf a sock!" His hand strayed gingerly to his head. "Never seed the beggar," he declared. "Goin' up to the garrich, I was, an' 'e caught me a fourpenny!" He winced when he touched the pad. "See a light in the garrich, I did. S'funny thing, I thought, I'd better 'ave a look-see. Then I slipped in the perishing snow, and then they conked me one. Who was it, Colonel?"

"We don't know yet," said Hamblin. "Are you sure there was a light in the garage?"

"No doubt about that," said Willing. "Them doors 'ave glass tops. I got a n'idea that somefink was up when the gennelman asked for the police, so I went to 'ave a dekko." He looked indignantly at Dawlish. "You might 'ave warned me."

"Mr. Dawlish insisted on going outside; but for that you wouldn't have been found until morning," said Hamblin, "and you would probably have died."

"Never mind my good deeds," said Dawlish. "We must have a look at the garage. Does it occur to you, Hamblin, that the snow was piled so high against the doors that no one could have got in from the front?"

"There's a side door," said Hamblin. "Still, you're right. Stay in bed, Willing, we don't want an invalid on our hands." He nodded to the man, and they hurried downstairs.

A faint snoring sound was coming from the sitting-room. Dawlish smiled as they went through the kitchen and into the back garden. They did not waste time going to the front doors, but went up a steep path by the side of the garage.

"It's been cleared of snow once to-night," Dawlish said.

"So I see. Here's the side door."

It was closed but not locked. The beam of the torch spread a ghostly light about the large timber garage, which struck surprisingly warm. A work-bench was placed against one wall, and beneath it was an electric fire. Damp footmarks covered the floor in front of the bench, and there were traces of dampness on the bench itself.

Dawlish looked at some iron filings beneath a small vice.

"Someone's been busy," he said.

"It's fantastic!" declared Hamblin.

"It's happened," said Dawlish, dryly. He found a switch and the garage was flooded with light. It housed Day's Austin 12, which gleamed brightly, and a woman's bicycle, as well as tyres placed about the walls and a variety of tools. "If you can tell me why, to-night of all nights, anyone came in here to file a piece of metal, it would be a help."

"I'm *completely* bewildered," said Hamblin, and in the light he looked older than when he had first entered the house. "There seems no sense in it at all, Dawlish—can *you* make any?"

"Yes," said Dawlish. "Day and his maid were spirited out of the house, and a man posing as a policeman was shot dead. Someone was outside when Willing came, and hit him over the head to prevent him from seeing what was happening in the garage."

"Yes, I know, but—"

"Come!" said Dawlish, a little testily. "Murder and violence, probably abduction, aren't crimes committed for nothing. There was probably robbery also. Day is a wealthy man and a collector of precious stones, among other things."

"Yes," said Hamblin. "I know. He—"

"He probably had a small fortune in jewels here to-night," Dawlish said. It was useless to evade the obvious, frankness was most likely to serve. He met Hamblin's gaze, and was not surprised when Hamblin asked abruptly:

"How well do you know Day?"

"I've known him for some years."

"You're not a stranger to crime, especially crime in London," said Hamblin. "I am telling you this in strict confidence, and I'm sure you'll observe it. I was warned by Scotland Yard that Day was suspected of dealing in stolen jewels."

Dawlish stared. "It sounds incredible!"

"I can only tell you what I was told," insisted Hamblin.

"The Yard is full of mistakes," Dawlish said, easily, "I shouldn't pay too much attention to that canard, if I were you. Anyhow, even if they are right—and I don't think so for a moment—robbery is robbery. This one is worse than most. The thieves—and murderers—are probably somewhere in the house or the outbuildings. What about those outbuildings, can we get to them fairly easily?"

"I'm not happy being out of the house," said Hamblin. "I think—Oh, all right! We'll look in the other places."

There were three outhouses, used for gardening tools and vegetable and fruit storage; all of them were empty. Because of the snow piled against the doors it was difficult to get into them, but Dawlish insisted on examining each one. Only then, more tired than ever and bitterly cold, did they go back to the house. Dawlish looked into the sitting-room. Felicity seemed to be asleep; Gordon opened one eye. Dawlish nodded reassuringly and went upstairs. Hamblin was coming out of Jane's room; Willing was all right, he said, and appeared to be dozing.

"I wish—" began Hamblin, and then his voice trailed off.

"We wish we could get our teeth into something," said Dawlish. "The truth is that we're stuck and the murderers are also stuck. They can get into the grounds but they certainly can't get away from Hurn until the snow goes—if you and Willing are right in your estimate of the situation."

"I am prepared to guarantee that no one in Hurn village and the little district surrounding it can get out for at least twenty-four hours," said Hamblin.

"But the telephone is still working in the village," said Dawlish. "I suppose you had a Home Guard platoon here?"

"A very good one," said Hamblin, surprised.

"Then why not telephone one or two of the leading members and tell them the trouble?" asked Dawlish. "They can't work to-morrow. They can watch and make sure that no one tries to get away from Hurn. That seems the best we can do."

"There is something radically wrong with me," said Hamblin.

"I should have thought of that a long time ago. I'll telephone Carter." He hurried to the telephone and lifted it. After a few seconds he began to bang the receiver up and down, but there was no answer. He tried for at least five minutes, and then Dawlish took the receiver. There was no sound on the line at all, and he replaced the receiver and said helplessly:

"That's the local line gone phut. There's a chance of going to see your friend Carter in the morning, I suppose?"

"Oh, yes."

"Then that will have to do," said Dawlish.

"You're so infernally calm about it!"

Dawlish smiled. "What good will it do if we get worked up? I'm as befogged and bewildered as you, but it's no use kicking against the pricks. I think it's time we called Sol Gordon and put him on guard," he added, "we can use some sleep ourselves." He looked at his watch. "By Jove, it's after four!"

"Four hours to dawn," said Hamblin.

Gordon opened one eye again when they went into the sitting-room, and Felicity stirred. Gordon got up, wrapped his dressing-gown more tightly about him, and assured them that he was feeling as fresh as a daisy. His eyes were bright, and he looked as good as his word. He admitted a little plaintively that he wished he had a gun, but cheerfully settled himself in the hall, where he could see the stairs and all the doors, and promised to stay awake until dawn. Hamblin, after some hesitation, decided that he would wait up with him. Dawlish went into the sitting-room and sat in Gordon's chair.

"Any results?" asked Felicity, opening her eyes.

"At once too many and too few," said Dawlish. "It's the oddest situation I've come across. Hamblin started off as if he were really intelligent, and has developed a complex or something which makes him too Poona for words." He gave her an outline of what had happened, and added: "He's right in one way, of course, there's nothing we can usefully do, and yet—" he broke off, to yawn.

"You're tired out," said Felicity.

"Yes. I shouldn't be."

"Don't be an ass," she said. "You were up at five this morning—yesterday morning, and that drive was a nightmare. You insisted on making me go to sleep, so—"

Dawlish laughed. "My own medicine, yes!"

New logs had been piled on the fire. He pushed his chair back, but the warmth made him drowsy and his bewilderment did nothing to keep him awake. He had an uneasy feeling that he had left something important undone, but could not give it a name. He was more than uneasy about Barney and Jane; it was easy to tell Hamblin not to get worked up, but inwardly he himself was thoroughly on edge. At least daylight would bring some relief, they would not feel entirely cut off from the world.

At daybreak Gordon came in, fully dressed, carrying a tea-tray. He pulled back the curtains and let the grey light in. The clouds were still leaden, and although the wind had dropped snow was still falling. Out of the window Dawlish could see the tops of the houses in the village, which was in a small dip. The square tower of the Norman church showed vaguely, but for the most part everything was white. The branches and bark of trees were coated white and it was difficult to see the road through the village. The only thing which showed up clearly was a narrow stream which meandered through the blanket of white, passed through the village, and disappeared behind a hill.

"A dreary prospect, my boy," said Gordon, brightly. "Not a question of every prospect pleasing, is it? I never did like snow; oh, no, I never liked snow!"

"I shan't again," said Dawlish.

"I persuaded the amiable Deputy Chief Constable to rest on one of the beds upstairs," said Gordon. "I promised to call him at eight-thirty, and also to find out whether the telephone was, by any chance, working this morning. I must perform my duties! The young man whom you rescued last night is fast asleep, I am glad to say, and there have been no more alarms, no more alarms at all."

"Splendid!" said Dawlish.

When the door closed he rasped his hand over his stubble, poured out tea, and looked again at the blank vista of the countryside. Only now could he fully appreciate the difficulties of the terrain, and realize that it had been almost a miracle that they had arrived at all. Beyond the village the ground rose to several hundred feet; Hurn was a little hollow completely surrounded by hills, which might have been mountains as far as travel in that snow-bound valley was concerned. Here and there smoke rose upwards from the chimneys, sometimes hidden by the snow which was still falling fairly heavily. Silence reigned.

"Well?" asked Felicity.

"Bath—shave—breakfast—business!" said Dawlish. "We'd better use the morning-room as a dressing-room until we've got the bedrooms sorted out."

Hamblin was struggling into his out-door clothes in the hall. He looked heavy with sleep and his hair was standing on end.

"I must go and rout out the Home Guard fellows," he said. "I'm astonished that nothing happened during the night—quite astonished. Do you think the men have got away from the house?"

"More likely they're lying low to see what we're doing," said Dawlish.

The water ran hot; he bathed quickly and went down to tell

Felicity the room was free. Then he shaved and dressed; the atmosphere was warm everywhere. Sol Gordon must have done an excellent job of stoking. He went into the passage and was outside Willing's room when he heard a movement. He tapped on the door.

"Are you awake, Willing?"

It seemed a fatuous question, and he expected a quick retort from the Cockney who had strayed into Dorset. He got none. He tried the handle, and pushed; the door was bolted on the inside. In sudden alarm he thrust his shoulder against the door, but the solid wood did not yield. He thought he heard another movement inside, drew back, and flung himself at the door, aiming to put most of his weight where he thought the bolt was placed. There was a loud crack. The door swung open, and he steadied himself on the threshold.

A panel in the wall closed with a snap!

He hurried to the bed, where Willing seemed to be asleep, but there was something in the man's stillness which brought alarm surging through him. It was not until he was close by the bed that he saw the red stain on the sheet; blood had soaked the sheet and the blanket on which the man was lying. He felt Willing's pulse; it was still.

No one came upstairs.

Felicity had gone to join Gordon in the kitchen; with the doors closed, it was unlikely that they would be able to hear the crash when Dawlish had forced the door. He hesitated for a moment, wondering whether to raise an alarm or to wait until Hamblin returned. As he stood by the bed, filled with a chilling horror, he heard a faint *crack!* He thought it came from outside, and ran to the window, which was open an inch or two at the top. He was in time to see Hamblin stumbling up the drive on his snow-shoes. A man muffled in scarves and overcoat was standing at the foot of the steep drive. He held a gun and fired towards Hamblin; a second *crack*! reached Dawlish's ears.

There was a heavy thud on the front door.

Dawlish swung round, raced down the stairs, and reached the hall as Felicity appeared from the kitchen.

"I thought I heard a knock," she said.

"You did," said Dawlish. "Keep to one side." He hurried to the door as the bell clanged once, and then fell silent. "To the side!" he repeated as Felicity came after him, and, alarmed by the tone of his voice, she flattened herself against the wall. He stood to one side and opened the front door. Hamblin lurched in, bringing with him a flurry of snow. He tripped up over the shoes, and fell headlong.

Dawlish peered round the door towards the drive.

The man was no longer in sight, only virgin snow seemed to be all about them.

He stepped on to the porch without heeding a warning from Felicity. As far as he could see there was only the whiteness; the gunman had disappeared completely. That was not difficult, he could have dodged behind any snow-covered hedge or mound. The stillness of the morning air was almost frightening.

He stepped back.

Felicity was bending over Hamblin, who was struggling to get up. His face was bleeding.

"It's only a scratch," he muttered; "only a scratch. I'm all right—help me get my shoes off, Dawlish!"

Dawlish bent down to do so. "What happened?"

"I got as far as the end of the drive," gasped Hamblin, "and a man came from behind a hedge and told me to go back. I—I refused, of course, and we came to blows. Someone else came and fired a gun. I—there was nothing else to do, so I came back."

"You would have been a fool to have gone on," said Dawlish.

Hamblin was obviously angry with himself, tormenting himself with the thought that he had failed in physical courage. "No Home Guard, then, unless someone heard the shooting."

"It would be muffled on a day like this," said Hamblin, still breathing heavily. He dabbed his cheek with a handkerchief. "Just touched me, that's all," he said, but blood was welling up from the wound; the bullet had carved a little groove in his cheek. "It's infamous, Dawlish."

"It's happening," said Dawlish, dryly. "They're still in the house, too. Willing has been murdered."

"Willing—" Hamblin's voice started loudly, then trailed off.

"Shot while asleep," said Dawlish, "and I didn't make sure the panel was blocked up!"

He ignored the alarm in Felicity's eyes and raced up the stairs. He caught a glimpse of Sol Gordon peering anxiously from the door leading to the kitchen. He reached Willing's room and approached more cautiously. He made sure that no one was behind the battered door, and stepped inside. The trouble in this house was that he had a feeling, amounting to certainty, of being watched all the time. A man might be standing behind the wall with a gun trained on him. The sounds he had heard when he had passed the room before proved that someone had been inside it, had not fired at Willing from the wall.

The panel that had moved was closed.

The only thing in the room which he could move with ease was the bed, with Willing's body on it. He exerted himself, and had lifted it as far as the panel when Hamblin and Felicity came in, with Gordon bringing up the rear.

"Stay in the passage," said Dawlish. "It's not safe."

A voice from the wall said:

"You're quite right, it's not at all safe. Dawlish, I want to talk to you."

They stared at the panelled wall. None of them moved except Sol Gordon, who backed into the passage. Dawlish thought he heard him padding down the stairs. He was disappointed in the fat man he had given him credit for more courage.

Hamblin burst out:

"Who the devil are you? What—"

"Save us the expostulations of a retired British officer," said the unseen man in the wall-passage. "I do not want to talk to you, Hamblin, nor to Mrs. Dawlish, but to Dawlish. We may come to a satisfactory arrangement. Go out, Hamblin, and take Mrs. Dawlish with you."

Hamblin stood quite still. "It is my duty—"

"*Get out!*"

Dawlish said: "You'd better go. I'll tell you what happens afterwards." He shot a smile at Felicity, who seemed undecided, and then hurried them both to the door. When they were outside he closed it; the bolt had broken and the screws had been pulled out of the woodwork; but apart from that the door was intact.

"You show good sense," said the unseen man.

"You show fine discretion," said Dawlish, ironically.

"Move the bed, and I will meet you face to face."

"No, thanks," said Dawlish. "Find another panel if you want to come in."

There was a moment's silence; it was uncanny to stand in the empty room, with only the dead man for company, and to know that the murderer was standing within a few feet of him, invisible and quite safe. He put his hand to his pocket for his cigarette-case; he thought he heard an exclamation, and reflected that the other probably thought he had a gun. He lit his cigarette, and flicked the match away.

"Dawlish—"

"So you're still there," said Dawlish.

"Listen to me. There are some jewels in this house, and I intend to get them. While you and the others stay on the premises, I cannot do so without injuring you. Persuade Hamblin and the others to leave at once."

"Your men stopped Hamblin from going," said Dawlish.

"That was at my instructions. One or two at a time is no use. You must all go—to the cottage in the next field."

"I don't know of any cottage," said Dawlish.

"There is one there. It is quite comfortable, and you can take provisions from this house. You will only be there for a day or two."

"I see," said Dawlish. "You propose to send us there, watch the cottage to prevent us going out, and make us wait until you have searched this house and got safely away. An attractive proposition," he added lightly. "It won't work, of course."

"Dawlish." The deep, not unpleasant, voice held a note of menace.

"At your service," said Dawlish, ironically.

"Day and the maid are alive and safe. They will not be unless you do what I say. You have a greater strength of will than any of the other people with you, and they will do what you advise. You had better advise them to do what I say and quickly. I want you all out of the house by ten o'clock—it is now half-past nine. Otherwise—"

Dawlish said with an effort:

"Otherwise what?"

"Day's maid will be returned to you," said the man behind the wall. "She will not be alive."

"I see," said Dawlish. His mouth was dry, and the cigarette seemed to burn his tongue. He remembered Jane, neat, trim, so fiercely loyal. He had seen enough of the work of the speaker to accept the threat as it stood. "You forget something."

"I don't understand you."

"Willing is dead, so is the policeman. I might persuade the others to make a deal with you if I see with my own eyes that Day and his maid are alive. Unless I see them, I shall do nothing of the kind."

After another pause the man said:

"Dawlish, you seem to forget this. I can shoot you where you stand."

"You can't," said Dawlish. "You had to come into the room to shoot Willing." When there was no reply, he went on: "Why did you do that? Senseless murder is always a step worse than murder with a motive."

"I had sufficient motive. I do not propose to argue with you. You have heard my terms."

"And rejected them," said Dawlish. "It's a pity, isn't it? If we knew for certain that we could save two lives, we might be persuaded." He tossed his cigarette into the fire-place and stared out of the window. He moved towards it. The soft, remorseless fall of the snow went on, and the blanket of silence was everywhere. Silence reigned in the room also. Yet he thought he could hear the man breathing.

How badly did the fellow want them out of the house?

How far dare he himself rely on the premise that the other could not shoot at him, or the others, *through* the wall?

The man said: "There is no way in which I can let you see them. It is not practicable."

"I'm sorry about that," said Dawlish.

He moved abruptly towards the door. His fingers were on the handle when he heard another exclamation. He held himself stiff; if they could shoot without hindrance, it was likely that they would do so then.

"Come here again at ten o'clock," the man said, "when I will try to meet your requirements."

"Nice of you," murmured Dawlish; he broke into a gentle perspiration.

He went out. To his surprise the landing was empty. He heard Hamblin speaking in the bathroom. There Felicity was putting a piece of sticking-plaster over a pad of lint on his cheek. Hamblin looked flushed, partly through anger, partly through pain and weakness; the wound must have hurt a great deal.

"What did he want?" he demanded, explosively.

"To parley," said Dawlish. He told them briefly what had happened, and to his surprise Hamblin did not immediately burst out with the statement that it would be impossible to accede to the request. He was by no means sure himself that they would have any choice except to go to the smaller cottage.

"We've half an hour's grace," he said, "and we can get a spot of breakfast before the next session."

"Sol's finishing it off," said Felicity.

"Sol!" echoed Dawlish, with a lift of his eyebrows.

"Oh, we're good friends! I'll be down in a few minutes," Felicity said. "There's another scratch on the Colonel's arm that wants attention."

Dawlish nodded and went downstairs; it seemed to him that Felicity had some reason for wanting him to go down alone. He was recalling Gordon's hurried departure from the scene of danger as he stepped into the kitchen, to be greeted by the cheerful sizzling of appetizing bacon and eggs, and the gurgling of the kettle. There was a broad smile on Gordon's face, and he whispered:

"Come here, Dawlish!"

Dawlish joined him by the electric stove.

"I asked your wife to arrange for you to come down alone,"

said Gordon in a conspiratorial whisper. "I have a present for you!" He took his hand out of his pocket, and to Dawlish's astonishment, held out a snub-nosed automatic. "That will give you reassurance, my friend! You are not robbing me, no indeed you are not! I have another. I hurried away just now to arm myself, and when I returned I realized that you were negotiating successfully, and came down again. Er—my dear boy, *one* request."

"Yes," said Dawlish, pocketing the gun thankfully.

"Say not a word to Hamblin about it," pleaded Gordon. "You know what officials are! The police, for some absurd reason, refused to renew my gun licence a year or two ago, but I must protect myself. You agree, don't you?"

"I've a licence for two," said Dawlish. "Let me give you a gun."

"Oh, my boy, my boy! What it is to have a resilient mind, to be able to rise to an emergency! Excellent! If I should need to show my gun, then, it will be agreed that you lent it to me! I feel much happier, much. Well, my dear boy, what did the man behind the wall have to say?"

While Gordon gravely turned over the bacon in the frying-pan, Dawlish gave him the gist of what had happened.

"Shrewd," said Gordon. "Very shrewd. If they show us Day and Jane alive, what will you do?"

"That depends on Hamblin."

"Oh, how wrong you are," said Gordon, hopping from one foot to the other and looking distressed. "How very wrong, my dear boy. Hamblin will be guided by you. He lacks the strength of character which such a situation requires. He has an impressive façade, of course, and pretends that he is in complete control of the situation, but he broke down under pressure—the pressure of circumstances. Even after he had seen the body, he was reasonably good. Not so calm as you, but good. Then he broke down. Something changed in him. You have noticed it, perhaps?"

Dawlish looked at him thoughtfully.

"What makes you think that?"

"Think?" Gordon patted his arm. "I do not think about a thing like that, my boy, I *know*. Hamblin is a changed man. I might go so far as to say a frightened man. There are the facts. Follow the facts and you will never go far wrong, that is what I always advise young men who come to me for help. Follow the facts!" His bright eyes searched Dawlish's face, and he laughed softly. "I am right, you see, and you admit that I am right—I can see it in your expression. Dawlish, one little word of self-commendation—I know men. It is my business to know men. There have been times when a wrong judgment, in the most difficult circumstances, would have led to a prison sentence, perhaps to worse. Oh, I know men and I do not believe that Hamblin will impose his will upon you. He may oppose your suggestions, but only querulously, and he will give way."

"Have you ever met him before?" asked Dawlish, slowly.

Gordon laughed. "My dear boy! Be yourself! What would the Deputy Lieutenant—no, Deputy Chief Constable, you see how confused age makes me—be doing with a fat old Jew pawnbroker from the East End of London?" He laughed again and patted Dawlish's arm. "It is just that I know men, and have long ears. I heard much of what you said when you were in the hall with him last night. But for you, no one would have ventured into the garden. There was a risk, oh, yes, a great risk. If your wife or I had been injured, you would have blamed yourself, and Hamblin's reluctance would have been justified. Instead, what happened? You found curious things, you saved Willing's life. True, that was of small service to him, poor dear fellow. Still, you saved it. Now don't ask me what I mean, my boy, use what common sense you have—and hush! They are coming!"

Felicity walked noisily along the kitchen passage, obviously to give warning of their approach. The table was set, the bacon now a little overdone. They sat down on kitchen chairs, and only Hamblin failed to do the food justice. He kept glancing at the ceiling, as if he were thinking of the two dead men and the unknown man who had uttered so stern a warning.

At five minutes to ten he broke a short silence.

"Well, what are you going to do?"

"See what our friend has to say this time," said Dawlish.

"It is my duty to be with you."

"He'll probably say more if you're not there, but you can stand outside the door," said Dawlish, off-handedly.

His manner was deliberately calculated to sting Hamblin into making a protest; it failed. Where many men in his position would have felt angry and slighted, Hamblin accepted without a comment. Gordon lowered one eyelid. Felicity, puzzled by Dawlish's abruptness, looked ready to pour oil on troubled waters, and was equally astonished at Hamblin's meek acceptance. Gordon was right; Hamblin had, for some unknown reason, completely changed his outlook.

"It is two minutes to ten," murmured Gordon.

"I'd better keep the appointment," said Dawlish. He dabbed at his lips with a table-napkin and stood up. "Are you coming, Colonel?" His manner was hearty now.

"I think, all things considered, you had better remain our spokesman," said Hamblin; "but you understand, of course, that you will agree to nothing without my consent."

"Of course," said Dawlish.

He went slowly upstairs, his preoccupation with Hamblin fading as he neared the rendezvous. Now that he was alone, reason and common sense seemed to recede; it was hard to believe that at breakfast they had behaved with such natural-ness, accepting a situation which had all the qualities of fantasy. None of them had boggled at the situation—at the fact that a party of men here was so daring, so heedless of consequences, as to commit murder and, in effect, blackmail four people.

What would happen if he refused to compromise?

He turned into the bedroom. It had become a grisly place because Willing lay there, staring sightlessly towards the ceiling. The sense of unreality was strengthened, normality was completely gone.

He stood looking at the wall from where the unknown had spoken. He waited for nearly five minutes, without moving, but reassured by the gun in his pocket. He was beginning to think that the appointment would not be kept when someone spoke. It was not the man who had talked to him before, but a woman, whose abrupt voice sounded familiar.

"He never lied, Mr. Dawlish, we *are* alive. We're okay, *if* you do what he says."

"Well, well," said Dawlish. "So you're there, Jane!"

"We're both here, Dawlish," came Barney Day's voice. He sounded weary. "I don't like advising this, but do as they ask. It is the only way to avoid further tragedy."

CHAPTER VII

STALEMATE

Dawlish moved restlessly towards the window, and put his hand to his pocket. He looked out at the white countryside, and then turned abruptly.

"You're probably right, Barney, but I don't think Hamblin will accept the ultimatum. Even if he would, I don't know that I'm justified in doing so. Two men have been murdered. If it were a question of robbery alone, I wouldn't hesitate, but—"

"I can only advise," said Barney.

"I know," said Dawlish. He forced himself to sound touchy and on edge. "The thing is, what will happen if we obey and go to this other cottage? We've no guarantee that you will be left alive—in fact, you probably know these people by sight, and they may decide that it isn't safe to allow you and Jane to live. I see no reason for accepting their word—do you?"

"I can only advise," repeated Barney.

"I suppose so." Dawlish stood staring out of the window, uncomfortably aware of the quickening of his pulse. "Before I decide, Barney, tell me this—who else is coming to the party? Whom can we expect to-day?"

"Don't answer that!" There was urgency in the voice of the man who had first spoken. "Don't answer, Day."

Barney said nothing.

Dawlish swung round.

"Jane! What time did I telephone yesterday evening?"

There was a short exclamation, but no reply, until the first speaker said harshly:

"Let's have no more of this nonsense, Dawlish. They are not here to answer foolish questions."

"No," said Dawlish. "They're not there at all. The voices are bad imitations. It won't serve," he added abruptly. "When I've seen them and know they're alive, I'll do what I can; I shall not be deceived by false voices."

The silence which greeted the words proved that he was right; there was stalemate, and he could imagine the anger of the man behind the wall. For the first time it occurred to him as likely that Barney and Jane were already dead. If they were, there was no point at all in leaving the house.

"Dawlish—"

"Produce them in person and stop fooling," Dawlish said. "I'll come back again at eleven o'clock."

His name was on the other's lips as he reached the door, but he ignored the call, slammed the door, and went downstairs. He was smiling with some satisfaction. The initiative had passed to his hands for the time being, at least, and the quandary in which the unknown found himself would take some escaping. The sudden change of tactics had buoyed him up and he was smiling broadly as he turned into the kitchen. Hamblin was standing by the window, and Gordon and Felicity were washing up.

"Well?" snapped Hamblin.

"We've another hour's grace," said Dawlish, "because they tried to pull a fast one. I think we ought to use that hour without wasting a moment. Felicity, put on your coat, will you, and go outside and walk wound the house, measuring the walls from corner to corner, or from doors to corners. The idea is to check up where the outside walls are substantially longer than the inside ones. I don't know what you'll do for a ruler—"

"I've a tape-measure," said Felicity, drying her hands and untying a flowered apron.

"I think we ought to get the two bodies out of the rooms they're in now," said Dawlish. "We know that the walls are double there. We can move them to the attic, or else to the garage—the garage might be better. Or else the morning-room, provided it hasn't a double wall."

"The others have access to the garage," said Hamblin.

Dawlish looked at him sharply.

"Yes, that's a point. All right, the morning-room, if it suits our purpose." He hurried to the door and called out to Felicity to start by the morning-room, and then turned back to the others. "It looks fairly certain that the entrance to the wall-passage is from underground, and that there is a tunnel leading from the entrance to the garage or one of the outhouses. Will you two check up where you can? You didn't bring a gun with you, Hamblin, I suppose?"

"No, I had no idea that one would be necessary."

"It's a pity," said Dawlish. "I've lent one to Gordon—you'd better share it between you." He nodded to Sol, who again lowered one eyelid, and then hurried into the morning-room. Felicity was standing by the window, looking very cold, but busy with the tape-measure. He opened the window. She gave him the measurements from the corner to a door leading to the side garden from the morning-room. The inside measurements were eighteen inches shorter.

"Nine-inch walls are reasonable," said Dawlish, "so this room will do for a mortuary!" He handed the tape-measure back, and she started on the other walls, while he examined the furniture of the morning-room. Two low-seated arm chairs with a pouffe between them, would serve as a bench for one of the dead men; three upright chairs with exceptionally wide seats would serve for the other. There was a sense of ghoulishness about the situation, but he resolutely ignored it. He hurried upstairs for Willing and wrapped sheets and blankets about the stiff body.

In twenty minutes both dead men were in the morning-room.

Dawlish closed the window and drew the curtains to prevent anyone from looking in, and then went out and locked the door, dropping the key into his pocket. He was perspiring when he finished. He put on the Wellingtons and the oil-proof cape and went out to help Felicity, whose hands were numb with cold. The snow was falling only lightly now, but the wind had sprung up again.

They had finished in five minutes.

Still wearing their out-door clothes, they checked the measurements of the downstairs rooms. Only the dining-room, which they had not yet used, showed any great discrepancy—one of nearly four feet along the narrower wall. Judging from that, a passage might run along the breadth of the room, which faced the outbuildings where Gordon and Hamblin were still busy.

"We'll sketch the layout and check upstairs," said Dawlish.

The dining-room was exactly the same size as the large bedroom upstairs, and it too faced the outbuildings. Next to it was the spiral staircase, then came Jane's room in which Willing had been killed.

"And next to that the bathroom and closet," said Dawlish. "We can check those walls all right." They were no more than nine inches thick, and he was satisfied that on that side of the first floor there were no more passages. Checking on the other bedrooms was more difficult, but he managed it by leaning out of the windows and holding a broom to gauge the length.

"That's the lot," he said, with satisfaction. "The only passages are those we already knew upstairs, and the one in the dining-room." He glanced at his watch. "We've a quarter of an hour to spare, let's see how the others are getting on."

The snow had settled a little on the ground, and had hardened; it was easier to walk, and they could see where they were going. The clearance which he had made during the night still showed; barely an inch had fallen since then. The fact that the path by the side of the garage had been cleared puzzled him, for there was no trail through the snow from the dining-room wall, and there was more reason to believe that there was an underground passage.

Hamblin and Gordon came out of an outhouse, both blue with cold.

"We have found nothing at all," said Hamblin. "Even the fact that the garage was used last night has been covered up, and those filings you saw have been cleared away."

"Good!" said Dawlish, and Hamblin gaped. "Of course it's good," he went on, "we know they can get to and fro easily, and our chief trouble is what we don't know. Let's get back to the house." He explained what he had done as they made their way to the kitchen, where Gordon took off his coat and went to the fire, spreading out his hands towards the warmth.

"What purpose have we served?" asked Hamblin.

"We don't know yet," said Dawlish, "except that we do know where they might spring out on us. I've locked the doors of the double-walled rooms, except the small bedroom, where they're probably waiting for me. Are you coming this time?"

"I had best leave it to you," said Hamblin.

As he went upstairs, Dawlish reflected on the oddness of human nature and the reflection made him grin. His first walk to the rendezvous had seemed unreal; this one seemed normal enough, as if he had done it several times before. It was a relief to enter the room without seeing Willing's body.

"Good morning," he said to the empty room. "It's eleven o'clock precisely."

There was no answer.

"Good-morning," he repeated in a sharper voice.

There was still no answer.

He did not know why this alarmed him so much; he had expected the man to be waiting for him, and the fact that he was not suggested that he had decided to refuse further parley. The consciousness of danger increased in this room, although there was some relief in the knowledge that those downstairs were now in no immediate danger. He stepped to the window, trying to compose himself. Except that there were more chimneys giving off smoke, there seemed no life in the village. He could not see the main street, but the smaller ones and the byways seemed empty. In a field near the church he saw cattle moving sluggishly, but that was all. The sky seemed darker than it had early in the morning, and the few flakes of snow seemed larger and more frequent; another blizzard would make the situation hopeless. A sudden gust of wind smote the windows, startling him by its violence. The snow on the ground was frozen so hard that none was blown by the wind.

He saw where the telephone wires were down—it was not far from the house. Probably the rest of the village could communicate freely. For the first time he saw the little cottage next door. It was nearer the road, almost hidden by snow-laden trees. Smoke wafted lazily from its chimney until seized by the wind and blown almost horizontally.

"*Dawlish!*"

Although he had been waiting for it, the voice made him jump. He turned and stared at the panelled wall.

"So you are not so much at ease," said the other, and there was a mocking note in his voice. "We have both been busy—I have been making holes in the panelling, through which I can if needs be shoot you. That is a cheerful thought, isn't it?"

"Shoot on," said Dawlish.

"That is senseless bluff—I shall shoot when I think it necessary, but I have no wish to cause further bloodshed. I have been thinking, Dawlish, and I can see your point of view. I will let you—*only* you—see Day and his maid. I hoped that my little trick at ten o'clock would work, but I should have known that you were no mean adversary."

"Compliments gratefully accepted," murmured Dawlish.

"How you must talk, to keep your spirits up! I can understand that, too. Now, Dawlish, listen to me. Leave the house immediately, and go to the cottage at which you have been staring. I will meet you there with the others. I give you my word that you will not be hurt, provided you do not make any further attempt to outwit me."

"I see," said Dawlish, heavily.

"If you do try to be clever, you will get hurt, and the other three here, I think, will be fairly easy to deal with. Come at once. I shall expect you in fifteen minutes."

"Is there a short cut?" asked Dawlish lightly.

"Yes, but I should not try it."

Dawlish forced a smile, but he was more than ever aware of the danger as he walked out of the room. The man might really be in a position to shoot; but he did not take the opportunity then. Dawlish hurried downstairs and found the others waiting for him in the kitchen, where Gordon had brewed tea. Hamblin, tall, pale, and now rather aloof, as if he realized that the others could not understand his change of attitude, was staring at the doorway, and Felicity, her face flushed from attending to the fire, looked up with relief.

"I'm going out," said Dawlish, "another stage in the parleying. If we can keep this up long enough we'll have a thaw, won't we?" He began to draw on the Wellingtons, and explained more fully. Dressed for the open air, he inspected the gun which Gordon had given him; it was fully loaded. He expected some protest from Felicity, but apparently she realized that there was no chance of making him change his mind.

He left by the kitchen door.

Normally it would have taken no more than three minutes to reach the cottage. It would take more than ten now. On some parts of the drive the snow seemed deeper and softer than at others, and he slipped and foundered, feeling annoyed with himself for not having thought of borrowing Hamblin's snow-shoes.

No one was near the drive from which Hamblin had been fired at.

There was a little gate leading to the cottage, and a path carved into steps, faintly outlined by the snow. The front door of the cottage had been recently cleared; brown, brushed snow was piled on either side of the path. He wondered how many other places in the village had received the same attention. From the cottage door he was able to see the sharp dip in the road which led to the village; it was probably six feet deep or more in snow at places.

He knocked at the door.

There was no immediate answer, but before he knocked again he heard footsteps. He prepared to face the newcomer, wondering if the man would be disguised, half expecting one of the lesser myrmidons.

The door opened.

Standing there with a hand on the door, neatly dressed and smiling as if there were nothing amiss, was Jane. Slim, dark-haired, with sharp features, Dawlish knew her so well that there was not the slightest possibility of a mistake.

CHAPTER VIII

JANE AND BARNEY DAY

.

It was only after the first shock of surprise that Dawlish, studying her carefully, saw that the smile was tense, as if turned on to order, and that her hands were strained and white where she held the door. She backed away for him to enter.

"Good morning, Mr. Dawlish."

"Hallo, Jane," said Dawlish with as much composure as he could muster. "I was afraid that dark things had happened to you."

"They—they *have*," said Jane, and her voice was unsteady. "Mr. Dawlish, please don't—"

"You were warned, my girl," a man said.

He was standing at the foot of a flight of stairs which led straight up from the narrow hall. He was tall and slim and well-dressed. His eyes flashed with an unnatural brilliance— a brilliance which Dawlish placed immediately; he probably took drugs. There was a casual air about him, and it was not surprising to see that his face, from the nose downwards, was covered with a red silk handkerchief. His voice was slightly muffled, but the words were audible enough.

Jane said: "Mr. Dawlish, don't—"

The man by the stairs raised his hand, and Jane cowered back. That in itself was astonishing; Jane, perky Cockney and afraid of no one, was terrified of this man.

"That is better," said the man. "Come in, Dawlish." He led the way into a front parlour, furnished with Victorian furniture so that every corner was crammed, and there was only just room to move round a small table in the middle—the table was covered with a green chenille tablecloth. Pictures, photographs, and china ornaments were everywhere on the walls, and yet the room seemed bright and cheerful, chiefly due to a log fire blazing in the hearth—a fire and fireplace much too large for the room.

In a saddle-back winged arm-chair was Barney Day.

He looked ghastly. Dawlish, shocked beyond measure, thought that he had aged ten years since he had seen him only a few months ago. He looked hardly the same man. His hair had been white for many years, but it had waved back attractively from his forehead; now it was quite straight and lank, like the hair of a man who has been through a serious illness. His cheeks were thin and there was no flush of health. His eyes were lacklustre. The fingers of his left hand were toying nervously with the buttons of his coat.

"Hallo, Dawlish," he said, and his voice was one of utter weariness. "It's good to see you."

It was so wrong, so hopelessly wrong. Barney had been so buoyant, so full of confidence, like a man who had found the secret of perpetual youth; now he looked ready for the grave. Of one thing Dawlish was convinced; this change could not have come suddenly. Barney had been undergoing some great ordeal for weeks, if not for months.

"You see, Dawlish, I told you the truth," said the man whose face was masked. "I am going to leave you alone with Day for a few minutes. He might persuade you to do what I want—he knows the necessity for it. I shall, of course, be listening." It was easy to imagine the smile on his lips, and his voice was silky.

The door closed on Jane and the man.

"Well, Barney," said Dawlish, quietly.

Barney smiled wanly. "I hardly expected to greet you like this, Dawlish. Things have moved fast in the past twenty-four hours, and the snow has made it worse, of course. I should have been frank with you from the beginning, but I was afraid that if I told you the whole truth you wouldn't come."

"You should have known better," Dawlish said.

"You would have been justified in staying away," said Barney, "and yet—well, let's face the situation as it is." His hand moved slowly to a box of cigarettes by his side, and he held it out. They lit up, and Barney, giving the impression that there was no need for haste, leaned back in his chair. "The situation as it is," he repeated. "Before retiring, I made one large purchase. Oddly enough—and you are one of the few men who will believe me—not one of stolen gems. True, they were smuggled into the country, but I paid a reasonable price for them and the seller was not dissatisfied."

"Are the stones well known?" asked Dawlish.

"They should be! They are part of the Alexis collection."

Dawlish said: "How big a part?" The collection was world famous, and familiar to him by name.

"Rather more than a third," said Barney with a faint smile. "The question, once I had the jewels, was what to do with them. The authorities did not even know they were in England, so there was no danger from the police. What I didn't know was that someone had been trying to get them while they were on the Continent, and they were followed here. They cost me a large sum of money—most of my available capital, nearly two hundred thousand pounds. There were one or two stones which I thought you would like, and I felt sure that the others would find a ready market. I had already made plans to retire and come down here, but I wanted to dispose of the jewels before I left London. Then I discovered that I was being closely watched, by the police as well as by someone whom I did not know. I was afraid to offer them. After a while the man you have met this morning showed his hand. He wanted the jewels—he offered twenty thousand pounds for them—and threatened to tell the police where they were if I did not sell. I defied him, of course. I had a visit from the police next day."

Dawlish said: "A curious mentality."

"Don't forget that he is listening," said Barney. "It wasn't so curious, after all. He knew that I would hide the gems where the police could not find them, and thought that by showing earnest he would have more success next time. He was wrong, of course, but from that time onwards I found things getting more and more difficult. There were many threats; Jane was attacked on three occasions, and seriously hurt on one—she has only just recovered. I could not go to the police, and—"

"You should have told me," said Dawlish, reproachfully.

"Knowing that you would get involved without losing a moment, and be mixed up with thieves?" asked Barney. "No, I didn't like the thought of that! I believed I could outwit the fine gentleman. I think I would have done but for one thing—you see what a wreck I am?"

"You look as if you want a six months' holiday," said Dawlish with forced heartiness.

"I look as though I've one foot in the grave," said Barney, "and so I have. They have been poisoning me for the last three months. I don't know what they're using. You see, as Jane was ill, I had to employ someone else. I didn't know that the new girl worked for the other side. I have been losing weight and energy, and there are times when my mind seems stagnant—to-day is a good day. I feel more like my old self."

Dawlish found nothing to say.

"I had selected *Timbers,* next door, and the shop in Shaftesbury," said Barney, "and I did not think the others knew about them. I planned to come down here, call a meeting of the most likely buyers, including you, and get the gems disposed of once and for all. The jewels were down here, you see—and they still are." He paused for a moment, and raised a hand helplessly. "The man here discovered at the last minute where I was coming. A great deal depended on what happened then. My whole future was in the balance. I had sunk much money into the shop and *Timbers,* and to keep going until I sold the Alexis Collection I had to call on the bank—except for the Alexis, I am insolvent now. I was not myself, you will not need telling that. I thought if I could interest one or two of the illegal buyers, I might get the whole thing settled and retire comfortably. I planned, of course, to tell you all the risks involved. Jane and I went into it, and finally decided that we could only really trust you and Sol Gordon—you to help, Sol to buy. All the other invitations were cancelled."

"I see," said Dawlish.

"The man outside learned, I did not then know how, about the house-warming. I told him about the cancellations, hoping that he would assume that the whole thing was off. At that time I knew nothing about his access to the house through the walls; that explained his prior knowledge and a great many other things which puzzled me. Before I knew of the danger from the walls this man had learned all my plans. The only thing he doesn't know is where I put the jewels. He knows they are in the house, and his original plan was to wait until I showed you and Gordon the gems. It would probably have worked but for my last minute discovery of the passages."

He stopped, but there was something on his mind, something he had not broached and which frightened him. There was some deep purpose in the mind of the man outside, or he would not have allowed this meeting to take place.

"By then you and Gordon were on the way," said Barney. "Quite frankly I didn't feel that I could face any more of it on my own. I wanted above all things to see you and tell you about it. I wanted Gordon to know, also—he is probably the wealthiest man of my acquaintance, and he is still in business. The Alexis collection would be a profitable purchase for him. Well, you know more or less what happened then. The man here bided his time. The snow came, and that helped him. He wanted to search the house from top to bottom—"

"What had stopped him before?" asked Dawlish.

Barney smiled. "A little trick about which he now knows. I brought two men from London, and I had a third man here on whom I knew I could rely—Willing, the taxi-driver."

Dawlish stared: "Surely he's been here for years?"

"Yes, but once he used to work for me," said Barney. "He reformed and bought the business in Hurn. There are some people on whom one can always rely. Willing was one, Jane is another—and the two other men who came down here to act, in effect, as my bodyguard, were in the same category. I dressed one of them as a policeman. I thought it would successfully bluff my adversary, and it succeeded up to a point, although, of course, my 'policeman' had to be careful of showing himself out of doors. The man who wanted the jewels had a tough nut to crack, you see. He wanted above all things to get the house empty for a few hours. I was equally determined not to leave it.

Then he tricked me, quite simply. He knew you were coming, and he telephoned a message which deceived me—I thought you were in the village early yesterday afternoon. I went to meet you. One of my men was shot. The 'policeman' remained and was here when I got back. I knew I needed more help, and I dared not telephone because I knew the line was tapped, so I went to see Willing. I was there when you telephoned from Salisbury. Jane, rightly, said that I wanted you to come at all costs. I had no difficulty in getting Willing to come to Gillingham for you, of course; but while he was gone, three men appeared from the spare room wall-passage. Jane and I were forced to leave the house, and brought here."

"How?" asked Dawlish.

"That question is *not* allowed," said a voice from the door. "Don't repeat it, Dawlish."

Barney said: "Apparently my remaining man thought he heard a sound behind the wall of the main bedroom, and actually opened the panel—it can be opened from inside the room, you see, from a press-button in the fireplace. I was told that he was shot, and that you found him there. When Willing eventually got back, he knew what the emptiness of the house meant, and I have no doubt that he went back to his garage, pretending to be satisfied, actually to consider the situation. Probably he hoped I would turn up, and didn't want you to know the truth too soon. I believe you telephoned for him. Willing saw that it was a question of my life, and decided to advise you to bring Hamblin—that, at least, is how I understand the situation. On his way here he saw a light in the garage, went to investigate, and was attacked. Hamblin was on the way then, however, and his attackers also wanted to find out what was happening inside the cottage, so they left him." Barney paused again, and then went on: "You know what happened after that. I have been told of his murder. He was killed, of course, because he actually saw something through the garage window—the face of the man who was in the garage. The others also saw the man's face, and they were killed. Three people have been murdered because of their loyalty to me. You can imagine the horror with which I think about it." His hand was gripping his coat lapel tightly, and his voice was barely audible. "It is unbearable! I cannot think about it with equanimity. But—*they* have been murdered. I do not believe that they were killed *only* for the sake of the Alexis jewels. There is—"

"You forget yourself," said the man who had been standing outside. He came in, and looked at Barney; his eyes were not so bright now, and there was something ominous in their dullness. "Dawlish, you now know that I intend to get these jewels. I have been fortunate. The village is isolated from the rest of the country and the house is isolated from the village. You cannot get help. It will be much simpler if you advise Day to tell me where to find the jewels—much, much simpler."

"There is more to it now than jewels," said Dawlish.

"Don't be a fool! I—"

"Three dead men," said Dawlish. "Three to be avenged, their murderers to be caught and hanged by the neck until they are dead."

"They'll never catch me! And if they did, how would it help *you*, or your wife, or Day, or—"

"You're getting incoherent," said Dawlish.

Barney said: "Dawlish, if I thought we could make an end to the business by letting him have the jewels, I would tell him where to find them now. There is more behind it than that. I cannot believe that any man would make such a set at jewels, would kill so ruthlessly, would work with such—"

"I said enough!" cried the man with the mask. He leaned

forward and struck Day on the side of the face, a blow which resounded and sent Day gasping against the side of his chair. It was a moment of unbridled fury, when Dawlish saw more clearly than ever before the danger of the creature to whom he was opposed.

He saw something else.

In that single moment of unguarded passion the man had laid himself open to attack, and Dawlish moved before he recovered his balance, caught his arm above the elbow and twisted him round so that he stood, gasping, pressing against Dawlish's body, and facing the wall. It happened so quickly that it was hard to believe that the tables had been turned, that there was a chance of getting Barney and Jane free while this man remained a hostage.

No one moved for several seconds. Barney lay back in his chair, his cheek red and angry-looking against the pallor of the rest of his face. Dawlish strengthened his grip. His victim was breathing heavily, as if he also realized the sudden change of circumstances; but he would not accept it without a fight, and there were others in this cottage.

Dawlish moved his position, keeping the other close to him, so that he could not be shot at from the window. He was opposite the door; any shooting from there would endanger the man whose breathing now grew hoarser and whose limbs were tensed as if he were prepared to struggle.

"You'll get hurt," Dawlish said. "Barney, can you walk all right?"

"Yes." Barney got up.

"Go into the hall, fetch Jane, and go to the house," said Dawlish, quietly. "Let anyone else in the cottage know that if they shoot at me they will injure their own leader, and that if you or Jane are hurt I will break his neck." The calmness of the words made them sound convincing. To emphasize the threat he put his free hand on his victim's neck, making the man gasp as he pressed against the windpipe.

Barney said: "I will try it, but what about you?"

"I'll manage," said Dawlish. "Don't waste time."

"Stay there, Day!" The man gasped the words, the muscles of his throat moved against Dawlish's fingers. "Stay there! Dawlish, I have taken no chances, I can finish *you* whatever happens to me."

"Off you go, Barney," said Dawlish. "Let him burble on."

"I tell you—" began the man in Dawlish's grip.

"Let me tell you something," said Dawlish. "The police will never rest until they've solved the mystery of the triple murder and hanged the murderers. And that's enough of that!" he added sharply, for his victim tried to back-heel. Dawlish tightened his grip on his throat, making his shouted words end in a choking gurgle. Barney hesitated by the door, but at a glimpse of Dawlish's face he went out.

He called Jane; she joined him.

Dawlish called: "Is there a key in the lock of this door, Barney?"

"Yes," said Barney.

"Lock it, will you, and push the key under the door," said Dawlish. He waited until the key slid along the polished floorboards, and then heard the front door open. By craning his neck, he could see Barney and Jane going down the little path. He knew that the other men in this house had heard what he had said, and were afraid to act.

He had not the faintest notion of what to do next.

CHAPTER IX

MAN TO MAN

It was a relief to know that the door was locked.

When Barney and Jane disappeared from view, looking shrivelled up with the cold and their hair blowing in the wind, Dawlish relaxed his grip—and the man took advantage of it, trying to back his elbow into his attacker's chest. Dawlish struck him a chopping blow with the side of his palm on the back of the neck. The man uttered a single choking gurgle and fell forward. Dawlish bent over him, ran his hands through his pockets and found an automatic and a spare clip of ammunition. He transferred them to his own pocket, then stood back in the corner. He was out of the line of fire from window or door, and it would be impossible for anyone to open the door without making some noise.

"I think I'll have a look at you," he said.

"Dawlish, if you—"

Dawlish bent down, snatched the handkerchief away, and then backed towards a chair. The man sat up. His lean, olive-skinned face was twisted with a fury which was not pleasant to see. The malignance in his eyes would have frightened many people. In a severe way he was good-looking; his mouth was well-shaped and very red, his chin was good, pointed and clean-shaven. Dark hair grew far back from his forehead.

Dawlish said: "So all who look on you die, do they?"

The man said nothing; he seemed to be possessed with a rage which prevented him from speaking, perhaps because of the acuteness of his disappointment. Dawlish was lulled for a moment into a dangerous mood of confidence and satisfaction.

"No Barney Day, no Jane and no jewels," he said.

"I've got *you*."

"Now, come," said Dawlish. He covered the man with Gordon's automatic. "Take out your wallet."

"Dawlish, if you—"

"Take it out!"

He was not as brave as he tried to pretend; and he was obviously badly frightened, for without further protest he took out his wallet. He tossed it towards Dawlish, on instructions, but lost the opportunity of using it as a missile. It fell on Dawlish's lap. He kept the man on the floor covered, and opened it, extracting several papers and visiting cards. He took a swift glance at one of the cards, and read: *Carlos Hotelan*—there was no address.

Dawlish raised his eyebrows.

"A gentleman with Spanish antecedents, I see." He paused, then added: "With Falangist or Republican sympathies?"

Hortelan said: "Dawlish, if you knew what you have done, you wouldn't sit there and grin like that." He got stiffly to his feet, but did not approach Dawlish. "That is an assumed name. I am one hundred per cent English, do you understand? One hundred per cent English, and—"

"You protest too much," said Dawlish, "and your real name is probably Smith." He was amused by the man's sudden descent from grandiose superiority to almost cringing eagerness to make his lie convincing. He wondered if Barney knew that the man had Spanish blood; other thoughts also were passing through his mind. The dangerous mood of confidence was passing, and he began to wonder what the other occupants of the cottage were doing.

"Very good, Dawlish." Hortelan drew himself up to his full height in a futile effort to appear dignified. Something not far removed from terror had filled him when Dawlish had discovered his name; yet he carried the visiting cards for anyone to see. Perhaps he had been supremely confident of avoiding capture or being robbed. "You have taken great risks, and the consequences will be more serious than you realize."

"Aren't you singing a different tune?" asked Dawlish.

"I *call* the tune," said Hortelan.

"Ah, yes." What *were* the others doing? Dawlish wondered. Were men creeping round the side of the house in the hope of attacking him through the window? Were they working at the door so silently that he could not hear them? Were they preparing for a grand assault on the door, hoping to overcome him by a mixture of force and surprise? "You've called the tune too long," he said. "I think we'll all go to Barney's house."

"You cannot—"

"Oh, but I can take you," said Dawlish. "You've trained your men well, haven't you? Obedience to your slightest order; murder on your instructions. Yes, they're well trained—and I hope they remain well trained, for your sake. Tell them that we are going next door."

"I shall do nothing of the kind!"

Dawlish shrugged his shoulders.

"In that case—" he broke off, and pointed the automatic at Hortelan's chest.

He did not think there was a chance in a thousand of pulling it off. He knew that he could never bring himself to shoot the man hoping to cow the others who were unknown and unseen. He expected Hortelan to call his bluff, and then he would be back at the same starting-point, not knowing what to do to get away from the cottage alive. The more he thought of it the less he thought of his chances—and yet as he looked into Hortelan's eyes, with their dark brilliance and clear whites, he recognized the fear, so near to terror, which had been in the man's expression when his name had been divulged.

"Dawlish, listen to me! It is important that I should get the jewels from Day; it is *essential,* do you understand? I will pay him for them, I am authorized to pay him—one hundred thousand pounds!"

"Half of what he paid for them," said Dawlish.

"I do not wish for all the stones, only for a selection."

"Oh," said Dawlish, blankly.

"You also can make good profit," Hortelan urged. "A very high profit, Dawlish. Here is a great chance to help Day and to help yourself. Nothing will happen to him if he sells me the jewels, that I swear. Nothing will happen to you, I will not take revenge." When Dawlish did not answer he stepped forward with his hands outstretched. He was perspiring freely, and there was no doubt about his sincerity; he was afraid that he would die, and yet it was not only fear of death that moved him. There was something much greater.

"Dawlish, listen to me!" There was a sob in his voice. "I have been given a mission, a mission which I hold sacred. I can only fulfil it if I obtain part of the Alexis collection. That is the truth. Arrange for me to buy that, and there will be no trouble for any of you. All I shall require is your promise to allow me to go free with them, and then—it shall be forgotten!"

"I see," said Dawlish, sardonically. "How do you know what jewels Day has?"

"I know what is missing, I can identify each piece."

"You're very proficient," murmured Dawlish. "There are over two hundred pieces in the Alexis collection. And you will pay a hundred thousand pounds for what you want?"

"Yes!"

"What will you use for money?" murmured Dawlish.

"It can be quickly arranged. I have other valuable gems here with me, of at least that value, and will exchange them. This is a matter of business, you will not be such a fool as to reject it!"

"I'm rather out of my depth," said Dawlish. "How do you propose we go about it?"

"I will send a man to Day to tell him to come here with the jewels." Hortelan stared wildly into Dawlish's face, and then added urgently: "No, no, you do not trust me. Very well, then! *I* will trust you. I will come with you, alone, to Day's house. I will rely on your word that you will persuade Day to sell and will allow me to leave in peace, with the jewels." Some semblance of confidence was returning to this man who was at heart so astonishingly afraid. "Now that is a gentlemanly offer," he went on. "You accept, of course."

Dawlish said: "No, Hortelan, not altogether."

"Then—"

"You forget the three murdered men and the tricks you have played on Day," said Dawlish. "It can't be done as easily as that, but—you are in danger of losing your life while I remain here, and I am in danger of losing mine unless I get back to the house. That's right, isn't it?"

"Of course. I am glad you see *you* are also in danger."

"Because I want to save my skin," said Dawlish, "I will come to some kind of terms with you. Come with me to *Timbers*. If you do that, I will see that you are allowed to come back uninjured."

"But—"

"The position will be as it was, except that you haven't got Day and Jane," said Dawlish; "but, on the other hand, you will be alive. You may think that is an advantage."

"I cannot do it!" cried Hortelan.

"If you haven't agreed in five minutes, I shall shoot you and take my chance of getting away," said Dawlish offhandedly. "Isn't the chance worth your life?"

Hortelan turned away from him.

Dawlish was surprised by two things. When the man's face had been concealed by the handkerchief, he had been full of self-confidence, and had given the impression that he was a man of thirty-five or forty. Now he seemed very young. That was negligible compared with the fact that he was so terrified of failing to get the jewels, that he let himself be forced into making such an offer.

Nothing had seemed real to Dawlish since he had reached Hurn; this was a development which made everything else that had happened seem almost normal.

The man's face was working. In the heat of the argument his English had been more stilted than when he had had time to consider what he had to say. He was not English, but he had probably been educated at a good English school. He looked well-bred; and he did not give the impression that he was a coward; yet fear was there.

What had he meant by a mission?

Why did he want only certain gems?

"The five minutes are nearly up," said Dawlish.

"It is intolerable!" snapped Hortelan. "Only half an hour ago I was in a position—"

"From which over-confidence has moved you," said Dawlish. He stood up, decidedly. "What is it to be?" He pushed the automatic forward an inch or two. He was listening intently, thinking it possible that Hortelan had been talking to gain time and to put him off his guard, but the remarkable silence continued. There was a pause of less than thirty seconds before Hortelan raised his hands hopelessly.

"We will go," he said.

"Call instructions," said Dawlish.

"Every word we have said has been heard," said Hortelan, "there will be no danger."

"Call instructions," Dawlish repeated.

Hortelan shrugged impatiently, and called out quickly. They were to be allowed to leave the cottage and to go to *Timbers* without being molested. Three different voices answered from the passage. Dawlish stepped to the door and opened it, suspicious of a trick; in fact he was prepared to have to shoot his way out once he reached the passage. He sent Hortelan out in front of him and told him not to go more than a yard ahead.

The man obeyed him.

There were three men in the passage. Dawlish saw them grouped round a doorway a little way along. They stared at him without speaking, all olive-skinned, slim, dangerous-looking men.

They did not move as Hortelan opened the front door. A blast of icy wind swept in, making Dawlish shiver; Hortelan gasped. Side by side they walked down the steps, slithering on the frozen snow. Nothing happened to impede their progress. They reached the drive of *Timbers*. A tall man was standing behind the bushes, wrapped in a fur coat, with an airman's helmet on, the flaps covering his ears. What little Dawlish could see of his face was olive-skinned.

He came forward hurriedly and *spoke in Spanish.*

"I will return," Hortelan said. He brushed the man aside and walked with Dawlish along the drive. The door of the house was open, and Felicity and Gordon were standing on the porch. Hamblin, Jane and Barney were pressed against the front-room window, all staring in astonishment at the sight that met their eyes. Felicity came hurrying to meet them, and Dawlish gripped her arm.

"You'll freeze, my sweet!"

"Pat, what—"

"An armistice," said Dawlish. He hurried forward, ignoring Hortelan, half-expecting the man to turn and run for the gates, but Hortelan continued to plod on.

Gordon's bright eyes beamed.

"A triumph for Dawlish, my boy! Congratulations!"

"Not due yet," said Dawlish. Felicity stepped into the hall, Dawlish stood on the porch and looked at Hortelan curiously. "What are you going to do now?" he asked.

"I wish to discuss the matter," said Hortelan. "You have given me your word I shall not be forcibly detained."

"I'm not a policeman, and not able to speak for the police," said Dawlish. "Colonel Hamblin may reverse my decision."

"I do not think he will," said Hortelan. He seemed to have regained something of his confidence, and again Dawlish felt that he did not lack physical courage. They stepped into the hall, meeting Hamblin, who came forward slowly. Jane and Barney were behind him.

Dawlish said: "On condition that Hortelan gave me safe escort here, I undertook to allow him to return to the cottage." He looked at Hamblin. "I hope you—"

"You went as my representative," Hamblin said, stiffly.

As they stood in the hall, Hortelan and Hamblin were the cynosure of all eyes. Hamblin was making a palpable effort to regain his authority. It was a queer business altogether. He succeeded, up to a point, and there was cold hostility in his voice when he spoke.

"It is a temporary arrangement, and I shall leave nothing undone in the future to secure your arrest." The formality of the words sounded natural enough.

"I am not satisfied with a temporary arrangement," said Hortelan. "In this house are some jewels which I wish to buy. I offer one hundred thousand pounds for a selection of them, Day." When Barney and Hamblin seemed too astonished to reply, he went on fiercely: "There is no reason why I should not have them—they are yours to sell, Day. Why will you not sell them to me?" When Barney, obviously greatly relieved that Hortelan made no accusations of illegally held stones, did not reply, he went on: "It is a matter of supreme importance to me. I wish no one any harm, only to obtain the jewels. Immediately I have them, I will go. My men will cause no more trouble. I will guarantee that."

Hamblin said: "Are you sane? You have committed three murders, and—"

"If men have died, it is not my responsibility," said Hortelan. "It need not have been so, but for Day's stubbornness. Understand this, all of you! You cannot obtain help. The house is surrounded at every point. The telephone wires will be further damaged. It is unlikely that anyone will try to get here from the village, but if they do so, they will be stopped. I shall not leave this village until I have what I require. If necessary, I shall attack the house without warning. None of you will be safe."

Into the silence which followed his words, Dawlish said with a sigh:

"A village in England, in this year of grace!"

Hortelan swung round on him. "That makes no difference! I

am not interested in what is right or what is wrong. I want those jewels and I will not leave here without them!"

"My dear young man," interrupted Gordon, raising his hands in astonishment. "What talk, what talk! There is a popular saying, I believe—'come and get it'. Eh, Dawlish? Well, well! To think that in this country I should ever hear such words, ever see a man who adopts such an attitude. My, my! Be off with you, young man, be off with you! We are law-abiding people, yes, law-abiding, we shall not condone such an attitude. Be off, I say!"

"You do not understand—" began Hortelan.

Hamblin said in an icy voice: "Unless you have left this house in one minute from now, I will arrest you on a charge of murder. Do you understand me?"

Hortelan drew back. "You fools! You—" he turned to Felicity, stretched out his hands as if in supplication. "You, Mrs. Dawlish, you know the folly of this thing, you do not wish to see more bloodshed, to lose your husband, perhaps to lose your own life. You can influence them!"

Hamblin was looking at his watch. Felicity made no answer.

Hortelan drew in a sharp breath and turned away.

"It is a question of ethics, my dear boy," said Sol Gordon, twinkling at Dawlish. "Should we have allowed such a scoundrel to go? The Colonel was very forbearing, you naturally made a promise which was necessary in order to save your own life, but should we have let him go? I ask you that—tell me, my boy, what do you really think?"

"If the Colonel had held Hortelan, his men would have come at once," said Dawlish. "There was no choice."

"Of course there was no choice," said Hamblin, harshly. "I know my duty, thank you, Mr. Gordon." He lit a cigarette from the stub of another—he seemed to be smoking all the time—and added helplessly: "It is an incredible situation! We are only a few hundred yards from help! Can he isolate us?"

"He has done," said Dawlish, laconically. "Shooting on a large scale will attract the people in the village, but they are not likely to come armed to see what's wrong, and we don't want to attract them—it would be luring them to their deaths." He tried to speak lightly, but the general effect of Hortelan's manner, and the knowledge of at least four men prepared to do his bidding, weighed heavily upon him. "We must stay here until nightfall, and then one or two of us must try to get out, warn the villagers of what is happening, and organize an attack. What about the Home Guard, Colonel—are their arms still in the village?"

"Yes, in store."

"So it's only a question of getting through a few hundred yards," said Dawlish. "Hortelan will know the danger of nightfall, though, and he'll probably try to force a decision by this afternoon. We're fairly safe inside—or will be if we have the doors of the passage-rooms properly barricaded. We'll have to watch from the windows, and take it in turns to rest. We're all right for food, from what I saw in the store cupboard."

Barney said: "We could stay here for a month, if necessary, we have ample supplies of everything." There was a tinge of colour in his cheeks, but he still looked a sick man. "Jane will be able to look after the food and the housework, there is no need to worry about that."

"What a situation!" cried Gordon, flinging up his hands. "My, my, what a situation! It is like guerilla warfare, isn't it, Dawlish? My, my!"

Hamblin looked at him sourly.

"You are right, Dawlish. I will look for the best observation posts." He strode up the stairs, and Gordon beamed after him.

"What a man, what a man!" he said in a hoarse whisper. "Well, now, what shall we do, eh? Barney, my dear fellow, I am grieved to see you looking so ill, very grieved, I assure you. Still, we must face the situation, as the amiable Colonel agrees, we must see what can be done. The Colonel does not know that the jewels which are in the house are smuggled, does he? . . . No, I hardly thought he would. We must keep that from him, we must only talk of that among ourselves! Hortelan wishes to persuade you to give them up, of course, that is why he did not talk wildly about stolen jewels; he is a man of curious mentality, that one. Most curious—a grown man who is a boy. Where else have you met grown men who behave like boys, Dawlish? Boys who imagine they have the right to cause death and destruction? Answer me that, where else have you met them?"

"If you ask *me*," said Jane, in an unsteady voice, "he's like a ruddy Nazi, that's what he's like. I'd like to—"

"Don't you think you should be preparing lunch, Jane?" asked Barney, quietly.

"I suppose I should," she said, abruptly. "Yes, okay, Mr. Day."

"Like a Nazi," Felicity said. She turned towards the kitchen. "I can't let her stay there alone."

"Keep the outside door locked and watch the windows," said Dawlish. When she had gone, he looked at Barney and Gordon, half-smiling, half-serious. "It's the queerest position I've ever met, but while we can keep Hamblin satisfied we shall be all right among ourselves. We'd better get the dining-room door barricaded, and then go upstairs."

Barney was too weak to do anything to help shift the furniture from inside the room to the passage to block the door. He stood watching, and they talked *sotto voce*. When that job was done they went upstairs. Hamblin was on the landing. His face was very pale, and Dawlish had an idea that he had been fighting an inward battle. He gave the impression of a man relaxing after a great struggle.

"The landing window and that of the bathroom make the best observation posts," he said. "One on duty there all the time will protect us from a surprise attack from outside. We must get the doors of the two dangerous bedrooms blocked."

"We've fixed the dining-room," said Dawlish.

"Then lend me a hand up here, will you?"

It was nearly one o'clock before they had finished everything to their satisfaction. Barney volunteered to watch from the bathroom for the next hour, and Dawlish raised no objection, thinking that it would be better to let him take a share in the general work. Gordon volunteered for the post on the landing. Both of them, thought Dawlish, had manœuvred so that he and Hamblin should be left together for a while. Barney had put some cigarettes in the sitting-room, and Hamblin absent-mindedly filled his gold case. Felicity came in from the kitchen to say that lunch would be ready about two o'clock. She went back, and Hamblin sat on the arm of a chair looking at Dawlish intently.

"Well, Dawlish," he said.

"To-night should see an end of it," said Dawlish.

"I doubt whether you seriously think so. These men are ruthless. The maid was right when she talked of them as Nazis. They behave in exactly the same way, they have the same blind fanaticism. I have met some of the worst of the Gestapo; I know what they are like. I am not at all sure that we shall escape from this house alive, Dawlish."

Dawlish stared at him in amazement.

"I have been trying to get my own thoughts in order," Hamblin said. "When I first arrived here last night, I had no idea what was happening. I have a very good idea now. I thought it was a matter of straightforward robbery with violence. With Hortelan in command, it is nothing of the kind."

"You speak as if you know him," Dawlish said.

"Yes. I do." Hamblin threw his cigarette away half-smoked, but lit another before he went on. "Dawlish, you're no fool. You must have noticed that my behaviour has been, to put it generously, rather less than authoritative."

Dawlish said: "I'll put it bluntly: you strike me as a man who is badly scared."

"I am," said Hamblin. "Not long after I got here, when I went upstairs for some first-aid equipment, Hortelan spoke to me through the wall."

Dawlish stiffened. "Yes?"

"I recognized his voice. I know him as Horlan. He has been a visitor to my house on several occasions—paying court to my daughter." Hamblin obviously found it difficult to get the words out, and he went on as if each one was causing him pain. "Phyllis had no time for him, of course, but he was persistent, and as he had been introduced to me by a close friend, I could not very well refuse him the house. He told me last night that if I did anything to obstruct him he would murder my daughter."

Dawlish stood up abruptly.

"Yes, it is startling," said Hamblin, grimly. "It nearly turned my mind, Dawlish. I was in no doubt that he meant what he said. I cannot be sure that my attitude to him downstairs will not bring about the—" He broke off again, and flung his cigarette away. When his voice was steady, he went on: "I have been wrong to put her safety above the other considerations, of course, but you can understand why I was glad to allow you to act for me. I hope you will continue to do so, as far as you can—I will, of course, support you in every way possible."

"Yes," said Dawlish slowly. "How far away is your house?"

"Little more than a mile," said Hamblin; "but it is on the other side of the hills, there is less chance of getting there than of getting into the village. Several times I have thought of making an effort to break through again, but I don't see that it will serve any purpose. All the same, waiting until darkness comes is almost more than I can do." He thrust his hands into his pockets and looked out of the window. "I have always suspected that Horlan—or Hortelan—was here for some other purpose than trying to pay court to Phyllis. I have always observed the curious domineering trait in the man—he was never able to take 'no' for an answer, and no amount of hinting would make him see that he was unwelcome. Since last night I've realized what he is, of course—he may be Spanish by nationality, but I think he is a type which has been thrown up by the world war, a completely ruthless and unscrupulous adventurer, a modern brigand." He uttered a harsh laugh. "Odd talk by a Deputy Chief Constable, isn't it?"

"It's reasonable talk," said Dawlish, slowly. "There is more behind Hortelan than mere adventuring, I think, or he wouldn't specify what jewels he wants. Obviously the jewels have some bearing, some importance which we haven't been able to fathom yet. Probably we won't know what it is until the whole business is over." He began to fill his pipe, looking at the other man's profile, understanding with deep sympathy all that was going on in his mind, He needed no further explanation of the change in him; it was easy to see, too, that he was quite sure that his daughter's life was at stake. Barney and Jane were no longer hostages, but Hortelan had known what he was doing when he had given Dawlish safe conduct.

"How many people are at your house?" Dawlish asked.

"Phyllis and two maids," said Hamblin. "The menservants went to Salisbury yesterday afternoon, and didn't get back.

She has no protection, and of course she has no idea of the danger. We cannot see from here whether Hortelan sends men out towards the house. If it were not for the men on guard, of course, we could get there."

Dawlish interrupted: "If it's over the hill, how can he get there now, and how could we reach the house?"

"The real obstacle to getting to Shaftesbury lies beyond my house," said Hamblin. He hesitated, and then turned round, decidedly. "I think I shall have to try to get through. If only I had brought skis instead of snow-shoes last night!"

"What can you do if you do get through?" asked Dawlish.

"My telephone is probably in order. In any case, if I can reach the village I can raise the alarm. I can't stay here doing nothing!" he added harshly, and swung towards the door.

CHAPTER X

SORTIE

"Steady a moment!" Dawlish called.

He caught up with Hamblin in the hall, and rested a hand on his arm. Hamblin looked at him, haggard-faced.

"Don't impede me now, Dawlish, I must try."

"Yes, we'll try, but we'll reduce the odds all we can," said Dawlish. "While it was a question of waiting here, with every hour in our favour, that was one matter. The issue's widened now. There will be many advantages in trying to get out," he added. "Hortelan is probably convinced that we will wait until after dark, and hopes to make his big effort in the middle of the afternoon. We shall have the advantage of surprise. Another thing—I shall have twice your chance of getting through, because I can probably move twice as fast."

"I can't let you—"

"We'll form a committee and leave the decision to them," said Dawlish lightly.

He led the way upstairs, passing Gordon who was sitting by the landing window, huddled in blankets and smoking a fat cigar. Gordon winked. In the bathroom, Barney was sitting on the edge of the bath, from which he was able to see the garage, outhouses and all the grounds on that side of the house.

"Barney," said Dawlish, "which way do the windows of the attic room face?"

"South—the front of the house," said Barney.

"I could have told you that," said Hamblin.

"We should be able to see more from there," said Dawlish, "and make sure that no one by the gates can do any harm. We can't see them from the landing because of the bushes, but the bushes aren't very tall. One of us is going to try to get out," he added briefly, and explained enough for Barney to understand.

"I insist on going myself," said Hamblin.

"Committee!" Dawlish insisted. "Who has the better chance, Barney?"

"You have, of course, but—"

"No 'buts," said Dawlish. "Didn't you play cricket before the war?"

Barney stared. "You know I did, but—"

"A fig on these 'buts," said Dawlish, obviously delighted. "Have you brought all your gear down here?"

"It's in the attic room."

"Couldn't be better," said Dawlish. "With luck I should be able to wear your cricket boots, and they should have spikes— have they?"

"Almost new spikes, yes," said Barney. "H'm. They will help you to get a grip on the snow, and you should be all right in them, but there isn't more than a chance in ten that you will get through."

"Let's find out what we can see from the dormer windows before we talk about the odds," said Dawlish.

As they went up the little spiral staircase, their footsteps sounding loudly, he wondered what Felicity would think of this.

She was probably expecting him to make some effort to break out; she had been afraid of it when they had been together in the hall. Now there was no choice; the sortie had to be made, whatever the consequences.

It gave him an odd feeling of exhilaration.

He had been wrong to rely on a system of passive defence; he should have puzzled out a way of making the attempt before. Once he reached the village, dozens of men would be within call, and there would be little chance of Hortelan holding off a concerted attack. The risk would have been justified, with or without Phyllis Hamblin's danger.

Barney went to a cupboard for the cricket gear, while Dawlish gently opened one of the dormer windows. Snow held it at first, but it opened with a crack as the coating of ice broke. He pushed it back. Snow fell into the room, and an icy blast of wind blew in. He raised himself up until his head and shoulders were outside. It had stopped snowing, but the wind was blowing in wild gusts and snow was flying from some of the trees bent beneath its fury.

The bushes by the gate had lost some of their covering, and he could see the man still standing there, hidden as he thought, from the house. Dawlish looked in all directions. There was another man not far from the garage, but he could see no one else. There was no point in trying to make a roundabout journey of it across the fields; if he were to get through, it would have to be down the drive and along the road.

Another sight cheered him.

He could see the village clearly. In the High Street dozens of people were working, shovelling or brushing snow so as to make a path to the village shop. Another little army was working on a path towards a huddle of farm buildings. Nothing else was being done in Hurn but that, and it would keep the villagers busy for a long time. He had only to get past the gate and the cottage next door, and then up the steep bank of that dangerous dip, to give a warning and to outwit Hortelan.

He dropped back into the room and closed the window.

"Well?" asked Hamblin, abruptly.

"It's a pity we haven't a rifle," said Dawlish. "If we had, we could pick them off before we started."

Barney said: "I *have* a rifle."

"That's our salvation!" cried Dawlish.

"It's only a small bore," Barney said. He went back to the cupboard and brought the gun out, together with a small box of cartridges. Hamblin seized it eagerly.

"I can pick anyone off at a hundred yards with this," he said; "it's exactly what we want." There was more colour in his cheeks as he put the rifle to his shoulder. Something of his excitement had communicated itself to Barney.

Suddenly a small plaintive voice came from the stairs.

"Gentlemen, is it fair? I ask you, is it fair to leave me in suspense like this? Please, please, what are you doing?"

"Penalty for deserting one's post, seven days C.B.," said Dawlish gaily. "We'll be down in a few minutes, Sol." He picked up Barney's cricket boots, and his eyes brightened when he saw the long spikes. Barney was a man to whom cricket was almost a religion.

"Will they fit?" Hamblin asked.

"They'll be all right," said Dawlish. He put them under his arm. "Hamblin, get on a table beneath that window, and when I call up from downstairs, have a shot at the man behind the garage and the fellow at the drive. The drive first, I think. I'll call loudly enough for you to hear, don't worry about that."

"Look here, Dawlish, you ought to let me—"

"Nonsense!" said Dawlish, "this is my job."

He went downstairs, with Barney close behind him, and called out to Gordon, who was now standing by the landing window but looking towards the stairs. They went together to the window, and Dawlish briefly explained his plan of campaign. Gordon's eyes gleamed, but before Dawlish went downstairs he asked softly:

"Tell me, Dawlish, what will your wife think of this?"

"Not much," said Dawlish; "and she isn't going to know until I'm on my way."

"Please," said Gordon, "please be very careful, my dear boy. I do not wish to have to break bad news to her. What plan is in your mind?"

"Half the village is clearing the snow from the streets," said Dawlish. "Once I'm there, the worst will be over." He patted the fat man's shoulder reassuringly before he went downstairs. Sitting on a hall chair by the front door, he put on Barney's boots. They were on the tight side, but not impossible to wear. He stood up gingerly. The studs bit into the old wood of the floor. Barney brought his mackintosh and hat.

"No hat," said Dawlish. "Lend me a cloth cap."

Soon, Dawlish opened the front door.

"Shout up to Hamblin," said Dawlish.

He was afraid that if he himself shouted, Felicity would hear it in the kitchen, and come hurrying to see what he wanted. He heard Hamblin's faint reply. He stepped on to the porch, his boots crunching the snow, and cautiously took half a dozen steps forward. Only the man at the drive gates could see him; the one by the garage was so far hidden from sight.

The *crack* of the small bore sounded very loud.

Dawlish thought he heard a cry, but did not wait to make sure. He tucked his elbows into his side, the stick beneath one arm, and went forward. The surface of the snow held surprisingly well. He went in no more than ankle deep, and the spikes saved him from slipping. He thought he heard Felicity call out from behind him. He heard two more shots, but nothing else, for a gust of wind, coming from the direction of the house, nearly pitched him forward on his face. He recovered his balance and went on. Twice he stepped into soft snow, nearly knee deep. Each time he heard the report of a shot. The feeling of help-lessness, trapped by the snow and not daring to move quickly for fear of becoming deeply imbedded, was frightening: he felt himself perspiring at the neck and forehead despite the intense cold.

The cold helped him.

It froze the breath from his nostrils and made his cheeks and ears numb, but the hard crust which it gave to the snow enabled him to make fair progress. He drew out his automatic as he neared the gate, but when he reached it he saw that the man on guard was lying on his side; near his forehead was a red patch in the snow.

Men were shouting near the cottage.

The reports from Hamblin's gun were sharp; the deeper bark of revolvers sounded not far away from him, and he was afraid that they were aimed at him. Then he reached the front of the cottage, *and saw that the men were firing towards the house.* A swift glance over his shoulder revealed Sol Gordon, Barney, Jane and Felicity, all outside the house, between the kitchen and the garage. He knew that they were deliberately drawing the fire, making a false sortie there to prevent the others from realizing where the real danger lay.

His fear for Felicity merged with that for himself.

It astonished him that he could make such speed, but as he passed the cottage, still safe from shooting, the ground dipped and he pitched forward. He fell heavily, breaking through the surface. For a few seconds he lay there. Precious time was flying, but the fall and the hurrying had made him breathless.

He got up cautiously and looked towards the cottage. A man had reached the gate and was looking towards the victim on the snow. He did not appear to notice the trail which Dawlish had made, but went to his fellow.

Dawlish crept towards the side of the road.

The snow was deeper there, and the crust less thick, but he was out of sight from the cottage and the gates. In front of him was a sharp dip; the gradient there must have been one in four. He pushed his stick well into the snow on one side, and gripped the snow-laden branches of the hedge on the other. Thorns pierced his gloves, but his hands were so cold that he did not feel the pain.

He reached the bottom of the dip near the little bridge.

If that were destroyed, he realized there would be scant chance of getting a rescue party over; repairs would be impossible under fire. He put the thought aside, and was scoffing at his fears when he reached the other side, still without pursuit. The village telephones would be working soon, someone would surely get out to repair them. Once a message reached Shaftesbury, the main danger was over.

Getting up the hill on the other side was trebly difficult. But for that effort on the part of the people still at the house, he would not have got through, for he could only move a foot at a time, and always had to stand still before he could put the other foot forward. At the top of the hill the road turned to the right, and there the high bank would give him protection.

He was nearly there when he heard the deep roar of a revolver. He felt nothing and saw nothing. He could not hurry, but pressed on, his teeth clenched. The revolver was fired again. A bullet tore through his coat; he felt the drag of it. The corner was only a few feet away, but in the seconds he needed to get to it a dozen shots could be fired.

A bullet went over his head and shook the snow from the hedge. He held his breath, and then plunged forward. He was buried in snow, but he knew that he had succeeded in the most difficult part of his job. He crawled forward a few feet, and then straightened up; the man behind him was completely hidden by the hedge and bank.

He peered round it.

His assailant was still on the other side of the bridge, making heavy weather of it. Dawlish dodged back out of sight; now that he was on the straight he would be able to move twice as fast as the other. He wondered how long it would take him to reach the village. He could see another bend in the road, but the village itself was completely hidden by a copse of trees which grew close to the roadside.

He rounded the corner; there in front of him, not a hundred feet away, were half-a-dozen men carrying spades and long-handled brooms. They were walking towards him in single file, and he knew that they had been attracted by the shooting. They stopped as he came in sight, and he motioned to them to stay where they were.

He drew level with the first man, an oldish fellow muffled up in coats and scarves and wearing waders. A pair of bright, suspicious eyes were turned towards him.

Dawlish said: "I have just come from Colonel Hamblin. He is being held a prisoner at *Timbers* with several other people, and the place is surrounded by armed men. I am being followed by one of them."

A man said: "I knew there was summat up, Tom."

"The Colonel wants me to find Mr. Carter—once Lieutenant Carter of the Home Guard," Dawlish said. "Where is he?"

"Back at the farm," said the oldish man. He looked suspiciously at Dawlish, but one of the others had gone forward and called back from the corner. "There he is!" On his words a shot rang out, but the bullet went wide.

"This isn't a hoax," Dawlish said.

"All right, sir," said the oldish man. "Tom, take the gentleman to Sam Carter, *I'll* look after un." He nodded towards the unseen gunman. Dawlish hesitated, not liking to let them run the risk, but the oldish man grinned suddenly, and said: "We've exercised in the Home Guard in worse than this, don't worry, sir."

"I won't," promised Dawlish.

A few yards further along a path had been cleared in the middle of the road. There were one or two isolated cottages, completely cut off from the village, outside which men and women were working so that supplies could be got to them. None of them seemed interested in the interruption, and all continued working. Dawlish, with 'Tom' for company, made good progress towards the centre of the village. Now curious villagers were staring at him, and he heard many questions in low voices. His escort paid no heed to the others, but pressed on. Outside a corner garage was a sign with the name 'Willing'; just inside the open double doors Dawlish saw the taxi in which he had been travelling the night before.

"How far away is Carter?" he asked.

"Not far now, sir."

The farm was only two hundred yards from the garage. It was approached by a road cleared for a yard in the centre, and there were hoof marks in the swept snow. The fact that he was with these people, with dozens of men pressing round him, was a relief the greater because an hour before he had not thought it possible. He was recovering his breath, and pressed on eagerly.

A burly man in a mackintosh and waders was standing by

the door of a cow byre. Dawlish liked the look of his stolid but intelligent face.

"Sam, a gentleman to see you from the Colonel," said 'Tom'.

"The Colonel?" Carter echoed.

"Aye—wi a funny story, Sam, a mighty funny story."

The problem was how to tell the story convincingly without wasting words. As he started, Dawlish realized the difficulties and wished he had brought a note from Hamblin, to make sure that he was accepted without suspicion. It appeared, however, that the shooting had been heard at the farm, and Carter showed no surprise at his story. Half a dozen people who had followed Dawlish gaped as he talked of armed men besieging the house, and gasped when he talked of taking a message to Phyllis Hamblin.

Carter shifted from one foot to the other.

"Did you ever hear the like?" he asked the crowd at large; and then, just when Dawlish was beginning to think that the man was less intelligent then he looked, he began to give orders. "Tom, round up a dozen or so of the old Home Guard, will ye? Here's the key to the hut, get out two Lewis guns and two automatic rifles and what else we need. Send four men wi' one Lewis here, fast." He turned towards the farmhouse as 'Tom' hurried off. "We'll soon have they out of this," he said, "don't worry, sir. You'll like to rest while we get Miss Hamblin."

"I'm coming with you," said Dawlish.

They eyed each other for a while, then:

"Oh, aye," said Carter. He led the way into the house, which smelt warm and comfortable, and then into the huge kitchen. A stock-pot was simmering on an open fire, and a woman was bending over the sink, washing clothes. "Martha," said Carter, "find this gentleman a bowl of soup, will ye, while I go upstairs for a minute."

Martha obeyed quickly. She was a raddled old woman with a roguish eye, and he could see that questions were nearly bursting out of her, but she restrained her curiosity until Carter came down. He was carrying three Mills bombs, and from the bulges in his pocket, Dawlish thought that he had more of them.

"Sam, what's all this?" burst out the woman.

"A bit o' trouble," said Carter, equably; "don't you worry yourself, old woman."

She snorted, but turned back to the sink.

"The others won't be so long," Carter said, and turned his patient eyes towards the door. "You'll want some gum boots, and I'll take up some milk and bread. We'd better be moving, sir." He led the way again, talking as he went. "If the Colonel's right, and there's danger for Miss Phyllis, they'll maybe cut across country to get to his house."

"Can they, in this weather?"

"Aye," said Carter, "if they've a mind to, they'll follow the river. So will we," he added comfortably. "Don't worry, sir. Are ye sure ye won't stay here?"

"Quite sure, thanks," said Dawlish.

Entering the farm gates were four men, carrying the weapons Carter had specified. The sight of them, and the knowledge that the whole village was warned and at arms, was the most satisfying thing Dawlish had experienced for a long time. He felt inordinately cheerful as he followed them across a field which had been cleared enough for cattle to be brought in to the byre, and soon they reached the river. The snow from the hills had melted in the water, which was a high level, but although it flowed fast, there was a suspicious thickness on the surface.

"Come night, it'll be frozen over," said Carter. Heavily laden with a small milk churn and a basket of bread, he led the small procession.

He plunged into the river. The water came up to his knees, but like the rest of them he was wearing waders. He turned left, and they walked against the stream, stumbling from side to side but keeping their feet. The bed was stony, and occasionally Dawlish stubbed his toes against a boulder, but someone was always at his side to help him keep his balance. The stream narrowed as they got further up the hill, and then it cut across a piece of flat land. Beyond that, they reached its source, and had only a few yards to go to reach the summit of the hill.

"Now we'll see," said Carter.

Standing on the crest, Dawlish looked over a shallow, broad valley. Two or three houses were visible, and smoke was rising from the chimneys. Apart from that, nothing but the expanse of snow met his eyes.

"We're in good time," said Carter with satisfaction.

Dawlish realized by then that the man knew every inch of the country.

Carter led the way towards the leeward of the hill, where the snow was little more than a foot thick, and then went straight towards the largest of the three houses. It was no more than half a mile away. Soon they were in the grounds, walking through a copse where the snow was comparatively thin on the ground. Beyond the copse they came upon a flower garden, where the bushes and rose pergolas were clearly marked. Here, on the flat, the snow was two feet deep or more, but it was not impossible to get across, and soon they were knocking at a side door.

CHAPTER XI

RESPITE

As the little party stood outside the door, waiting for an answer, Carter gave instructions in a level voice, calling all the men by their Christian names. The four went off, singly, to various parts of the grounds, and Dawlish was relieved that Carter took nothing for granted.

He was on edge again; it seemed a long time before footsteps sounded in the room beyond.

A girl opened the door.

She was tall, not over-thin, and flushed as if she had been bending over a fire. Her eyes were bright, and she looked at Carter with obvious astonishment.

"Why, Sam, I didn't thnk anyone would get through to-day."

"Well, Miss Phyllis, here I am," said Carter. He kicked the snow off his waders, and stepped into a small scullery, putting down his load. "Are ye all right here?"

"Lucy has a filthy cold," said Phyllis Carter, "and Mrs. Mead is trying to clear a path to the coal-shed, we've only enough to last for an hour or two."

"I'll give her a hand," said Carter. "This is Mr. Dawlish,"

he went on, "wi' a message from your father, Miss Phyllis." Obviously he knew his way about, for he walked across the scullery through another door, and Dawlish heard him calling to someone who was out of sight. The girl looked puzzled as she led Dawlish along a wide passage and into a small room where a fire was blazing. There were small-bore and shot guns on the walls, one or two trophies of the hunt, a roll-top desk and some worn leather chairs. "We had the fire put in here," said Phyllis, "it's the best room to get warm." She indicated a chair.

"Thanks," said Dawlish.

He was faced with the same difficulty as he had met with Carter—how to explain a fantastic situation. But he liked the look of the girl. She had common sense, and she would not fly off into a panic. She was attractive without being beautiful; her fair hair was unruly, her full lips were like Hamblin's, and she had a good chin. The knitted woollen dress she wore clung to her figure; its dark green suited her.

"Is something wrong at Mr. Day's house?" she asked.

"Badly wrong," said Dawlish, "but I don't think there's any need for alarm now. It's a long story, and I'll keep it as short as I can. A party of men planned robbery on a large scale and hoped to cut the house off. I managed to get away for help. Your father, Mr. Day and several other people are there, under some pressure at the moment, but they'll be relieved very soon—if, in fact, they're not already relieved."

He ran his hand over his hair. The bare recital of the situation reduced it to reasonable plausibility. It was only then, as she looked at him incredulously, that it dawned on him that relief *was* imminent. The other rescue party should have reached the house by now.

"Well," said Phyllis, after a pause, "I certainly didn't expect *this*. Be frank, please. Is my father hurt?"

"He was quite all right when I left him," Dawlish assured her, "except for a scratch."

"Then why did you make the journey here?"

"A man you know as Horlan gave us cause for alarm," said Dawlish, lightly. "We wanted to make sure that you weren't molested here."

"*Horlan!* That—" she broke off, but her eyes were blazing. "He telegraphed me early this morning, wanted me to go to see him to-day! I thought he was crazy, but—"

"He probably is," said Dawlish. "You've known him for some time, I gather?"

"For some time too long," she said.

Dawlish concealed a smile, and went on: "You may be able to help the police by recalling anything he has said at any time about his reason for being here, but we needn't worry about that now. Will you come back with us, or shall we leave a couple of men to make sure you're all right?"

"I'll come," she said quickly, "but someone will have to stay. I can't leave Lucy and Mrs. Mead on their own." She lit a cigarette, staring at him incredulously. "It's still so hard to believe. How—how many men has he got?"

"Five or six," said Dawlish, cautiously.

"I knew there was something wrong with that man," said Phyllis. "I—" she broke off again, and looked alarmed. "You know we can't get out of the valley, don't you?"

"There are enough men in the valley to look after Hortelan," said Dawlish.

"I suppose so." She fingered her lips, then smiled absently and said: "I'll go and see Sam Carter. Will you wait here?"

Carter had lost no time clearing a path to the coal-shed. When Phyllis came back she told Dawlish that the farmer had gone to bring the men in, and to make sure that no one else was approaching. She took the whole thing with remarkable calm, almost with nonchalance. He asked her about the difficulties of getting out of the valley, and for the first time he was given a detailed story. Whenever there was a lot of snow, they were isolated from all the neighbouring towns—Shaftesbury, Salisbury and Tisbury, the last the smallest of the three. Sometimes it was only for a couple of days, but she had known them cut off from the rest of the country for a week or more. To illustrate her point, she showed him an ordnance map of the district. Beyond the grounds of Hamblin's house there was a steep descent into a narrow valley, then another range of hills; it was the same all the way round. He was completely convinced, for the first time, that they could not get help from outside except by air and that could only be summoned by telephone, which was out of the question at the moment, or by radio. It was just possible that someone had a private transmitter in the village or could assemble one to send out a rudimentary S.O.S.

There was a respite but no relief.

It worried him that he could not feel more optimistic. He estimated Hortelan's party at half-a-dozen strong, and one of them at least was out of commission. He was not convinced, all the same, that Hortelan was beaten yet. It should be a simple matter of hemming him and his party inside the cottage, and waiting for the thaw before rounding them up, but the man's curious confidence made it difficult to think that it would be as simple as that.

Carter came back. He had arranged for two middle-aged men to stay at the house; the others were to go back. By then, Phyllis was dressed for the journey, wearing a mackintosh over a Persian lamb coat, Wellingtons and a knitted hat pulled low over her ears. She seemed excited at the prospect. Carter seemed to have no anxiety about taking her, and she proved more sure-footed than Dawlish on the return journey to the village.

At every vantage-point, Carter scanned the countryside towards *Timbers*. No one moved against the white background. Hortelan appeared to have boasted of more than he could do. There was even a chance that by the time they reached the house he would have given up the game.

Men in the village soon disabused him.

The man who had fired at Dawlish had been caught, and was now in the village hall under guard. A small party of men had managed to get through to *Timbers*. Passing the cottage was dangerous; apparently Hortelan and his gang had withdrawn into it, and were by no means finished yet. From the windows, they were sniping at the men who now surrounded the cottage, and also at *Timbers*.

"It will be dark in an hour's time," Carter said. "We'll wait until then. I think, Mr. Dawlish, it'll be safer."

"Yes," said Dawlish. "Meanwhile, what can we do to get word outside?"

"Nothing," said Carter, bluntly.

"Is there a radio mechanic in the village?"

"There was," said Carter. "Willing. You say he's dead. He might have got a message through, but no one else in Hurn can, that I do know. What we do we'll have to do ourselves, Mr. Dawlish. Not that there's much need for fear," he added, reassuringly, "we outnumber the rogues by four or five to one, and we're better armed than they are. It's a good thing the Colonel didn't send back those arms right away!" He gave a slow smile, and led them into the huge, bare living-room, where Martha had laid high tea. The room grew dark. Oil lamps were lit, for the electricity supply to this part of the village had failed, although it still worked in others.

"We're in for more snow," Carter announced, suddenly. "We'll have a night of it, I reckon."

"I didn't know it ever snowed like this in the south," said Dawlish, chilled by the thought.

"Once every ten years or so we get a blizzard as bad as this," said Carter, "but this'll be worse than most if I'm right about to-night. Ten days is the longest we've been cut off. That reminds me," he added, "they'll be wanting flour and bread as well as milk at the house. I'll get it."

"Can we collect my luggage from Willing's garage?" Dawlish asked.

"No trouble in that," said Carter.

By the time darkness fell, a little after five o'clock, the snow was coming down fast. A party of men, seven strong, with an armed man at the head and the rear, made their way along the road which had been cleared as far as Barney Day's drive. Two or three guards were walking up and down, trying to get the cold out of their systems. Carter murmured something about two-hour duties, and mumbled to himself. With a further sense of unreality, Dawlish walked up the drive. There was no attempt to stop them. The curtains had been drawn at the windows of *Timbers*, only a little slit of light showed from the front door. As they reached the porch, however, the front door opened.

A torch shone out.

"No lights, please!" snapped Carter.

The crack of a shot from some way off was followed by a sharp sound as a bullet hit the wall. A second followed. They hurried into the hall, scattering snow all about them, and Dawlish saw Felicity standing by the wall, a torch in her hand.

"Do ye want us all shot?" demanded Carter severely.

"I'm sorry," said Felicity. "I—"

"My turn," said Dawlish. He stepped towards her, and felt the tense pressure of her hand on his. "Sorry about it, darling, but I dare not lose time."

"It's all right," she said, with a catch in her voice. "It's all right." She turned her face away from the curious gaze of Carter and his men, and added in a muffled voice: "You'll want something to eat?"

"We've just feasted," said Dawlish. "All well here."

"Sol was slightly hurt, but nothing to worry about, that's all. I made Barney go to bed. He had a sleeping draught, and he's been asleep for several hours. Everything else is much the same. Pat, is it over?"

"It's getting on," said Dawlish, "but we aren't quite through yet."

Hamblin, his face aglow, was talking to Phyllis and Carter. Suddenly he broke away from them, stepped to Dawlish and, without a word, wrung his hand. Dawlish smiled. Carter began to talk in a firmer voice. Now the villagers were here, they might as well take things into their own hands, and everyone at the house obviously needed sleep. If the Colonel would tell him the exact position—

Hamblin did so.

Soon Dawlish and Felicity were in a small bedroom, which Jane insisted they should have to themselves. The attic room was left for Hamblin and Gordon; others who wanted to rest or sleep were accommodated in the sitting-room. Dawlish felt a sense of anticlimax, and Felicity seemed tongue-tied. It was not reproach for what he had done; he knew she would understand why he had avoided seeing her before that desperate venture. He wondered if something had happened to depress her, beyond the general circumstances, and when they were in bed, with a subdued light between them on a small table, she said slowly:

"Pat, I'm afraid that Barney is going to die."

Her words and the tone in which she uttered them made him go cold with shock.

"Surely he—"

"He says that he's all right," said Felicity, "but he's been ill for so long, this damnable poison has destroyed something in him. He's nothing but skin and bone. I didn't say anything downstairs, I didn't want to start a general alarm, but—"

"Go on," he said, when she paused.

"Pat, Hortelan *isn't* finished. He must have known that this might happen, so what else will he do?"

"Aren't you changing the subject?" asked Dawlish.

"Yes and no. If we can't get out of the valley to fetch a doctor for Barney, we can't, and that—well, we'll have to do what we can. But can they poison *us?*"

"Now, come!" chided Dawlish.

She had put a new and ugly thought in his mind, all the same. Hortelan had had access to the house for some time; he could have tampered with any and everything in the larder. They had felt no ill-effects yet, but then it had been a slow process with Barney. Hortelan might, at the last moment, speed up the process. He took the idea seriously enough to go downstairs and tell Carter, who, more authoritative and in many ways more capable than Hamblin, immediately decided to send for supplies from the village at once, and to ban eating any of the stores apart from those which had been brought up that night. It was a relief to feel that they were in this man's hands. Carter looked on it as a job of work to be performed thoroughly and conscientiously; he would show no fireworks, but he could make no serious mistakes. Whether he was the right man to match his wits against Hortelan was a different matter, but as yet there was no immediate need for a battle of wits.

"And I'll see what I can do about a doctor," Carter said. "Dr.

Mordell is the nearest, out Tisbury way. I'll see what I can do, sir; you go and get some sleep and don't worry, we'll be all right now."

"Thanks," smiled Dawlish. "I'm certainly tired." Upstairs he said: "Carter doesn't think you're crazy."

"Now that I've got it off my mind, it seems absurd," said Felicity, "but I can't get the thought of Barney out of my head. He's aged twenty years in the last few months. Pat, does *he* know something more than he's told us?"

"Almost certainly," said Dawlish. "He couldn't tell me when Hortelan was listening, and he hasn't had a chance of speaking freely since. He knows why Hortelan wants the jewels, I think. The jewels," he added, swinging his feet to the floor and staring at her. She had a green chiffon scarf about her head, and had cleansed the make-up from her face; she wore a bed-jacket as well as pyjamas, and looked a little over-dressed but snug and warm. "Jewels," repeated Dawlish, softly. "Do you know, my sweet, this is the first time that it's really registered on my mind that we are sitting pretty on a very valuable cache of precious stones, their value almost incalculable, and that Barney hasn't yet told us where they are."

"I wonder if he's told Jane," asked Felicity. "They haven't really mattered until now, but—" she broke off, got out of bed and put on a dressing-gown. "I'll speak to Jane," she said, and hurried out.

She was soon back. All Jane said she knew was that the jewels were somewhere in the house. Barney had never told her where, but had always been confident that they could not be found.

Dawlish found it hard to be as confident, and yet Barney had nearly proved his point. Hortelan had been in the house more than once, but had failed to find them.

"I don't think that we've ever been in such a mess," Felicity said, when she was back in bed. "I wish we could call on Tim or some of the others," she added, wistfully.

"Yes," said Dawlish. "But we might as well wish for the moon."

'Tim and some of the others' had been in his mind more than once. All were close friends of Dawlish and some of them had worked with him in the same Department at Whitehall. Others had been with him when he had adventured without the approval of the police in pre-war days. All of them were reliable in every way, any one of them would have been invaluable at *Timbers*. That was the chief trouble—they could not be sure of anyone, not even of Gordon. Hamblin sometimes seemed hostile, Carter was undoubtedly reserving his opinion. Barney had misled them about the reason for the house-warming, and yet that was understandable. He had felt the need for help, and a man of Dawlish's reputation was exactly what he had needed—a man in whom he could confide, who knew the ropes, and who could, in an emergency, put a different complexion on the affair for the benefit of the police. It had out-run such possibilities as that, yet it was still necessary to try to save Barney.

He grew drowsy, but questions still passed through his mind. They merged into one, which was all-important; *why* did Hortelan want those particular gems?

He had talked about a mission—he had offered to buy but had murdered to try and steal them—he was prepared to go to fantastic lengths to get possession of them. True, a quarter of a million pounds was a prize worth any adventurer's time, but would any man risk so much for money. He might make an attempt, but against such odds as were now brought against him, would retire. He couldn't retire easily, of course, for it would be difficult for him to get away from the cottage—unless he made a retreat under cover of darkness.

They might wake up to find that the emergency was past.

Heavy footsteps sounded in the passages and up the stairs. Men talked in subdued tones, gradually lulling Dawlish to sleep. Felicity had been asleep some time before he dropped off. His last waking thought was that of all the people here, Carter and Sol Gordon were the most natural and the most likeable.

Dark grey clouds were scudding across the sky when he woke up. The wind was howling, making a hideous cacophony, but it had stopped snowing. Dawlish looked out of the window, and shivered at the bleak prospect. The paths were covered again; it would be some hours before anyone could get to *Timbers*. Probably the path between the house and the cottage was impassable again. There had been no alarm during the night, however, or he would have been called. Felicity looked at him sleepily, and drew the clothes up over her chin.

"Is it as cold as it smells?" she asked.

"Worse," said Dawlish. "I hope they got those supplies in before the snow came down."

On his words there came a tap at the door. Sol Gordon squeezed through the doorway, carrying a tea-tray. He was in his woolly dressing-gown, a little fluffy ball with a bright smile and mischievous eyes.

"Good morning, good morning!" he said, "a pot of the cup that cheers—is that what they say? No, no, Mrs. Dawlish, let me have the pleasure of pouring out for you." He poured out. "There! A beautiful cup of tea, brewed and poured by the same hands. Well, Patrick, my boy! Another dreary prospect. It has been snowing all night."

"Did they get the provisions?"

"Can you imagine them failing, under the eye of a martinet like Carter? Yes, yes, they got the provisions, and brought many other useful things—more cigarettes for the Colonel, for

instance. Well, what a business it all is, indeed, a most astonishing business, but we are all snug and warm and comfortable
up here, aren't we, without a care in the world!"

"Don't be silly," said Felicity.

Gordon roared with laughter. "You see, my boy, she tells me
off as if she were my own wife! All the world over they are the
same, these logical women! Well, then, what are our troubles?
Not Hortelan, I hope, we leave him to the admirable Carter. It is
a matter of action only, Carter will tell in a moment if they are
trying to get in by their secret way. He has already been talking
of finding that way and getting in to *them*. I did not discourage
this, I left that to you, if you think it wise. Other things, then?
Poor Barney, I am grieved about him, he is a very sick man and
there is no hope at all of a doctor to-day, no hope at all."

"Is that certain?" asked Dawlish.

"I am afraid so, my boy. You should see from the windows—
yesterday it was a bright spring morning compared with what it is
now! So we shall have to do our best, and I hope we shall succeed
in saving poor Barney. Well, then, what next? The jewels—don't
tell me you haven't been giving them a lot of thought."

"Some," said Dawlish.

"Some!" chortled Gordon. "You pull the wool over old Sol's
eyes—don't you believe it! Well, where are they? Jane does not
know. She is up, Hamblin is up, he has interviewed her. Barney
is still asleep—no, no, Mrs. Dawlish, do not alarm yourself!"
He patted Felicity's arm. "Jane has told me that it is usual for
him to sleep for a long time, twenty-four hours sometimes,
and then he comes round, always very weak. She is afraid to
wake him, and I should not like to take the chance; he looks as
if he is in a coma, the poor fellow. So, it is *our* responsibility,
Patrick!"

"What is?" asked Dawlish.

"What a joking man you are!" beamed Gordon. "The jewels, and where they are." He looked preternaturally solemn. "Imagine, now, if you please! A great fortune in jewels in this house, and many men—twelve besides ourselves, I have counted them—wandering at will. He who finds might keep. Honest men like you and I, Patrick, would not, but then—" he shook his head sadly, "would you trust *every* man as you would yourself?"

Dawlish laughed. "Sol, you're an incorrigible scoundrel! The answer is 'no'. I will not help you to find them and will not share the spoils when I do."

"My, my!" said Gordon. "What an honest man! But Patrick, you upset me, really you upset me. I am a friend of Barney's. The finding of them is a matter of importance for him. They are his. Now these other men may all be strictly law-abiding and not carried away by the sight of such jewels, but—the *police* might have heard of them. They were smuggled, Barney says. Well, my boy, you and I are old in the ways of the police, isn't that so? We would be fools to think that the police have not heard that they have reached this country. Hamblin might have read a description of them—oh, it is possible, do not shake your head as if I were a schoolboy, I am a grown man! Answer me, is it not possible?"

"It's possible," conceded Dawlish, slowly.

"Well, then, is our duty not clear? We must prevent the police from finding those jewels. If they do find them, Barney may not wish to recover, because he will go into jail. My, my, what friends we would be to allow that to happen, wouldn't we?"

"Are you sure Hamblin is looking for them?"

"Quite sure, but I do not think he will find them without help. Yet he is the authority and is feeling stronger now that he is supported by Carter and the others. He will try to question

Barney when he comes round. Now Barney will be in a weak condition, very weak, my boy, and perhaps he will tell at once. So, Patrick, it is up to us to make sure he tells *us* first. How are we going to make sure of that, eh? Answer me that, how?"

CHAPTER XII

CRISIS WITH BARNEY DAY

"One of us could be with him most of the time," said Dawlish, thoughtfully, "but we may not be there at the moment when he comes round."

Gordon looked at him, bright eyes rounded.

"Patrick, Patrick, what is the matter with you? I had always thought you were a man to whom a hint was enough, that just a little word to show the way my thoughts were running would bring light in your eyes and understanding to your mind. Has the snow affected you, my dear boy?"

Dawlish laughed.

"I don't know what we would have done here without you! Perhaps the snow has atrophied my mind, but I don't see what you're getting at this time."

"My, my!" mourned Gordon, darting a comical glance at Felicity, "what a mighty fall from a pedestal, never again will the great Patrick Dawlish be so great to old Sol Gordon, never again. Patrick, my boy!" He stepped forward, took Felicity's wrist and Dawlish's arm, drew them towards him. His voice fell to a whisper. "Listen now, both of you. Hamblin was an efficient

136

man, Hamblin lost his efficiency, Hamblin regained it. To-day he is a new man, I give you that assurance. The reason does not matter—"

"It's simple enough," said Dawlish, and explained.

"Well, well," said Gordon, grimacing. "It is a pity, after all, because I thought it was to do with his conscience; I always prefer to deal with a policeman who has an uneasy conscience, somehow it affects efficiency. Well, it makes our situation worse, and there is no point in denying that. You must *not* interrupt with questions, please; I have my own way of telling a story, let me do it my own way. Attend! There are jewels. I believe that Hamblin suspects that our dear friend Barney not always traded honestly. He might even suspect *me*. I do not believe that he suspects you, Patrick, and yet he may do. Well, then: he will expect, perhaps, that one of us will look for those jewels, and *we* will be watched. How, then, are we to make sure that we learn what we need to learn from Barney, and then get the jewels and so prevent the police from realizing that he has no real right to them?"

"But he has a right," objected Dawlish.

"Nonsense! They are smuggled. You might say that all he need do is to pay the duty on them, but I doubt very much whether they would allow that to pass with such a man as Barney. The police have been trying for forty years to catch him red-handed, poor fellow, and they would not lose an opportunity of bringing him into court on a charge of smuggling. They are not great-hearts, my boy, not great-hearts at all. Clear your mind of illusion. It is a difficult position, and a dangerous one for our good friend Barney Day."

"Why not leave the jewels where they are?" said Felicity. "They seem to be well hidden."

"Oh, please!" said Gordon, in great distress. "I have been at great pains to tell you that I think they will question him as soon as they know he has come round, and that in a weak state he might tell them. Have no doubts, Patrick, Barney is suspected, I am a marked man, and you—well, my boy, although you were recommended to Hamblin by Trivett, bless his heart, it is a strange fact that you are in the company of suspected rogues. We must remember that."

"You're really alarming me," said Felicity.

"I am sorry, my dear young lady, but there are the facts and they must be faced. Oh, I am not greatly worried *yet*. If the worst should happen we can always declare that Barney did not know the jewels were smuggled. It means a tussle, that is all, and we have the advantage of knowing that Hamblin and the admirable Carter are preoccupied with Hortelan. You see, all men, even bad men, have their uses! Be prepared, though, to be watched with great attentiveness when you go downstairs. I have warned you!" He patted Felicity's hand. "Don't worry, my dear, don't worry at all—when your husband and I put our heads together we shall find a way of evading this danger, so don't worry."

He padded out of the room.

"Is it as bad as he makes out?" asked Felicity.

"Probably," said Dawlish, judicially. "He's right in one way, too, the snow must have done something to me; I hadn't realized clearly how it might work out. I could only see as far as Hortelan."

"That isn't quite true," said Felicity.

He looked at her with a twisted smile, and then stroked the bridge of his broken nose. She was right. He had not let the other thoughts gain too firm a hold, but they were passing in and out of his mind all the time. Felicity had sensed them.

"What is worrying you?" asked Felicity.

"Guess," said Dawlish, and then went on before she had

a chance to try. "Hortelan isn't English. Someone's already mentioned the Nazi streak in him. Nazi or Fascist doesn't matter. He's Spanish. These jewels came from Spain." He paused, and then added with a less strained smile: "You see, thoughts all haphazard, vague ideas that flash to and fro, but—it's suspiciously like a job for Intelligence."

Felicity said nothing.

"That, above all things, means that we've got to see it through," said Dawlish, "even if we upset Hamblin and his men. I don't know that I'm right, but I think bigger things than we thought of are at stake. The question is—does Barney know? Did he send for me because I was attached to Intelligence? Does Gordon know the whole truth?" He paused, and then added with a harsh laugh: "We're doing well."

"Whatever is behind it, you can't do more than you are doing," said Felicity.

"Doing!" exclaimed Dawlish. "My sweet, I've never known a time when I seemed to do so little."

"You're doing plenty," said Felicity, confidently. "Supposing you knew more? Supposing there is work for the Intelligence, what could you do other than you have?" She paused, and then answered for him: "Nothing."

"Let's say you're right," said Dawlish.

"I *am* right." Felicity was almost serene in her confidence. "And at least there's something more to fight for, we aren't just saving—well, saving Barney's skin. Although," she added, contrarily, "I think I'd rather save Barney's than Hamblin's. I don't really like that man. And I don't like his daughter—she sits and reads, the lazy—"

"Hush!" said Dawlish, but he was frowning. "Odd, that a grown woman can just sit and read with all this going on about her."

"It's almost as if she knows she's all right," said Felicity.

After a while, Dawlish said: "We're probably fancying things. The sensible thing for Phyllis Hamblin to do is to keep out of the way as much as she can. I wonder how Barney is?"

"You can inquire," said Felicity, practically.

Dawlish nodded, and went across to Barney's room.

The door was unlocked, but he was conscious of a lengthy stare from a man on duty nearby. When he went in, he was startled by a whispered voice:

"Who is that?"

A man was sitting in an easy chair near Barney's bed. Dawlish recognized him as one of those who had gone with him and Carter to Hamblin's house. He was a middle-aged, comfortable-looking fellow, now very much on the alert, but he smiled more freely when he recognized Dawlish.

"Day nurse?" inquired Dawlish, brightly.

"A bit more than that, sir," said the man. "We're hoping that when he wakes up Mr. Day will be able to tell us more about the hidden passages and other odd things in the house. A few minutes might make a lot of difference, so we're having someone with him all the time."

"I see," said Dawlish. "I'll have to take my turn of duty." He stood at the foot of Barney's bed, looking hard at the man and appalled by the pallor of his face. Felicity was right; he looked sick unto death and hardly appeared to be breathing. The dark bags beneath his eyes had an exaggerated effect because of shadows cast by a bedside lamp. His lips were set tightly, as if even in his sleep he were in pain.

It was a drugged, not a natural sleep; so much was obvious.

"How long has he been like that?" asked Dawlish.

"All night, I think, sir."

Dawlish nodded and went out. He was preoccupied while he

bathed and shaved, after telling Felicity what he had seen. Her fears of the previous night came back, grew into a dread that Barney would not come round.

Downstairs, Jane was working in the kitchen with an oldish man acting as kitchen-maid. She was tight-lipped and sharp, her appearance sour, her voice an acid expression of her anxiety. She was even sharp with Dawlish, but apologized soon afterwards and asked with tears in her eyes whether it were really impossible to get a doctor.

"We won't lose a moment that we can help," said Dawlish.

There was something disquieting about the fact that men were stationed at every vantage point in the house. Last night they had given security and reassurance; this morning, after Gordon's warning, they seemed almost menacing, and Dawlish never felt free from their gaze.

It seemed, too, as if Carter and Hamblin were avoiding him.

After breakfast, he went with Felicity into the sitting-room. Hamblin and Carter were sitting at a small table which had been used as a desk. Hamblin looked up, nodded, and pointed to chairs.

"Sit down, won't you? We've had some luck, Dawlish." His tone and manner were crisp and decisive.

"In what way?" asked Dawlish, as Felicity dropped into an easy chair and pretended to be interested only in the fire.

"We've found the architect's plans of the reconstruction of *Timbers*," said Hamblin. "Carter is an amateur architect, and knows a little about plans. He says the indications are that there is a passage leading from the dining-room to the garage—below ground of course. The sewage drain is here—" he indicated a point with his pencil on the tracings of bluish paper in front of him, "and the electric cable here—"

"I thought the electricity supply was overhead," said Dawlish.

"It used to be, but underground cable was laid later, and

the overhead serves as an emergency. Then there is a well near the cable, and the ground slopes sharply there. Carter doesn't believe that they would have built the tunnel under sloping ground like that—they would have to go too deep to make it safe. Probably a ladder is used to enable them to get up to the passages on the first floor."

"What are you going to do?" asked Dawlish.

"Find that tunnel," said Carter, in his slow voice.

"Aggressive defence," murmured Dawlish.

"We're not on the defensive now—Hortelan is," said Carter, and Hamblin nodded.

"Of course, this is a police job," he said. "I've sworn-in all the men here as special constables, Dawlish, and you're relieved of any responsibility."

"Oh," said Dawlish. "Services no longer required."

"No, don't take it like that," said Hamblin. "You have done far more than your share already, and it's only right that we should take over."

"I suppose so," said Dawlish. He lit a cigarette and sat on the arm of a chair, looking out of the window. He had made Hamblin and Carter feel uncomfortable, and in spite of Hamblin's words it was clear that Gordon was only too right; they were prepared to be suspicious of him, this move was to make sure that he could not interfere with what they did. The change from the first day and night was startling; but for the possible consequences, he would have found a sardonic amusement in it.

"You do understand, don't you?" asked Hamblin.

"Yes," said Dawlish. "You're the boss, you know!" He smiled, freely enough. "Still, I hope I can voice opinions."

"Oh, yes! We'll welcome them!"

"Then don't try to get through to the cottage," said Dawlish. "Wait for Hortelan to attack, and keep on the defensive."

"I don't see why you say that?" said Carter.

"Hortelan knows exactly where we might get at him," said Dawlish; "and you can be sure of one thing—he is determined at all costs to get safely away. He is quite ruthless. There are such things as mines, you know."

"You don't seriously think he'll do anything like that!" exclaimed Hamblin.

"I do," said Dawlish.

"I don't hold with sitting tight and doing nothing," said Carter stubbornly.

"I can't say that I like it," said Dawlish; "but it seems to me that you'd be much wiser to get men outside, as soon as possible, to fling a cordon round the cottage and to prevent Hortelan and his men from getting away easily. That would be precaution number one, if I were in command." He smiled, and his voice was amiable. "Then I would sit back and wait for a message from Hortelan."

"You yourself imply that he will use force," said Carter.

"After he's presented his newest demands," said Dawlish. "Don't make any mistake about Hortelan. He thinks of himself as a being protected by the All Highest, and that nothing can go seriously wrong with anything he attempts. This set-back is quite unexpected, and he's already explained it away by now. He's full of bounce, and he may even send an emissary."

"I doubt it greatly," said Carter.

"Supposing he does, what would you do then?" asked Hamblin.

"Gain time," said Dawlish, promptly. "Promise an answer in an hour, or two hours, and meanwhile see whether anything can be done to raid the cottage itself."

"Surely it would be an advantage to raid the cottage both from below and outside," said Hamblin.

"It would, if it could be done safely," said Dawlish. "Of course, I may be raising an unnecessary scare."

Carter made it plain that he thought that was so.

One of the great disadvantages in the situation was that there was so little opportunity of getting away from the men in the house. Dawlish would have given a lot to get outside for half an hour, but it was impracticable. He raised the question once more of sending for medical help, was assured by Carter that not a moment would be lost, and then sat down in an easy chair in front of the fire for half an hour. Hamblin and Carter talked in undertones, but made no particular effort not to be overheard.

Suddenly Felicity stood up and went to the radio in a corner.

"We haven't had this on once," she said.

"Connection with the outside world," murmured Dawlish. "What time is there a news bulletin?" It was then nearly ten o'clock. "There's one on a regional station at ten, isn't there?" They got the right wave-length, heard a few minutes of light music, and then the formal voice of the announcer.

"Hallo, we're started!" murmured Dawlish.

"The great blizzard which raged over most of Southern England and the Midlands during the night has caused great dislocation of traffic. At London termini it was learned this morning that some trains are already more than twenty-four hours overdue, and there is little prospect of their arrival until the weather moderates. Fresh falls of snow were reported from most districts during the night, and the temperature in parts of Southern England has fallen to some degrees below zero, the coldest known there for over fifty years. Wiltshire and Dorset appeared to be most affected, and many small towns, villages and hamlets are completely cut off. Two Cabinet Ministers are among the people held up in the isolated areas."

"High Company! Do we want any more?" asked Dawlish.

"Yes, leave it on," said Felicity.

Most of the bulletin concerned the blizzard. There was cold comfort in the knowledge that it was widespread and sufficiently serious to take up that much of the news; the fear that Hurn might be cut off for ten days or more was strengthened. Restlessly, Dawlish got up and went to the window.

He stiffened. "I think—" he began, and then broke off. Carter and Hamblin, attracted by the tone of his voice, joined him.

Two men were walking up the drive, which had been cleared in the middle, making progress fairly easy. One of them was a villager; Dawlish thought that the other was one of Hortelan's men. As they drew nearer, he felt sure, and Carter turned and looked at him in some astonishment.

"Did you *know*?" he demanded.

Dawlish smiled. "Envoys under a white flag aren't exactly new departures," he said. "Am I in this?"

"Yes, please stay," said Hamblin.

Carter went outside. There was a mutter of voices in the hall, and then the door opened and Carter led the envoy in. He was a tall, olive-skinned individual, with a supercilious expression, and he gave Dawlish the same impression as Hortelan had done—that he felt that he was under the protection of some divine right.

He saluted, and clicked his heels.

"You are Colonel Hamblin?" He looked at Hamblin coldly. Hamblin nodded.

"I have brought terms," said the man, and drew a sealed envelope from his pocket. "I am instructed to tell you what they are and to leave this copy with you. You will withdraw from this house within two hours—by noon precisely. That applies to *all* the people here except Day and his maid. *All*, please understand. You will withdraw men from the gates and the roads and allow us freedom of action and of movement. There are no other terms."

Hamblin began to turn red.

"What the devil—" he began, but checked himself, then said harshly: "They are rejected."

"Otherwise," said the envoy, with remarkable nonchalance, "*Timbers* will be destroyed. It is already mined."

Carter shot a startled glance at Dawlish. Hamblin's eyebrows met together, and he looked as if he could strike the man—but there was something more in his expression, a fear that this man was not making idle threats. The silence which followed was tense. Clearly the envoy did not seriously anticipate further refusal; it was beyond his understanding that the men who were at *Timbers* would defy such threats.

"No *Timbers*—no Alexis collection," murmured Dawlish.

The envoy swung round on him.

"They will be found! It is understood that they are not in the house!"

"I wouldn't like to chance it myself," said Dawlish, "but have it your own way. Without butting in, I suggest we promise Hortelan an answer by a quarter to twelve," he said.

"The answer must be given *now*!"

"Oh," said Dawlish. He looked at Hamblin, whose hands were clenched by his side, and Carter, who seemed stupefied by the extent of the threat.

Hamblin spoke in a low-pitched voice.

"I will send an answer at quarter to twelve, and not earlier. That is all."

"I tell you—"

"Utter another word, and I will detain you!" snapped Hamblin, while Dawlish silently applauded.

The envoy looked as if he would make a further protest, turned to stare malignantly at Dawlish, and then stalked to the door. It closed with a bang. There were more voices outside, and then they watched the man returning down the drive under escort. Dawlish lit another cigarette and broke the tense silence which followed.

"Thanks," he said. "At least we've gained time."

"They'll never do it!" said Carter.

"I wouldn't like to bank on that," said Dawlish.

"Then what are we to do?"

"If we're really helpless we'll have to go," said Dawlish. "You've heard from the radio what our chances of getting outside help are. We can't be here and outside too. We can surround the place at a distance, as we've plenty of men and arms, and hope that we can cut them off when at least they try to get away. They'll go by night, of course, but we could organize a series of beacons, or man-handle all the cars in the village to the vantage points and keep the headlamps on after dark. We need something like that, anyhow. The chances are that if we stay here we shall be blown to little pieces, and I don't like the thought—do you?"

"But this is *Eng*land!" cried Hamblin.

"Unfortunately Hortelan isn't English," said Dawlish, dryly. "Taken by and large, you'll agree that it's better to live and to have a chance of stopping him later, than die and be finished with the whole business."

Carter said, with slow heat:

"Mr. Dawlish, do you *want* this man to succeed?"

Dawlish looked at him levelly. The countryman's eyes were clear and candid, but after a few seconds he flushed and turned away. Felicity, getting up from her chair, stepped across the room and looked at the others with a scorn which delighted Dawlish. Carter seemed to be getting more and more embarrassed.

"Of course he wants Hortelan to win," Felicity said. "That is why he came to the village, risking—" She broke off, abruptly, and swung round. "I should let them do as they like, Pat; but if it's necessary, *we're* going."

Carter said: "I'm sorry, Mr. Dawlish. Just for a moment I couldn't understand how you guessed what they would be up to."

"Forget it," smiled Dawlish. "There are limited ways and means, you know. It isn't likely that they know exactly how many men we have here, so two or three could stay behind. We can't leave Day in their hands without giving him a fighting chance—even if he's got that now," he added.

"Ah!" said Carter. "*That's* an idea, Mr. Dawlish!"

"You'll want volunteers," Dawlish said. "The Colonel and I can't stay, because they'll know us. Miss Hamblin, my wife and Gordon can't stay—we're all too easily identified. Whoever stay must be men who came here by dark and haven't shown themselves outside. I—"

He was interrupted abruptly. The door opened and a man hurried in, wide-eyed with alarm, breathing heavily. He was without a hat or coat, and as Dawlish stared at him his heart missed a beat.

The man gasped: "Colonel, Day is in a fit, he's shouting and raving; Tomkins is trying to hold him down, but—"

Dawlish was out of the room before the sentence was finished. He took the stairs three at a time and ran to Barney's room, hearing the sound of a struggle, afraid of the possible consequences of this attack.

An oldish man was trying to stop Barney from getting out of bed. Barney's eyes were wide open and staring, glassy bright. His lips were turned back over his teeth, he was gasping for breath and striving to throw off the restraining arms. The bedclothes were in a heap on the floor, a table was on its side and a water-jug broken.

Dawlish said: "Leave him to me."

The man released his hold.

Barney seemed taken by surprise, and failed to take advantage of it. Dawlish put an arm about his shoulders and gripped his wrists with his other hand. Barney struggled again, butting at his chin, but Dawlish tightened his grip and spoke quietly:

"It's all right, Barney, you're with friends. It's all right, no one will harm you." He spoke close to Barney's ear as he fought against the man's convulsive efforts to break free. He felt quite sure that Barney could not see the others who streamed into the room, he did not think that Barney would recognize him, and he could only hope to quieten him by unyielding pressure and the constant, soothing words. He talked as he would to a feverish child.

Felicity came and stood by the bed, while Barney shouted incoherent, unintelligible things, and half a dozen men, Hamblin and Carter among them, stood helplessly by.

CHAPTER XIII

ULTIMATUM EXPIRES

"Steady, Barney!" murmured Dawlish, "there's nothing to worry about now, you know. You're quite safe. So is Jane, so is Felicity, even old Sol Gordon, he's here with us and as ebullient as ever!" The words seemed inconsequent, but they had some effect, for Barney quietened a little; Dawlish gently laid him back on the pillows. His eyes were still glaring, but his lips were normal.

Then there was a disturbance outside. One or two men's voices were raised in mild protest. A man nearly fell into the room as Jane pushed her way in, approached Barney, and held out her hands towards him. She was ashen pale.

"He's better now," Dawlish said.

"Better!" The word nearly choked her. "They'll kill him before they've finished with him; they'll kill him!"

Barney held out his hands towards her, as if he recognized her voice and in some queer way wanted to comfort her. They gripped hands. Dawlish nodded his head towards the door, and all but Felicity and Hamblin went out. Gordon sent Dawlish a warning glance, as if to make sure that he remained alive to the dangerous possibilities, before he tiptoed out.

The door closed.

"Has he ever had an attack like this before?" asked Dawlish.

"Twice," said Jane. "The devils! When are you going to kill them? When are you going to stop them torturing him like this?" Her voice, pitched low, was fierce; she spoke to Dawlish as if putting all the responsibility on him. "He thought you could save him, that's why he wanted you to come. You mustn't let him down, you mustn't." When Dawlish did not reply immediately, she repeated in a louder voice: "You mustn't let him down!"

"I will do everything I can," Dawlish said, quietly. "Don't make things worse by getting hysterical, Jane."

"I'm not hysterical!"

Dawlish plunged off at a tangent.

"Isn't there any way in which you can help us? Don't you know the underground way from the house to the cottage?"

"No, I didn't know there was one until now." She was breathing heavily, as if afraid that in the extremity of her fear for Barney she had gone too far. "I'm sorry, I wish I could help. He knows something, he found something out, they don't only want the jewels. They'll let him live until they find them, that's all, and then they'll kill him, unless you do something."

It was Felicity who soothed her.

When Barney's paroxysm had spent itself and he lay back, exhausted, deep breaths making his whole body shudder, Felicity took the maid out, leaving the men together. Carter came back to the room.

"I wonder if she's right?" Hamblin asked.

"What about?" asked Carter.

Hamblin told him. Carter now seemed out of his depth, and they did not speak again, but looked at Dawlish as if waiting for him to give a lead. He was staring at the sick man's face, and coming to a conclusion with which he believed the others would agree, but which might cause disaster.

"We can't leave him or Jane here," he said. "The probability is that they'll give him a stimulant to bring him round for a little while, get what they want from him, and then kill him. We must make sure that he has a fighting chance." He lit a cigarette, and got up from the bed. "We'll have to carry him out, dressed in the clothes of one of the other men. As for Jane—"

He paused, and Hamblin said: "They'll know in a moment if she goes out with the crowd; we can't hide the fact that she's a woman."

"No," said Dawlish. "How long have we left?"

"A little more than an hour."

"Stay here with him, will you?" said Dawlish.

He did not think there was any likelihood of Barney coming round for a long time, except with the help of an artificial stimulant, and he had no idea what to give him. He waited outside the door for a few seconds, watched by curious men, and when he moved towards the stairs one of them said:

"Your wife and Mr. Gordon are in your room, sir."

"Thanks," said Dawlish.

He went in to them. Felicity was standing by the window, motionless, her head raised; outlined against the frosty glass, she looked so lovely that Dawlish stopped for a moment, and silently stared at her. She turned and smiled, her whole face lighting up. Sol Gordon, from the depths of an easy chair, puffed out cigar smoke, and for once did not cast a roguish glance upon them.

"What are you going to do?" asked Felicity.

"Accept the ultimatum up to a point," said Dawlish. "We can't do otherwise. We can take a risk with one or two, but not with the whole crowd. Barney mustn't stay, but a woman must." He looked at her steadily. "I must, too."

"I *shall*," said Gordon.

Dawlish looked down at him. "I don't see how you can help, Sol. There's no need to alter the terms of the ultimatum too greatly, but—"

"I insist on staying," said Gordon. "That is that and all about it." He paused. "Hamblin will also want to stay."

"Unless I'm greatly mistaken, Hortelan is more afraid of the police than he pretends, and would much rather deal with us than with Hamblin and Carter," said Dawlish. "We must make Hamblin go. I think we can manage it. The thing is—" He broke off, looking at Felicity.

"How can you help?" she asked, levelly.

"I don't quite know," said Dawlish. "I do know this. Much more than we yet realize is at stake, and I won't be justified in not trying to work it out. That is putting aside the danger which we know threatens Barney."

"Yes," said Gordon. "Yes, you are right, Patrick."

"Jane can take my clothes," Felicity said. She smiled humourlessly. "They'll be deceived by the mink, that's certain! That's what you want, Pat, isn't it?"

Dawlish said: "It's what I think will be best. Hortelan believes that Barney and Jane could say or do something which would be fatal for him, that is why he has stipulated that they should stay here. We know nothing, and are therefore in less danger. We won't be entirely defenceless, anyhow. Hortelan won't necessarily kill for the sake of killing, but is more likely to want to use us as hostages, to get his own way with the police. I don't think there is any immediate risk for us, and when they're outside, Carter and Hamblin can organize a really powerful cordon to make sure that there is no escape from either place. If we gain a few hours for them to do it, we won't have failed entirely. We might even save days."

"Yes," said Gordon. "Good, Patrick! The danger for your wife is undoubtedly less than that for Jane, poor child. How awful she looked when she came up the stairs, as ill as Barney himself, I thought."

"She's shared the tension and the torment," Dawlish said. "Well, are we agreed?"

"Will Hamblin and Carter *let* us stay?" asked Gordon.

"I'll go and see them," said Dawlish.

As he went downstairs there seemed to be a heavy weight pressing on his chest. Was he justified in letting Felicity take this risk? That she would in any case prefer to be with him needed no saying, but if he insisted on her going she would not stand out against him. Was it right to release Jane and let Felicity stay? He had encouraged her to make the offer, influenced at the moment by what he thought was right, but now he was tormented by doubts. Was it really certain that Jane's danger here would be greater than Felicity's? She had maintained that Barney had told her nothing, and Hortelan probably knew that.

Hamblin and Carter were conferring with other men in the hall. They broke off at sight of Dawlish's set face, and led the way into the sitting-room, which had become headquarters. The fire had burned low and the room struck cold. Dawlish threw on some logs.

"I am staying in Day's place," he said abruptly, "and my wife in the maid's. Gordon insists on staying because he is a close friend of Day's. We could make him go, but I think we should let him stay. We can send word to Hortelan that I shall be here with Gordon. You and Carter ought to go, I think, and leave two of your men here to hide, if you think it's wise."

"I—" began Hamblin.

"I must stay!" said Carter.

Dawlish gave a tight-lipped smile.

"I know we all feel very heroic," he said, "and I'm at one with you about that, but some things are too obvious to need emphasis. Hortelan wants two things—to keep Day and to get rid of you as the official representatives of the police. We can deceive him on one count, but not two. If we try to do more than I've suggested, we shall fail altogether. If Hortelan thinks that you are here, Hamblin, then he will probably try to prevent anyone getting away. The only way to the village is past his cottage, which means that the whole party will be under fire if he chooses to give the word."

There was a long, tense silence after he had finished. It was some time before Hamblin agreed, and Carter, looking oddly at Dawlish, muttered his agreement.

Hamblin led the way out, Carter brought up the rear. Between them were, in all, eleven men and two women—Jane and Phyllis. The forces in the house were larger than Dawlish had realized. Two men remained; they were in the kitchen, and planned to hide in the attic room as soon as the last of the party was safely away from the cottage. Until then, they remained at the windows and doors, to start shooting if an attack were launched.

One man left the party opposite the cottage, and was admitted. He carried the terms of acceptance, saying that Dawlish was to stay. Walking slowly, muffled up in the mink coat, Jane passed without attracting any comment. She had said little when they had told her what was decided, was apparently interested only in Barney. He was carried between two men, muffled up so that it was impossible to recognize him from a distance. There was a danger that Hortelan would suspect that he was Barney, but there was no indication that he did so.

The messenger came away from the cottage.

The party passed on the way to the village, crossed the little bridge, and was lost to sight.

Dawlish and Felicity, standing by the sitting-room window, saw them go. They had their arms linked together. Gordon was sitting in front of the fire, and kept muttering:

"Don't be morbid, now; don't be morbid."

"They've gone," Dawlish said. "I—"

His words were cut short; he caught a glimpse of a great upheaval on the road near the bridge. First snow, then smoke and flame leapt upwards, and fast upon it the boom of an explosion reached their ears and made the doors and windows shake. It had not died away before there came another roar even louder. Smoke billowed up, blotting out the road; debris was falling, gaunt black objects against the distant whiteness, then lost against the smoke.

Gordon bounded out of his chair.

"It's all right," said Dawlish, with a twisted smile. "They've blown the bridge. Hortelan kept his word, he let them get across."

"We're *more* isolated!" exclaimed Gordon. "Oh my, oh my!"

"We should have expected it," said Dawlish. "Well, we'd better get busy before the visitors come!" He went out into the hall, and met the men from the kitchen. "You know what you're to do," he said. "Stay in the attic until there seems any emergency or one of us comes for you, and have the guns and ammunition ready. Carter left some bombs, I hope?"

"All ready upstairs, sir," said one of the men.

He was the 'Tom' who had led Dawlish to Carter's farm-house. A short, wiry, live-faced man, with bright eyes and a slow, drawling voice, whom Carter had said was the best man he had known in the Home Guard in an awkward situation. His fellow was tall and well-built, a shrewd-looking man who did not seem to know what fear meant. Carter had told them exactly what they were to do. The attic had been chosen because there was a large built-in cupboard there, in which they could hide, if there were a cursory search of the room. Hortelan would suspect some such move, Dawlish thought; the main job was to outwit him. In real emergency, Tom and his companion—who was addressed as 'Les'—could get out of the dormer windows and, during the emergency, stay on the roof. It was unlikely that the house would be watched from the outside while it was being searched.

"Well, here we are," said Gordon, when Dawlish rejoined him and Felicity. "Goats for the sacrificial altar, eh, Patrick! No, no, I am not serious, I think we shall have a chance of beating that creature, I do really. *Bluff,* Patrick. I have been thinking about the reason for his obstinacy."

"I don't suppose anyone else thought of doing that," murmured Dawlish.

He was staring towards the cottage, wondering why there was as yet no sign from Hortelan. The grounds were deserted. All they could see was the trail which the party had made on the snow and, farther along, the dark mass where the bridge had been blown up. The water was already above the level of the road, making a lake which grew visibly larger. The stream was more like a torrent now and quite impassable. He wished he had thought of the probability that they would blow up the bridge before; it made him uneasy about what next trick they might attempt.

"No, Patrick, no sarcasm at this stage!" protested Gordon. "We know they are like Nazis. We know they are Spanish. *I* know that the Alexis collection was smuggled from Spain. What a relief to be able to speak freely."

"Are you sure?" said Dawlish, sharply.

"Oh, quite sure, my boy, quite sure! I am not a politician, but I am not blind and I read the newspapers, and I know that things are not all well in Spain. I know that two or three different parties are trying to gain power; wasted efforts, perhaps, because they will surely have a people's Government again, but that does not matter, it does not matter a bit. This is *political,* my boy. So, with Hortelan, perhaps we shall pretend to know more than we do—"

Dawlish rested a hand on his curly hair.

"Wake up, Sol!"

"Now what is there wrong in that," demanded Gordon, indignantly. "Don't you agree, Mrs. Dawlish?"

"I hope not," said Dawlish. "We're banking on our chances of escaping without too much trouble because we know nothing. If we start pretending to know a lot, off go our beads!" He laughed at Gordon's expression. "You can't be right all the time, you know!"

"Oh, my, oh, my!" cried Gordon, mournfully. "I—"

"They're coming!" cried Felicity.

Four men had appeared from the cottage, and were soon at the foot of the drive. One was Hortelan. They walked slowly, in single file, and they all carried weapons, as if they fully expected an attack. The snow on either side of the drive would be cover enough for them, and they were running no great risk after the first shots. It flashed through Dawlish's mind that it might have been wise to have tried to shoot them up, but the idea went almost as soon as it was conceived.

"Let's welcome them," he said.

He stood by the open door, with Felicity, now in Jane's heavy winter coat, and Gordon wrapped up like a little ball. Hortelan walked more boldly. At the same time, men appeared from the side of the house and from the cottage, and out of the corner of his eye Dawlish saw another man come from the other side of the house. They were closing in with great caution, but now they appeared satisfied that there would be no direct attack.

Hortelan took the lead.

"Greetings!" called Dawlish, and raised a hand as if in welcome. Hortelan ignored the frivolity. Dawlish stepped back, and soon the others were in the hall, holding their guns. Dawlish kept his right hand in his pocket; Gordon followed suit.

Hortelan looked at Felicity, and said:

"I understood that only you would remain, Dawlish."

"My wife and I count as one," said Dawlish, mildly. "We have one or two other shocks for you, Hortelan, and you may as well know that at once. Day and Jane have gone."

Hortelan stared at him: Dawlish tightened his grip on his gun—and was then astonished at the smile which curved Hortelan's lips. It made him look remarkably handsome; in this mood he seemed much more mature and capable.

"How remarkable, Dawlish! Having made a point that they should be allowed to stay, I hardly expected to find them here! You are surprised, are you?" He put his gun into his pocket, and laughed. "I shall have many surprises for you, I expect. Barney Day will not live out this day."

Dawlish said: "You mean—"

"He was poisoned before he left the cottage," said Hortelan carelessly. "A slow-acting poison—he has already had fits, perhaps? Yes! He will have more, then they will culminate in his death Jane the maid, she does not matter, only Day could have dispensed information, and I know one thing—he would not do so when the police were within earshot." His English was excellent now, and he might have been taken for a native. "What else did you attempt, Dawlish?"

"Nothing else," said Dawlish, slowly.

"Indeed! How many men did Hamblin leave behind to spring a surprise on us?" Hortelan laughed again. "You see, I am not the fool you imagine, my friend. I did not expect to have the ultimatum accepted in good faith. What mattered was that I should gain possession."

"Joint possession," murmured Dawlish.

"I do not understand you."

"We three are here."

"I am not worried by *you*," said Hortelan. "Oh, I am not even a little worried by you, Dawlish. If you had been sensible from the first we need not have had this trouble and this difference of opinion. That is the pity of having a reputation which must be maintained, is it not? All I need is *some* of the jewels, particular ones. I am not interested in the others. You and Gordon may share them between you."

"Oh," said Dawlish, blankly.

"You see, I am generous," said Hortelan. He smiled again, but there was something new in his expression, a hint of the malignant menace he had shown before. "But understand this, Dawlish. If you make any attempt to interfere with me and my men, if you are foolish enough to continue to work for the police—*death!* Of course, I do not expect you to be so foolish as to do anything directly," he went on. "That would not be wise of you, Dawlish, and I know you are not altogether a fool. You will perform a service for us when we have finished. You will negotiate for free conduct for us! On the whole, I am glad that you allowed your wife to stay with you, men are always more amenable when their womenfolk are in danger. Don't you agree?"

"Possibly," said Dawlish, in a strained voice.

"So Hamblin and the others, when they have become almost stiff with cold by surrounding this place, will find their sacrifice useless, because you will again find some way of getting me what I want—as you have done here. Well, Dawlish—what do you think now? Have you been so clever?"

"I was never clever," murmured Dawlish.

"Such modesty!" Hortelan rubbed his hands, and added, looking at Felicity: "It is a pity if we remain on bad terms. I hope we shall sink our differences while we are forced to stay here together, as we will be for a few days, and be friendly. I wish we could get out earlier," he added, "it is a pity, this snow. Without it, I would have got safely away yesterday." He took out a cigarette case and handed it round, and then said amiably: "Let us go into the warm and sit down."

"Aren't you anxious to find the jewels?" Dawlish asked.

"Oh, that is a matter of time only, and it will not take long. You see, Dawlish, when Day last had a fit and came round from it, I talked to him. He told me where to find what I want. Oh, he does not know that he did, and therefore he could not tell you, but I am prepared to say that within one hour my men, who are already searching, will have found the jewels. A very neat hiding-place, Dawlish!" He sat on the arm of the chair, thrusting his hands towards the fire and thoroughly enjoying the sensation he was creating. "In one of the beams in his bedroom, the main bedroom—a beam which can be moved from the ceiling and in which there is a secret drawer. My men are already working there, as I say, and I expect to hear from them within an hour. Well, Dawlish, what do you think of the situation now?"

CHAPTER XIV

THE ALEXIS JEWELS

How much was true?

If everything that Hortelan said was true, Dawlish reflected, then he had been hopelessly outwitted and outclassed; and there was a ring of confidence in the man's voice which made him think that Hortelan was not exaggerating. His manner, too, was subtly different; before, when he had not been taken completely by surprise by Dawlish's attack, he had the swaggering confidence of a man who believed he would get what he wanted. Now he had the complacent appearance of one who had got it. There was less bluster and arrogance, as if he realized that the need for that was gone. When he smiled he was an attractive-looking fellow with quite an air. Watching him as he swung his leg to and fro and beamed upon Felicity, as if to make her realize what a fool her husband proved to be, Dawlish remembered the different phases through which he had passed. The man was a good actor, even a superlative one; probably his changes of mood had been to get Dawlish in two minds. Now he was thoroughly pleased with himself and no longer needed to create an impression.

"You cannot find words," he said, with a shrug. "I quite understand how you feel, Dawlish. From what I know of you, you are not often bested. Come—admit that this time you are!"

"If it pleases you—I admit it," said Dawlish.

"Splendid, my dear fellow! Now we shall get on much better than before, and there is no reason why we should not enjoy our enforced stay here. I see you have brought in fresh supplies of food—perhaps you thought that the other stores had been tampered with. A wise precaution, but unnecessary; they were not touched." He stood up. "You see, Dawlish, I bear no umbrage. You must admit that I am a forgiving fellow."

"Apparently," murmured Dawlish.

"Oh, it is more than apparently," declared Hortelan, "it is a fact. If it were not so I would take revenge on you for the trick which you played on me, but I shall do nothing of the kind. Now, what of your friend Sol Gordon? You should be more careful of the company you keep; he is a great scoundrel. Tell him, please, that we have agreed to armistice terms."

"Armistice," murmured Dawlish. "Hostilities suspended, but not permanently stopped. All right, I'll tell him."

"And bring him here with you, so that I can have the benefit of two expert opinions on the gems."

"He'll come," said Dawlish.

He gave Gordon a gist of the conversation, and confessed himself at the end of his resources. Gordon looked thoughtful and grimaced comically, but he made little comment. When they reached the main room, Hortelan had gone out. The radio was tuned in softly and Felicity was listening to a concert by a light orchestra.

"How music can console," said Gordon. "I am glad you thought of that, Mrs. Dawlish. Well, we must see what happens next. At least there appears to be no immediate threat to our safety, and we should be grateful for that. I must remark upon one thing, you know." He patted her hand and beamed at Dawlish. "Our Patrick is a very good fellow, he has taken a beating with admirable *sang froid*. I do like a man who smiles in defeat—especially when I know that behind his smile he is concealing an active mind seeking a way of turning the tables. Eh, Patrick?"

"My mind's completely inactive," said Dawlish.

"Oh, no, no, my boy! Subconsciously it is very busy indeed just now. You will not gladly allow a man guilty of three cold-blooded murders to escape the consequences of his crimes! I will admit," he added, "that I am surprised to find Hortelan so gracious and his men so incurious. I feel that I am watched less closely by them than by Carter's men! I—"

He stopped as the door opened.

One of the olive-skinned members of Hortelan's party entered, carrying a small oilskin bag. They stared at it. Hortelan spoke to someone outside, then entered with an air, smiling broadly. The first man put the bag on a table, and withdrew. Hortelan stared at it for a few seconds, and then slowly, as if carefully calculating how to get the best effect, picked it up and opened the top, which was drawn together with string. He pulled out a roll of cotton-wool, three inches in diameter, seven or eight inches long. He held the wad in his hand and looked gaily at Dawlish.

"You see, I allow you to be in at the kill!"

Slowly he unwound the wad. A couple of inches of wool lay straight on the table, and then something caught the light and sparkled brilliantly. Hortelan's eyes reflected the brilliance; he was almost hugging himself. Three diamonds of equal size, pear-shaped and tinged with pink, rolled free from the wool on to the table.

"Please, please!" protested Gordon, "be careful how you treat such things as those!" He advanced slowly, and under Hortelan's smiling eyes picked up one of the jewels and weighed it in his hand. "Beautiful!" he breathed. "Beautiful!"

"It is indeed," said Hortelan. "Now let me see what else I can find."

Two smaller diamonds, a sapphire pendant, an emerald the size of a pigeon's egg, soon added to the brilliance. Dawlish and Felicity watched in fascination as the pile grew. Like a glittering, fiery mass the jewels were heaped upon the table, several dozen gems, each of them remarkable for its size and brilliance. Gordon's eyes seemed to be popping out of his head. Dawlish wondered what would happen if he drew his gun then and tried to hold Hortelan up, as he had done before; he knew that he would not have the same success, Hortelan would not be caught twice by the same trick.

The Spaniard took a wallet from his pocket, extracted a slip of paper, and unfolded it. It was larger than it looked at first. On it were ink drawings of precious stones, drawn by a man who had contrived to capture something of the appearance of the gems which were now on the table.

Hortelan looked at it, picked up a diamond, and put it on one side. He referred to the paper again, selected another, and then did the same thing time and time again until half the stones were in one heap. Obviously he was familiar with gems, or he could not have made his selections so easily.

"There are *all* those I want," he said. "We shall have to come to an arrangement about the others—a reward, perhaps, for your help a little later!"

"What would I not do for those lovely things," breathed Gordon. He picked up a rose-tinted diamond and carried it to the window reverently, his lips pursed, his eyes protruding.

He held it between his thumb and forefinger and looked at it against the light. "Beautiful," he said, dreamily; "a lovely, lovely thing. Come, Patrick, come and look at it!"

Dawlish joined him, taking two other stones as he went. As he reached Gordon, he was aware of a slight pressure against his ribs—deliberate, not accidental. Gordon was not looking at him, but was gazing at the gems. He took those from Dawlish's hand, and gave them the same reverent treatment; he looked like a fat priest worshipping at an altar.

The pressure was repeated.

Dawlish knew why; he stood there straight-faced, trying to emu late the awe which Gordon stimulated, but finding it hard not to show his astonishment. For those jewels, brilliant though they looked, *were paste*! He knew enough about precious stones to be sure of that.

"I have no doubt at all what happened," whispered Gordon, later. "Hortelan thought that Barney was in a state of mind when he could only tell the whole truth, but Barney deceived him, the brave fellow. False gems, Patrick—we still have to find the real ones! And Hortelan, for all his superficial knowledge of stones, does not know the difference between the real thing and paste. He deserves all he gets, doesn't he, my boy?"

"Yes," said Dawlish, abstractedly.

They were sitting together round the fire. Hortelan had gone out, taking with him those jewels which he said he wanted, leaving the other jewels where they gleamed upon the table.

"And now you have some place to start from again," said Gordon. "You are not beaten yet, thanks to Barney's cunning."

"Does it make such a difference?" asked Dawlish.

"Yes, yes, because it gives us new hope," said Gordon. "You will see that as time goes on. What we must do now, of course, is to continue to regard the fakes with awe, to show greed and avarice and great desire for them. Hortelan will believe what I have already implanted in his mind, that we will come to terms with him for the same of the residue which he does not want for himself."

"There's something that doesn't ring true," said Dawlish. "If the residue were real, what would it be worth?"

"A hundred thousand pounds, my boy, not a penny less even on the wholesale market."

"I see. How many men would willingly turn aside from a hundred thousand pounds?" asked Dawlish.

"I don't follow you," said Gordon.

"I'm not so sure that he believes them genuine," said Dawlish. "Oh, he has what he wants, but—"

"I think you give him more credit than is justified," said Gordon. "And you do not judge him from the right viewpoint. He is not doing this for money or for gain, but for a cause. Oh, yes, he has a cause, he believes in it, he is one of those *herren-volk* individuals. All of his men are the same. What a wonderful thing, this blind sense of superiority! How fortunate that they carry it to excess, for that is their downfall always. Well, Patrick, what are you going to do?"

Dawlish shrugged. "What can we do?"

"Just as I say, I hope."

"Plenty of hope," said Dawlish.

"Good! Now, my boy, I am going to say something which I know will perhaps upset you, but you are a sensible fellow, and I hope you will realize why I say it. This Hortelan, he is a handsome, upstanding man, with an eye for the ladies. That is why he was so fond of Phyllis Hamblin, perhaps. Well, I do not imagine he is indifferent to any woman's charms, and we have in this room one of the most charming ladies in England!" He shot a bird-like glance at Felicity, then looked back at Dawlish. "I do not think the day will pass before he has endeavoured to impress Felicity with his handsomeness and his cleverness—do you?"

"Go on," said Dawlish, grimly.

"All I ask, my boy, is that Felicity should not be *wholly* antagonistic. She is a clever girl, she can fool him—any woman can fool any man if she so requires. She might, perhaps, learn more from Hortelan than you or I could do. Of course, do understand me, it would all be very frivolous, a *little* hero-worship, perhaps, especially as her husband has been discredited—what do you think, Patrick? Would you object?"

"It might show results," said Dawlish, with a quick smile at Felicity, "and it would give Felicity some fun."

She made a *moue* at him.

"What understanding people you are, to be sure," said Gordon. "Where other people would get angry and be most indignant, you make faces at each other and consider it as if I had said a mere nothing. Good! That is our plan of campaign, then—Felicity shall worm herself into Hortelan's good graces, although he will make all the advances, and you—Patrick, do I go too far? Could you pretend to be a jealous husband?"

"He could," said Felicity, smiling, but she looked thoughtful. "What good will it do?"

"Come, my dear! One day we must find out why Hortelan is going to all this trouble. We do not believe it is for a very good purpose, do we? Then the more we know, the better for us! It is agreed, then? I shall derive much enjoyment from it, I assure you of that." He beamed at them, and then suddenly sat back in his chair and rubbed his stomach. "I am feeling hungry. I do hope it will not be long before we are offered some lunch, we must sustain ourselves!"

Soon afterwards a man came in and asked permission to lay

a table in the room. He was polite, almost servile, and Dawlish was more than ever puzzled. He went upstairs with Felicity, talking in undertones about Gordon's suggestion, neither of them taking it seriously, each seeing the possible advantages. They reached the landing—and then Dawlish missed a step. He gripped Felicity's arm tightly, and she stifled an exclamation; they walked on. Inside their room, with the door closed, Dawlish gave out a long, deep breath.

"Well, what do you think of that?" he demanded.

"It's—" she started, and then broke off helplessly.

A man had been standing by the door which led to the attic room, and they had seen what he was doing; a padlock was being fitted to the door of the spiral staircase. *The men up there could not get down into the house.*

Hortelan lunched with them.

He had ceased showing off as a man with a mission, and set himself out to be pleasant. He succeeded. He had a good turn of phrase and a pretty wit, and there were moments during the meal when Dawlish almost forgot the real circumstances. One of his men was a good cook; out of tinned foods he had made a repast good enough to satisfy Sol Gordon, who seemed interested only in his food.

There was something uncanny about the fat man's cunning.

More and more Hortelan's attention turned towards Felicity. It was cleverly, even subtly done. A joke directed towards her, a quick glance from his fine eyes and watchfulness for what she needed. Before the meal was over there was no doubt that he was trying to draw her attention; it was something subtler than flirting, something more than table-talk.

Now and again Gordon caught Dawlish's eye, and lowered one lid.

Felicity responded skilfully, even occasionally looked at Dawlish as if uncertain of his attitude. Dawlish drew more within himself, taking little part in the conversation; it became almost a *tête-à-tête* between Felicity and Hortelan, and Hortelan blossomed out, a gallant with a courtliness beautiful to see.

Was it simply inability to resist an attractive woman, Dawlish wondered? Or did Hortelan hope to gain her confidence and plan to play her off against him?

He would have paid more attention to that but for the discovery of the padlocked door. Hortelan had said nothing about it, and it was almost as if he *knew* that the two men were upstairs. The only good thing about it, as far as Dawlish could see, was that they had been given ample provisions, and could last a week if need be.

Other thoughts pressed urgently on his mind.

If Hortelan had known they were there, how had he discovered it? Was that knowledge connected with his lack of surprise at finding Dawlish there and Barney gone? Had he, in fact, known exactly what to expect?

The idea strengthened.

He had found it hard to believe that Hortelan guessed so much; that he would be prepared for a trick was obvious, but he appeared also to have been prepared for everything that had happened. Certainly he had not seen what had taken place in the house, but there were two ways in which he could have found out.

Sitting back in an easy chair and drinking coffee, Dawlish looked at Sol Gordon. Gordon had been out of the room several times and *could* have passed a message on. There was no guarantee that he was as genuine as he seemed to be. He had a great love of jewels and a greater love of money—even his best friends knew that. His amusing roguishness *might* be calculated to set

Dawlish's mind at ease. The thought was disloyal, and Dawlish felt uneasy about it, but he could not entirely dismiss it from his mind.

There was another possibility.

Hamblin and Carter had prepared a written note which a messenger had taken to the cottage. Either of them might have added the information; or the messenger could have passed it on verbally. The possibility that Hamblin had told a plausible lie when he had talked of the danger to Phyllis had not to be considered; his indecision might really have been prompted by a different motive. If Hamblin were excluded from the list of suspects, Carter and the messenger remained. Hortelan had been in the district for some time, according to Hamblin, and he might have made contact with some of the villagers. It was much easier to suspect Hamblin than Carter, but if the view that Hortelan knew more than he should were accepted, then someone must have got word to him.

There remained the outside possibility that there was a means of hearing all that was said in the house. Possibly dictaphones or some simple system of wiring had been installed, but Dawlish thought it unlikely that any system could have been devised by which *everything* could have been heard. If he refused to accept that possibility, then he had to face the fact that Gordon, Hamblin, Carter or the messenger had betrayed them.

And I might even be trying to excuse my own failure, he thought, watching Hortelan lean forward towards Felicity, resting his hand lightly on her arm. If Gordon were the informant, Hortelan might know of the plot to let Felicity pretend an interest in him.

Gordon began to yawn, and after a few minutes said that he was going upstairs to rest. Solemnly, he apologized because of his advancing years. From the door he winked at Dawlish and beckoned him. Half an hour earlier Dawlish would have been amused at the blatant ruse to leave Felicity and Hortelan together; now his new suspicions made him reluctant. Yet there was no point in assuming the worst, and suddenly he got up and said that he wanted a book from his room. Did Felicity want anything?

"Not now, darling," she said, absently.

Dawlish smiled a little grimly to himself as he went upstairs. He expected Gordon to be in his room waiting, but no one was there. He went out to look at the locked door, then returned to his room, selecting a book from the slim volumes he had brought with him. He refilled his cigarette-case, glanced out of the window towards the village, and saw the people moving to and fro. There was no one on the road which led to the cottage or *Timbers;* they would lie low during daylight, of course. Now he was haunted by the fear that Hamblin or Carter was working in league with Hortelan; he could not make himself confident of anyone.

There was no point in reproaching himself for what had happened, and yet he wondered whether if he had handled the affair differently from the start, he would have been in a better position now. The snow had caused the trouble, of course— snow, and the fact that Barney had given him no warning of danger. Even then he should have realized, from Jane's distress on the telephone, that an emergency might come about.

The issue had been too confused from the first, and was certainly no better now. It was impossible to concentrate on any one factor: his mind kept shifting from contemplation of the possibility of treachery to the problem of Hortelan's mission and the false gems. He was in no doubt as to that; and it was in Sol Gordon's favour that he had drawn attention to them so quickly.

The most puzzling and disturbing feature of the whole affair was the behaviour of the police. He had expected serious trouble with Hamblin when he had suggested accepting the terms of the ultimatum, and yet Hamblin appeared to have dropped back into the indecisive, leave-it-to-someone-else attitude which he had shown soon after coming to *Timbers*.

"Oh, I'd better get downstairs!" he said aloud.

He turned and went to the door—and was startled because it did not open. He tried the handle again, thinking it had stuck; it was more than that, for the door moved slightly; it was held by the lock.

Then he noticed for the first time that the key was not on the inside of the door.

CHAPTER XV

TURNING-POINT

Dawlish stood quite still.

Alarm surged through him. His thoughts flew to Felicity, he saw her sitting in the easy chair, talking and laughing with Hortelan, confident and, he had believed, quite capable of handling the situation. The complacency with which he had agreed to Gordon's suggestion was now quite gone, and he realized that Hortelan, by his disarming manner, had reduced his defences completely. He had allowed himself to be locked in, like any tyro; he was incapable of doing anything to help himself, Felicity or Gordon.

He felt very cold.

His hand was on the handle of the door, and he turned it again and pulled, without result. He released it, turned away, and lit a cigarette. From the window, the bleak expanse of white countryside seemed now to hold far greater menace than ever before. Hurn, only a few hundred yards away, might have been on the other side of the county.

In spite of all that, it was the turning point.

Vague uncertainties, speculation and confusion all faded from his mind. Here was a job to do, one he could do, one he must. Hortelan had made one mistake; he had allowed him to keep his automatic. He took it out and examined the chambers; it was full and seven bullets would be a help in real emergency.

He sensed the change in his own attitude, was conscious of a new determination and a new confidence; that there was nothing to justify it did not alter the fact that it was there. One immediate task was easy, and helped to bring him back to an awareness of the immediate needs of the situation and the fact that he could deal with this move.

The lock on the door was simple.

Years before such a lock would have baffled him completely; now forcing it was a matter of five minutes' work; that was a fact which troubled policemen who knew his ability.

The problem was to make sure that no one was on the landing outside. There was a set smile on his face as he tapped lightly at the door but received no response. He tried again; no one answered. He took a pen-knife from his pocket, one with many blades, each with a particular purpose. He spent two minutes examining the lock, and within three minutes had it back.

He stepped out to the passage.

No one was in sight, the first floor was silent. He closed the door and used the tool to lock it again from the outside. There were no scratches visible on the lock, no one would know that he was out of the room unless he were seen.

He went to Gordon's room.

He tried the handle and pushed; that door too was locked. A faint snoring sound came to his ears, which satisfied him that Gordon was asleep. He was relieved in one way; it looked as if both of them had been locked in, and Gordon was surely absolved of any complicity.

With his hand in his pocket about his gun he looked in the other rooms; all were empty.

He went downstairs. The quiet was uncanny.

It was the first time since he had returned with Carter that there had been no one standing at the vantage points, and keeping a close watch on all that happened. Apparently Hortelan was now confident that there would be no attack until dark; probably he felt sure that no one would be able to ford the river near the bridge.

No sound came from the sitting-room.

The door was ajar and he went in to an empty room. Hortelan and Felicity could not have stayed there more than a quarter of an hour after he had left. The fact that there was no sign of anyone was puzzling; a short while before he would have found it bewildering, but his mind was clearer now, tuned up to the needs of the situation. The issue had become vitally personal because of Felicity.

He turned and looked along the passage towards the dining-room—and for the first time he realized that the furniture blocking the doorway had been moved, not just shifted farther along the passage, but taken out of sight. He looked into the dining-room; the sideboard and two heavy chairs were back in position, and the panelled wall seemed untouched. He went out and locked the door, dropping the key into his pocket. Next he visited the morning-room where two dead men were lying—

Had been lying! They were gone; the room was orderly again, and there was no sign of Willing or the pseudo policeman. Dawlish felt coldness gripping him, but he did not waste time there. He turned away, leaving the door unlocked, and went to the kitchen.

It also was empty.

In a quarter of an hour, he discovered what he most feared; Hortelan had gone with all his men and with Felicity.

He went back to the sitting-room.

On the table was a small heap of paste jewels, surprisingly bright, excellent fakes, so good that he looked at them again to make quite sure that there could have been no mistake.

He opened the kitchen door and walked to the garage. The snow had stopped but it was still freezing hard. The surface crunched beneath his feet, but he did not sink far, because other men had trodden a path before him. The garage was unlocked, and no one was inside. The outhouses were empty of people. He looked at the cottage, where a few hours before smoke had been curling towards the leaden skies, but there was now no sign of smoke.

He returned to the house, and stoked up the kitchen fire and that in the sitting-room. He lit a cigarette and stood looking out of the window: he seemed to be doing that interminably. The answer to all questions was clear enough. Hortelan thought he had found what he wanted, and had taken Felicity as a hostage, convinced that when the time came Dawlish would do his bidding.

He went upstairs, picked the lock of Gordon's door, and went in. Gordon stopped snoring as the door opened, and looked at him with one eye closed. He sat up abruptly at sight of his face, and Dawlish told him briefly what had happened.

Half an hour afterwards they reached the front door of Hortelan's cottage. It was shut; no one was in the grounds, and no one came when Dawlish picked the lock and stepped inside. It was deserted. He doubted whether anyone had been there since Hortelan had left to take over *Timbers,* for the fires were out and every room struck cold. Gordon seemed dumb, and uttered no word as they completed the hurried search. Not until they had finished and were at the back door, looking towards *Timbers,* did the fat man speak.

"Patrick, my boy, I cannot express my sorrow. It was my fault, entirely my fault, I suggested—"

"Nonsense!" said Dawlish, roughly. "They would have had an opportunity of doing this sooner or later." His suspicion of Gordon was quite gone now.

"But where *are* they, Patrick?"

"Underground," said Dawlish. "I—Great Scott, I've forgotten Carter's men!"

He led the way back to *Timbers* and they hurried upstairs. The padlock was simple enough to break open, and Gordon watched him in fascination, amazed at the ease with which he worked, the quick, dexterous twists of his fingers as he manipulated the knife-tool.

The door swung open.

"And I cannot get up, I just cannot!" wailed Gordon.

"I won't be long," said Dawlish. He raised his voice. "Ahoy, there! It's all safe!"

"*All—safe!*" His voice came back to him, echoed by the thick wooden walls, and seemed much deeper. There was no other reply. The door in the ceiling was open, and he hauled himself into the room, not now surprised that there was no reply, but disturbed by what he might find.

There was no sign of Carter's men!

The dormer windows were closed, and before he gave up hope of finding some trace of them he opened the windows and looked out on the roof. The snow there was untouched, no one had been out that way. He dropped back to the floor and went to the stairs, calling down to Gordon. One thing was certain; the men had not been removed while he had been in his room before being locked in. They had been taken while he had been at lunch, or else when he and Gordon had gone across to the cottage.

He turned and went downstairs, and then caught sight of a piece of paper pinned to the door leading to the stairs. It was a folded note, with no writing on the outside. He took it off and slipped it into his pocket.

Gordon was standing, tense-faced, looking at him.

"*Everyone* gone, Patrick!"

"Everyone," said Dawlish. "Let's get downstairs to the fire."

When he stood in front of it getting warm for the first time since he had made the discovery, he took out the note. He felt an odd reluctance to open it, and Gordon stared, pop-eyed. At last Dawlish unfolded it, and his heart contracted, for it was covered with Felicity's handwriting, a hurriedly-written, pencilled note. Briefly, Felicity said that Hortelan had promised her that she would come to no harm provided Dawlish and Gordon made no attempt to leave *Timbers;* and, she added, she did not know where Hortelan was taking her, but it was not to the cottage.

"And there is nothing we can do," wailed Gordon; "nothing at all, Patrick. My dear boy, how you must feel!"

"Feel?" said Dawlish, harshly. "I'm incapable of feeling!" He tossed away a cigarette, and stared at the letter. "She can't be far away," he muttered. "There may be a tunnel beneath the garden, but it can't lead far. There isn't another building nearer than the village."

"There is the hill at the back," said Gordon. "It is steep, something could have been built into it—or am I thinking in wild terms?"

"You might be right," said Dawlish. "Sol, there must be a reason why they deserted the house and the cottage. It wasn't a whim. Hortelan had to get away, probably because he had work to do elsewhere. What work would it be?"

"My boy, how can we guess, what good will it do if we do guess?"

"It will give us something to think about," said Dawlish. He laughed. "Oh, you're right, but one thing is certain—I am *not* going to stay here and do nothing."

"We could look for the real jewels," Gordon murmured. "Now that would give us something with which to occupy our minds, my boy, and we cannot tell what we might find apart from the jewels. I—" he broke off, for Dawlish was looking away from him, towards the radio, and on his face there was a new expression. "Patrick, what is it?"

"Jewels," said Dawlish, very softly.

Beneath the radio-set, only visible because he had been sitting on the arm of a chair, were several of the paste stones. He took them out. One diamond, one emerald and one sapphire, all pieces which Hortelan had set aside, pieces which had corresponded to the drawings on the sheet of paper. He held them in his hand, frowning—and then he saw a smear of red on one of them.

"Patrick—" wailed Gordon.

"Lipstick!" said Dawlish. "Felicity's shade, too!" He peered closely at it, and went on: "It's too thick to have come from her lips, she must have daubed it from the stick. What do you think that might mean, Sol?" There was a note almost of jubilance in his voice, and when Gordon said nothing, he went on: "She managed to get them from Hortelan, she smeared the lipstick on to tell us that she had done so, and she knows that he'll be back for them. She's given us something we can fight with, and we'll fight!"

"Remarkable!" breathed Gordon, "really remarkable, but— oh, my boy, what are you doing? What *are* you doing?"

"Experimenting," said Dawlish. "You've told me a lot of things about jewels, real and false. Remember?"

He took a log out of the box in the fireplace, put a paste

diamond on to it, picked up the poker and struck the gem. Pieces of the paste flaked off at the third attempt, and the main piece slipped.

"Hold it firm with the tongs, will you," Dawlish said, and when Gordon did so he struck more firmly. Three blows were enough to crack the piece into several pieces and to show that it was not solid. There was a small cavity inside, and from the cavity there rolled a tiny ball of paper, the size of a small pea.

"Well!" cried Gordon.

"Hortelan's mysterious motive," murmured Dawlish tensely.

The paper was so tightly compressed that at first he could not unfold it. He held it on the shovel in front of the fire, warming it through; and with the warmth the outer fold loosened. He pulled it gently. It was a single piece of paper, and as it unfolded and grew larger, Gordon hopped from one foot to the other. At last it lay flat on Dawlish's hand, a piece of paper about six inches by six, thin but tough and durable, and covered on one side with faint writing. He turned his back to the window, so that the light did not glare on it, and after a few seconds he looked up.

"Do you know Spanish, Sol?"

"I wish I did, my boy, I wish I did!"

"So what it says remains a mystery," said Dawlish. "I wish we had some powder here to make a paste diamond. We might make Hortelan think he'd the real thing."

Gordon said in a thin voice: "I *have* the stuff, Patrick. The question is, can we make the oven hot enough to bake it? How hot does an electric oven get? Oh, my boy! Why didn't you take a sketch of it before you broke it in two, why didn't you? We can only guess, now."

"A guess will probably be good enough for Hortelan," said Dawlish. "Get the powder, Sol, I'll switch on the oven."

He did not ask why Sol Gordon, not only a pawnbroker and fence but an expert in manufacturing paste gems—in, as he was always careful to explain, the most legitimate fashion—had such materials with him.

Sol scurried upstairs. Dawlish went to the kitchen and switched on the oven hot-point. When Gordon came down he carried a small attaché case, which contained two canisters of powder and several bottles of treated water, a pestle and mortar, a little shaping tool and small steel vice. Dawlish watched his stubby fingers as they worked, swiftly and surely. In ten minutes the rough shape of a pear-drop diamond was fashioned; in twenty, the dull white thing lay on the kitchen table on a small sheet of asbestos also taken from the case.

"All that matters now is the oven and two precious hours," said Gordon. He slid the sheet in and closed the door. He was perspiring freely, and dabbed at his forehead with a damp tea-towel. "It will be quite dark by then, Patrick; we shall be lucky if we do not have a visitor before."

"That depends on when Hortelan discovers that three jewels are missing," said Dawlish. "Have you any pliable asbestos?"

"A little, yes."

"We'll put the other gems in the sitting-room fire," said Dawlish, "they should stand the heat wrapped in asbestos. Don't you think so?"

"There is a risk, my boy; they are good fakes, but I do not know what heat is needed for the paste of which they were made. It would be a risk, I think, a great risk—but there is a simpler hiding-place where there is no danger."

"What's that?" asked Dawlish.

"The snow, my boy. Snow outside—or on a window-ledge or over a porch. We had better use the side door, they cannot see us from there."

They chose a spot outside the side door, and dropped the fake gems there. Each made a small hole which gradually filled up as they pressed the snow gently about them. When they had finished there was no trace of holes or of the fact that the snow had been disturbed.

Darkness was falling.

Darkness brought back the wind, and the windows and door shook beneath its onslaught. The house, so empty now, seemed full of noises. They made some tea, took it into the sitting-room and tried to behave normally. That Hortelan would come back was beyond question now, and they could bargain with him; but—

Did he set as much store by those three paste jewels as Dawlish did by Felicity?

The clock in the hall struck six.

"Six o'clock," said Gordon, struggling to get up from his chair. "We may as well prove that we are not alone in the world, my boy." He switched on the radio, and as it warmed up the last of the six *peeps* of the time signal came clearly. The announcer's dispassionate voice read the weather report, and then said:

"*At the end of the news there will be a special police message, of particular interest to the people of Dorset and Wiltshire. The blizzard which . . .*"

CHAPTER XVI

POLICE MESSAGE

"Will he never stop this news?" cried Gordon. "Will he never stop talking about things which do not matter?"

They were standing in front of the radio, staring at it as if by their concerted will power they could make time fly and more quickly reach the end of the bald recital. Blizzard news had been the biggest item, now there was talk of food conditions in China. On and on it went, almost interminably, until it came almost as a surprise when the announcer said:

"*That is the end of the news. Here is the police message of particular interest to the people of Dorset and Wiltshire. It has come to the knowledge of the police that a small group of men, suspected of murder, have taken refuge in some part of the county of Dorset or Wiltshire. The region to which they are known to have gone is marked by the towns of Salisbury, Sherborne and Tisbury in the north, and Blandford and Dorchester in the south. Information lodged with the police suggests that these men have had their residence in a small village near Shaftesbury—the name of the village is Hurn, spelt H-U-R-N—but there is no way of telling at the moment, because of the complete standstill of*" *traffic and the dislocation of communications, whether they are still there or whether they have moved to a different district. It is known that they could not have moved outside the region indicated in this message. The leader of the group is known sometimes by the name of Horlan, sometimes Telan and sometimes Hortelan. As far as is known, all the members of the group are aliens, natives of a south European country. The public is warned that they are armed with a variety of weapons and will not hesitate to commit violence. It is of the utmost importance that these men should not be allowed to escape from the district mentioned, but all civilians, as well as police and military personnel, should use the utmost care in dealing with any persons whom they may suspect of being members of the group. I will repeat the districts to which this message particularly applies."*

"Enough!" cried Gordon.

"More than enough," said Dawlish, slowly. "I wonder if Hortelan heard that?" In his mind were the suspicions he had spoken of to Felicity, of great interests at stake, perhaps endangered by Hortelan. Would such a message have been broadcast for any usual crime?

"Does it matter, my boy?" said Gordon. "Isn't it enough that the police consider them so dangerous and of such importance that this message has been broadcast? Oh, Patrick, Patrick, what have we stumbled across, what hidden horrors are there behind this awful gang? I have known gangs, many gangs, but this—imagine, Patrick! Our unimaginative police force compelled to word a message in such a way, does it not tell you how perturbed are the authorities?"

"Not only the authorities," said Dawlish. "I—"

He paused, straining his ears, for he thought he heard a sound from inside the house. He stood up and stepped to the door, taking out his gun. The sound was repeated; it came along the passage from the dining-room. He tiptoed towards the door, while Gordon hurried down the kitchen passage to his precious 'diamond'.

Dawlish heard the sound again—a tapping on the door of the dining-room. It was soft and regular; he imagined that someone was using a hammer and chisel. He waited for a few seconds before he spoke in a deep voice.

"That's enough, Hortelan."

The tapping stopped. He heard a whispered consultation, followed by the sound of footsteps. He wondered if the snow piled up against the dining-room windows was enough to stop the men from getting out that way and through another window; with only himself and Gordon to work, every window and door could not be protected.

Gordon came up. "It is finished, Patrick—a beauty! Congratulate me!"

"Congratulations," said Dawlish. "Watch the sitting-room windows, will you."

"At once," said Gordon. He hurried off, and after a long time voices were audible in the dining-room again. They fell silent, and Hortelan spoke.

"Is that you, Dawlish?"

"Yes, and properly armed," said Dawlish.

"You are in no position to talk of being armed. You will do exactly as I tell you, or else your wife—"

"Don't finish your threat," said Dawlish, "but listen to this one. Unless my wife is allowed to return to the house within half an hour the three faked jewels which you dropped will be smashed and the pieces burned."

The silence which followed was a sufficient indication of the effect on Hortelan. It lasted for so long that he was afraid that the Spaniard had gone away, but Hortelan spoke in a low-pitched voice.

"What guarantee have I that you will not do that even if I send her back?"

Dawlish's heart leapt. It had worked! "My word on it!"

"That is not enough," said Hortelan, who sounded as if he were speaking under great emotional strain. "Dawlish, I will do one thing. I will return your wife in exchange for the jewels. They must *not* be broken, but intact. I know, of course, that they are paste."

Dawlish said: "You can have one of them first, as an earnest, and the others when my wife is back."

"I cannot rely on your word," said Hortelan.

"Either you rely on it or lose the fakes," said Dawlish, with a lighter note in his voice. Obviously those stones were a bargaining weapon beyond price. "Go out of that room now, and in ten minutes I will put one gem on the dining-table. My wife must be released and allowed to come through the dining-room, and you must make no attempt to get into the passage with her. Is that clear?"

"Dawlish—"

"*Is that clear?*"

Hortelan said: "How shall I get the other gems?"

"I will put them in the garage afterwards."

There was another silence, a sound very like a sigh, and then an urgent whisper at Dawlish's side. Gordon, standing on tiptoe, pulled at his sleeve and whispered again:

"Not outside, Patrick, not outside—they will be able to shoot you on the way; don't take risks, my boy!"

"No risks, no results," murmured Dawlish. "We do want to see an end to this, don't we?"

"What are you saying?" Hortelan called out.

"I'm saying that I'm tired of waiting for you," said Dawlish.

"I must have some guarantee that you will surrender the

gems, I cannot take your word for it, Dawlish. Give me them first, and—"

Dawlish said: "The first gem will be on the dining-room table in ten minutes' time, if you go out and leave the room empty. When my wife is back, the other two will be left on the garage bench. That is my last word."

"Patrick," pleaded Gordon, "what risks you take, what terrible risks you take!"

There was no reply except a sound of light footsteps followed by the closing of a door. Silence ensued. Dawlish looked at his wrist-watch, while Gordon stood staring at the door with his hands clenched and veins standing out on his forehead. But for Gordon, Dawlish would not have felt the tension so acutely, for he believed that Hortelan would accept the terms. Gordon put doubts into his mind. The seconds seemed to drag like minutes; the silence grew more intense.

After eight minutes there was another sound inside the room. Gordon gave a deep, agonized sigh. Dawlish waited until the ten minutes were up, then unlocked the door, making no effort to deaden the sound. He pushed the door open an inch, standing to one side so that he could see into the room. Gordon put the new paste gem into his hand; it was still wrapped in asbestos, and Hortelan would take it for granted that it had been hidden in the fire. He did not even look at Gordon's product.

"Careful, careful," said Gordon in an agonized voice. "Oh, the risks you run!"

No one was immediately opposite the door as it opened more widely. Dawlish kept pushing with his left hand, while he covered the room with the gun. Soon he could see three parts of the walls; no one was visible. He pushed the door back against the wall abruptly, expecting to find someone hiding behind it; it hit the wall and swung back slowly.

"Stay there, Sol," he said.

Gordon was holding his gun; he looked unsteady, and was more frightened by this attempt than by anything that had gone before. Dawlish himself stepped forward, feeling as if he were being watched, wondering if slits had been carved into the panelling but were invisible from the room itself. He shook the gem from the asbestos to a wooden mat on the dining-room table. In spite of his tenseness he was startled by its brilliance, by the mastery of Gordon's handiwork. It looked exactly like the diamond he had broken into pieces.

He pushed the mat to the centre of the table and backed away, still covering the panelling opposite the door. He could not see where it opened, and he could not hear a sound. He reached the passage safely, left the door ajar, and wiped the perspiration from his forehead.

"My boy, I never thought you would be allowed to come out alive," said Gordon. "I could not bear the thought of being left here alone! What is the matter with the man, does he not realize that without you I am in a helpless position?"

"He wants those gems," said Dawlish.

He stood opposite the door, his ears strained to catch the slightest sound. The silence, broken only by their breathing, lasted for a long time, and was suddenly broken by the whirring of the grandfather clock, before it struck seven. He started, Gordon exclaimed in alarm, and then they looked at each other with sheepish grins.

Five minutes passed.

Dawlish stirred restlessly. The muscles of his face seemed stiff, and his throat was dry and taut. A nerve in his forehead began to twitch and made his eyelid flicker; he could not stop it. Another five minutes passed, and Gordon spoke in a low-pitched, broken voice.

"They are not going to do it; they are going to demand the other stones, and then—"

"Hush!" exclaimed Dawlish.

He heard the opening of a door inside the room, the same sound as he had heard before. He went forward a pace. There was a muffled sound of movement, and then the unseen door closed. The one to the passage remained ajar.

Dawlish widened it, covering the room with his gun.

He saw Felicity!

She was sitting in an easy chair, her hands resting on the arms, her face pale, her head lolling back, and her eyes closed. She looked unhurt. Dawlish's heart almost turned over. He had to restrain the temptation to rush forward, and made sure that no one else was hiding there before he stepped to her side. Her breast was rising and falling, her breathing shallow but regular. Her eyes flickered, but remained closed.

Pinned to her coat was a slip of paper.

Dawlish unpinned and read it; Gordon passed him and raised Felicity's hand, feeling her pulse. Dawlish brushed his hand across his forehead, and said:

"She's all right, Sol. He says it's a shot of morphia, that's all." He stood staring down at her for a moment, and Gordon, much more himself, raised one eyelid.

"Yes," he said, "the pupil is dilated, it could be morphia. Pulse slow—you see I am almost as good as a doctor! Patrick! Stir yourself! We must get her out of here!"

Dawlish lifted his wife in his arms. Gordon covered the room with his automatic.

Nothing happened to impede them.

In a few minutes Felicity was lying on the settee in front of the sitting-room fire, which Gordon stoked busily, while Dawlish was putting on a kettle for hot water-bottles and coffee, to have it ready as soon as she came round. While the kettle was heating he hurried upstairs and collected half a dozen blankets. With them piled on her, Felicity's pallor faded and warmth began to give colour to her cheeks. Hot water-bottles made her perspire gently.

"She will be all right, my boy," said Gordon. "I cannot understand the man; he was a fool not to have stood out, he must have realized that you would not have sacrificed your wife for those jewels."

"There's a feeling abroad that the English are funny that way," said Dawlish. His relief was so great that he felt like shouting, but, he restrained himself, lit a cigarette, and stood staring at Felicity, who was now so flushed that she looked as if she were in a fever.

"She mustn't get too hot," said Gordon, "not too hot, my boy. Take the bottle away, there is a good fellow, otherwise she will be baked, and you won't want that!" He gave a high-pitched laugh, an indication of his own tension. "What about the other gems, Patrick?"

"Will you get them from the snow?" asked Dawlish.

"You *are* going to return them?"

"I don't think they'll be much use without the one we've broken," said Dawlish. "And I'm going to carry out my part of the bargain—good faith will be useful if we need to parley again."

Gordon raised his hands helplessly, but pattered off. Dawlish stood looking down at Felicity, hoping she would come round before he left for the garage, but she was still unconscious when Gordon came back. He was shivering with cold, and said he thought it was getting even colder. Dawlish slipped the gems into his pocket and hurried through the kitchen passage and to the back door.

Had he stopped to calculate the value of the imitation gem which Gordon had made, he would have realized the advantages of making duplicates of all three instead of the one. It was too late to hope to do anything like that now, for more than he realized might depend on convincing Hortelan that his word could be relied on.

In spite of his heavy coat the cold seemed to bite into his bones before he reached the garage. The only light was from the window of the kitchen.

The garage door was still open.

He put the two gems on the corner of the bench nearest the door, and then returned to the house. No one molested him. He stood by the kitchen door, waiting, hoping. He must have been there for a quarter of an hour when Gordon came pattering along the passage.

"Patrick, what is keeping you?"

"I want to see where they come from when they fetch the gems," said Dawlish.

"Oh," said Gordon. "Yes, yes, of course, my boy!"

Another five minutes passed, and then Dawlish became aware of a faint light shining along the garden. He drew back as far as he could while keeping the garden and the garage door in sight. He heard the crunching of footsteps on the snow. The dark shape of a man, visible against the light of his torch, approached from the far end of the garden and entered the garage. He was shorter than Hortelan, and he was alone—or so Dawlish thought at first, until he saw two other dark figures by the outhouse farther along the garden.

The first man reappeared; he called out in Spanish, and rejoined his companions hurriedly.

Dawlish stepped into the garden.

He could still discern the dark figures. They went up the

steep path to the back garden, and he followed with Gordon at his heels. He was at the top of the slope in time to see them enter the little garden shed, the last of the outhouses. A door closed. For five minutes they waited, but heard and saw nothing more.

"It's time we went back," said Dawlish.

"Yes," said Gordon, "yes, it is certainly time, Patrick. So we now know that they can get into that top shed—a great help, my boy, a very great help!" He stood warming himself in front of the kitchen fire while Dawlish took off his hat, coat and Wellingtons. "I must admit that I am surprised Hortelan has behaved like this. His need for the jewels is remarkable."

Dawlish put his head on one side.

"Not really!"

"Oh, you know what I mean," said Gordon. "It is an obsession, nothing must be allowed to interfere with it, he must not take the slightest risk. I am beginning to think that now that he has them he might leave us unmolested, that his talk of wanting us to make sure that he has safe escort is all bluff."

"I shouldn't rely on it," said Dawlish.

"If he is not going to do that, why has he disappeared? Why does he not break into the house from the hidden passages without worrying about what noise he makes? He could have shot that door to pieces, and could destroy the bedrooms to which he has access, my boy, and yet he lets us keep the doors locked so that we have some semblance of security. Even when we are out of the house for ten minutes or more he does not force his way in. Oh, it is a remarkable business!"

"We'd better make sure that he hasn't sent men in," said Dawlish.

The house was deserted but for themselves and Felicity.

She was sleeping more naturally, and the flush had gone from her cheeks. Once or twice in the next half-hour she stirred.

Gordon volunteered to heat some tinned soup and to cut some bread. He was gone for more than half an hour, and came back wheeling a dinner-wagon on which were several dish covers. Under one was bacon and eggs, under another toasted cheese, under the third soup which had splashed over the edge of the tureen and caused him much dismay. He beamed at Felicity, as she stirred again—and for the first time opened her eyes.

She could tell them little.

Not long after Dawlish and Gordon had left the room, Hortelan had bent over her as if to whisper confidentially, and she had felt the needle which he thrust into her arm. When it was done he clapped his hand over her mouth to stop her from calling for help. The drug had worked quickly and she had felt herself losing consciousness almost immediately. She remembered coming round once, in an unfamiliar room, furnished with poor quality furniture, and very warm; the only thing she remembered about it was that there were no windows. One man had been with her, and had put another hypodermic needle into her arm.

"And now this!" she said.

Dawlish laughed. "In future, we are all to be kidnapped together, not one at a time!"

"What shall we do to-night, Patrick?" asked Gordon.

"Stay in this room with the door locked and barricaded," said Dawlish; "there's nothing else we can do. If you feel energetic we could move down beds from upstairs."

"I am not as energetic as all that," said Gordon; "but why not bring down some mattresses, my boy? They are very comfortable, and will be better than easy chairs."

A little before nine o'clock they brought the mattresses

down, with some more blankets, and settled down to wait until midnight, when they would take turns in sleeping. Felicity was a little heavy-eyed, but otherwise her normal self. She switched on the radio as the hall clock struck nine; they had told her of the police message, and it was repeated, word for word as in the six o'clock news.

"Well, we know they'll get here as soon as they can," said Felicity. "They won't wait for trains and free roads, they'll probably send by parachute."

"As soon as we can get word through and they know exactly where to come, they'll be here," said Dawlish. "Meanwhile we can only hope—"

He did not finish, for the stillness of the night was suddenly shattered by the staccato chatter of a machine-gun not far away, followed in a few seconds by an explosion near enough to make the windows shake.

CHAPTER XVII

VAIN EFFORT

"We'll try the landing window," said Dawlish.

Gordon, already half-way to the front door, swung round and bolted up the stairs. Dawlish gave Felicity a hand. When they reached the window and looked out, they saw what Felicity had expected—gunfire. The rattle of machine-guns continued, and, in lulls, the sharp crack of rifles was audible: as they stood by the window the brilliant orange and yellow flash of an exploding mortar bomb twice illuminated the whole scene.

The fight was by the bridge.

Two machine-guns were placed on the opposite bank, and the yellow tracers they were firing carved light in curving lines across the river. The guns seemed to have been placed behind walls of snow. Farther behind them was the mortar, obviously a relic of the Home Guard armament.

When the vivid flashes came, the shapes of men on both sides could be picked out. There seemed to be a dozen this side of the river, and Dawlish was surprised that Hortelan had so many men; his forces were apparently strong enough to hold out for a long time.

Dawlish knew now why no attempt had been made to force a way into the house. Hortelan had been expecting this attack from the village, and had been preparing for it. His men were protected by snow ramparts, and had placed their main positions so that the village forces could not easily shift them. Much depended on whether the mortar succeeded in silencing the machine-gun emplacements.

It was an eerie sight.

The only sounds were those of the guns and the occasional roar of the mortars, which were badly aimed and landed their bombs half-way between the bridge and the cottage. During the next half-hour the firing never stopped for more than a few seconds, and all the ammunition used was of the tracer kind; red and yellow streaks passed to and fro. It was fascinating to watch; they hardly felt the bitter cold of the landing and did not speak until Gordon suddenly exclaimed:

"Why do they not get the range with that heavy gun?"

"Mortar," corrected Dawlish.

"What does it matter what we call it?" demanded Gordon, testily. "They are wasting every shot, the fools!" He darted a quick, almost furtive glance at Felicity. "What a pity we cannot attack Hortelan's men *from the rear,* Patrick!"

"The moment we went out, we'd be shot," said Dawlish.

"But they could not see us, they are fully engaged already. Patrick, it mihgt be a wonderful opportunity. I will come with you, my boy."

"Now who wants to take risks?" asked Dawlish, dryly. "No, Sol, it's the wrong time for it."

"I cannot believe—"

He broke off. Twenty yards down the drive the flame of a match showed a man lighting a cigarette; it also showed a machine-gun which was placed behind a wall of snow. The gun was trained on the front door of *Timbers*. Gordon gulped, and patted Dawlish's hand.

"You were right, my boy; how often you are right! But it is horrible to have to stand here and be able to do nothing."

"I'm enjoying it too," said Dawlish, sarcastically.

The shooting seemed to slacken, and for some minutes there had been no heavy explosion. Then one came. They just heard the moaning whistle of the bomb, and saw it burst within a few yards of one of Hortelan's machine-gun posts. The flash showed men flinging themselves into the snow, and for a moment the machine-gun was silent. The light faded. Then came another whistle, and another bomb, which exploded a little further away from the post.

"That's better, that's better!" howled Gordon. "Just one or two more like that and they will be finished! We might be relieved to-night. To-night!" His face was radiant. "It would be wonderful! I did not realize what a strain this was until now, when I see the chances of rescue!"

"I doubt if they'll make it," Dawlish said.

"Oh, you pessimist! They—"

A flash from this side of the river made him stop; with it came a *boom* as loud as anything they had yet heard—and they saw a shell burst on the opposite side, high up in a snow-covered field. The flash of the explosion revealed the mortar and its crew in vivid detail. The men were flinging themselves down, just as Hortelan's men had done. Swiftly there came another shot, then a third and fourth—and, with the last, they saw a direct hit on the mortar. In the flashes from other shells which followed they saw the pieces of the gun flying in all directions, the gun itself on one side and several figures near it, lying motionless in the snow. There was something ruthless in the shooting from Hortelan's gun, which was a heavier piece than anything else used that night.

It made them silent.

They pressed against the window, watching the quickening machine-gun fire, but now Hortelan's men were using several heavier guns and maintaining a stream of small-arms fire which Dawlish thought could only have one end. The answering fire slackened. Soon Dawlish saw from the big flashes that the villagers were retiring, leaving only a small rear-guard; it was as if they feared that Hortelan's men would press forward now, and try to cross the river. There was no movement of water, although it had been torrential during the afternoon.

It was frozen over, Dawlish realized.

Before long the shooting stopped altogether. The beams of torches replaced the light from the guns. Hortelan's men were walking to and fro along the river bank; as far as Dawlish could see they made no attempt to cross. They would have been help-less if they had tried to climb the hill on the far side of the bridge.

"They'll take no chances," Dawlish said. "All they want is to make sure that they are safe here."

Gordon gulped. Felicity turned away from the window, and they went downstairs. The excitement of the first few minutes, when the hope of rescue had loomed so large, was completely gone. They were silent and depressed, even Gordon could find no quips with which to enliven them. After a while he said that he would make some tea. He went off, and Dawlish sat in front of the fire with his wife, who stared into the flames, which danced brightly in her eyes and on the waves in her dark hair.

"It hasn't seemed real from the moment we got here," she said, "and that battle made it ten times more unreal."

"I don't know," said Dawlish. "Realism at its height, I would say. I didn't expect much else, although I hoped for it."

"Can we do anything?" asked Felicity.

"Just keep on hoping," said Dawlish. "Relief *will* come, you know; I can't believe that in an emergency like this one of Hamblin's men won't get as far as Shaftesbury, where they'll surely be able to get a message out by radio. There's one new thing in our favour."

"I haven't seen it yet," said Felicity.

"The clouds are thinner," said Dawlish. "I saw some stars once or twice. I think we're in for a spell of heavy frost, but frozen snow isn't so likely to stop men moving about."

"Hortelan will realize that," said Felicity.

When Gordon came in with tea he was more cheerful than when he had left. He hurried out, to return with a small bottle of whisky, which he held up proudly.

"I always have it with me, Patrick; I thought we would find things a little less depressing with a spot or two inside us! I have been everywhere, but failed to find any wines or spirits in the house; that is unlike Barney, isn't it?"

"Most of what has happened is unlike Barney," said Dawlish. "It's been out of character from the very beginning. Hortelan caused that, of course." He put a tot of whisky in his tea, insisted on giving one to Felicity, and sniffed appreciatively. "We'll have to ration ourselves with this," he said.

"One tot a night," said Gordon. "Yes. I wonder," he added, suddenly solemn, "how many nights will pass, my boy? I wonder—" he broke off, abruptly. "But I am getting melancholy, and that won't do! Two tots for the first night, eh?"

Dawlish took the first watch.

The settee, for Felicity, was pushed further away from the fire, and Gordon rolled himself in blankets and lay down on one of the mattresses. Soon he was snoring. Felicity fell asleep quickly, and Dawlish switched off the light and sat in the firelight, trying to get his thoughts in order, but forced to acknowledge the hopelessness of their position unless they received outside help. Even the satisfaction of knowing that the tunnel led from the house to the shed at the top of the garden was short-lived.

The astonishing thing was that they had the freedom of the house. For how long would Hortelan let them stay?

Not for many minutes once he discovered that the jewel was a 'new' one. Dawlish's thoughts shifted. Jewels—jewels containing messages or secret information. There was nothing new in that, but one thing that was hard to believe, perhaps harder than anything else—the inference that Barney Day had bought the Alexis gems without knowing they were paste.

Gordon, of course, would insist that he had bought the real ones and the fakes had been substituted. Dawlish admitted the possibility of that if it were admitted that Barney had known the importance of the false gems, and had gone to such trouble to hide them. There were questions arising which that explanation could not answer, however.

If Barney had bought the real jewels, *why* had he also bought the false ones?

If he had known what was in the fakes, *why* had he tried to conceal them, instead of reporting to the authorities?

If he had realized what might follow, why had he planned the 'house-warming'? If he had been nervous of confiding in the police, why had he not told Dawlish the truth? His explanation at the cottage had helped a little, but it was far from satisfying, because much had been left out on the orders of Hortelan.

Could he have been victimized for as long as he said, and withstood the strain, without turning to someone for help?

The mystery of Barney's behaviour seemed to Dawlish to be one of the major problems, second only to the question: what was written on the paper inside the jewels? The police broadcast left no doubt of the great importance of the affair. Gordon was almost certainly right when he suggested that it was political, perhaps a matter of international politics in which Spain played an important part.

It was useless to try to stop thinking about it; when he tried, he found himself dozing. He washed his face and hands in a bowl of water brought in for the purpose, and settled down again nearer the fire, trying to rest. He could not concentrate. After the first half-hour he was less on the alert for sounds from the rest of the house. He had almost taken it for granted that Hortelan would leave them alone for the night.

At four o'clock he went across to Gordon, and shook him gently. Gordon peered up at him with one eye, then sat up, yawned and rubbed his hands.

"I've had my ration of sleep, have I? Very good, Patrick, I will take over. No alarms, I assume, or you would have called me earlier."

"No alarms," said Dawlish.

He was asleep within a few minutes. Gordon promised not to leave the room without calling him, and sat with a book in front of the fire. The house was silent except for logs falling in the grate as they burned.

Dawlish, always a light sleeper, was conscious of a touch on his shoulder. He opened his eyes, and heard Gordon whisper:

"Wake up, Patrick, wake up! Don't make a noise, please, but wake up. Ah, that's good!" He backed away as Dawlish sat up, with a hand raised. There was a sound from the window, not from the passage—a gentle, insistent tapping.

"Is it a trick?" murmured Gordon. "Are they trying to get in that way?"

"Listen," said Dawlish.

The tapping continued, growing a little louder. There was no other sound. The curtains were drawn, and Dawlish knew that if he pulled them back with the light on everyone inside the room would make good targets. He put a hand carefully beneath the curtain, and tapped back.

After a pause, the tapping outside started again.

"Keep the window covered, Sol," said Dawlish, "and pass me a blanket, will you." He put the blanket round his shoulders and stepped softly across the room. The air in the passage was like ice. He unbolted the front door and stepped out on the porch, then on to the frozen snow. It crackled beneath his feet so loudly that he was afraid of being heard.

There was a faint glow of light coming from the front-room window, and in it he saw the figure of a man, crouching low, still tapping with his gloved hand. Dawlish drew nearer cautiously, and then suddenly shone his torch.

The man at the window turned round, without a sound.

It was Carter!

He stood quite still, one hand about a gun which pointed towards the ground. He was muffled up in heavy clothes, but there was no mistaking his face. Obviously the torch light blinded him so that he could not see Dawlish.

Dawlish whispered: "Are you alone?"

"Dawlish!" Carter spoke too loudly, then dropped his voice to a whisper. "No, there are three men with me; we managed to get across country. Are you all safe?"

"Yes."

"Wait here," said Carter.

He turned from the window and disappeared towards the corner of the house. As he went Dawlish's suspicions of him returned; his conviction that someone had given Hortelan information had never altered and he was doubtful whether anyone could have got through the guard without being observed. He could do little about it, whatever the truth; the man had to be taken on trust.

Carter reappeared with three other men. They made little noise despite the hard crust of the snow, and in a few minutes they were all standing in the hall, their faces blue with cold. One of them began to shiver. Dawlish pushed open the sitting-room door, and Gordon covered him with his automatic.

"All safe," said Dawlish, smiling.

Felicity was sitting up, flushed with sleep; Sol had warned her of the interruption. She swung her legs off the settee as the men entered, making for the fire and speaking in whispers. The man who was shivering could not keep still, so Carter took off his coat and began to pummel him. Gordon, with a shrug of his shoulders, went off to the kitchen. He was back soon with tea, and as the door closed behind him the hall clock began to strike.

"Seven!" said Gordon. "Well, not too bad, Patrick!" He stared at Carter, who was sitting back in an easy chair and beginning to look less frozen. "How did you manage it?"

"We started across the fields when the main attack was made," said Carter. "The river was frozen so we were able to get across. Things are bad in the village, I'm afraid, there were several people hurt before we left. We did not come straight here, thinking the house would be closely watched, but managed to find a way to the back. Once we were stuck for three hours, I thought we would never get here, Mr. Dawlish." He sipped hot tea as he spoke and his ruddy face was glowing. "You're glad to see us, I'll be bound!"

"Overjoyed," said Dawlish, trying to speak warmly.

"What has happened here?"

Dawlish told him, omitting only the fact that in his pocket was the sheet of paper taken from the jewel. Carter heard him out, nodding from time to time, and when he had finished one of his men said:

"It is remarkable that they do not mind you being here, Mr. Dawlish." He was younger than the others, and his voice was pleasant; Dawlish judged him to be from one of the larger houses.

"I think they mind a lot," said Dawlish, "but they think we're too weak to cause much damage."

"Can they hear what is said in this room?" asked Carter.

"I don't think so."

"Then we can take them by surprise when the opportunity comes," said Carter. He accepted a cigarette and sat back, comfortable but looking very tired. "The Colonel is going to attack again to-night, at dusk. We shall go in from the rear." He paused. "We *must* get them, this time! Did you hear the news last night?"

"Yes," said Dawlish.

"Astonishing, isn't it?" said Carter. His calm voice was in itself remarkable, he took it all so much for granted. "We dassen't fail, and that's all there is to it."

"What about a messenger to Shaftesbury?" Dawlish asked.

"The Colonel is trying again to-day. It is not easy, Mr. Dawlish, but with the snow hard it might be done. If there is a thaw we cannot hope to get through for a long time, and if we have more snow it will be hopeless, but if the frost holds we *might* get a message through. The Colonel will do all he can, don't fear that."

"No need for fear," murmured Dawlish.

He tried again to put a note of jubilation into his voice, but it was difficult. He did not feel elated at the arrival of the party, and he did not feel sure that he could trust Hamblin. Common sense told him that Carter and the others must have told the truth about their journey, or they would not have got so cold, but even then he wondered if Hortelan had known they were coming and let them through by arrangement. Hortelan might suspect that there had been trickery with the jewels, and—

Felicity exclaimed suddenly.

"Pat, we've forgotten Barney!" She looked at Carter. "Is Mr. Day—"

"Better, I would say," said Carter, reassuringly. "There is a qualified nurse in the village, she has been looking after him, as well as his maid. She's a faithful one, that maid—she won't leave his side! He was violent again, Mrs. Dawlish, had another fit you might say, but it did not last long. He was sleeping naturally when I last saw him."

"So we've a chance of saving him," said Felicity.

"Has he talked intelligently?" asked Dawlish.

Carter shook his head. "Not yet, Mr. Dawlish. When he *can* talk, what a story he will have to tell!" He gave a gentle chuckle, and put his feet up on a pouffe. "If you're sure we're not likely to be attacked, an hour's sleep would help all of us. Dare we take it, d'ye think?"

"We'll wake you soon enough if there's trouble," said Dawlish.

The unreality of the situation seemed to increase. He went out of the sitting-room with Felicity and Gordon, leaving the four villagers together, two on mattresses and two on chairs. There was no sign that Hortelan had made any attempt to break in during the night. The doors of the rooms were locked, and upstairs the furniture was still in position as they had placed it to make sure that there could be no easy break through. In the kitchen Felicity and Gordon started to prepare breakfast while Dawlish, clinging to habit, had a quick bath and shave, then changed his clothes. The suit in which he had slept was crumpled and faded-looking; the change made him feel much better and helped him to forget that he had slept so little. When he got downstairs an appetising smell of frying bacon was coming from the electric stove, and Felicity and Gordon were laughing.

The eight o'clock news brought a repetition of the police message; there was nothing else of note in the bulletin. None of the villagers stirred when Dawlish came in to listen. He went back to the kitchen where breakfast was ready. He was ravenously hungry, and Gordon chuckled as he ate. The bread was stale, but there was enough left for two days, thanks to the provisions Carter had brought on his first trip.

Outside, for the first time since they had arrived, the sun was shining from a sky which looked like hard blue glass. There was little warmth in the sunshine, but it sparkled on the frozen snow and gave to it a beauty which the dark clouds had hidden. The village seemed quiet. A few people walked in the streets, but on the whole there was little movement. From the landing window they could just see men manning the earthworks which had been thrown up at the top of the hill—a wall of snow had been built for several hundred yards, and it was doubtful whether Hortelan would ever be able to break through that way. Hortelan's men were manning the posts by the river; all of them were clad in furs, almost as if they had expected the struggle to come during this spell of weather.

The river was still frozen; it looked like a grey, glassy ribbon winding through the hills and meadows, and the valley it ran through was a king of no-man's-land.

It was while Gordon was shaving and Felicity and Dawlish looking through the landing window, that they heard the sound of an engine, distant at first, but gradually growing louder, until they knew that it was an aeroplane, flying up from the south.

CHAPTER XVIII

HORTELAN MAKES A MISTAKE

Soon they were able to see the machine.

It was flying low, no more than two thousand feet, a two-engined carrier-plane. It flew almost straight along the course of the river, then circled several times round the village. Suddenly a column of smoke rose from the centre of Hurn, rising almost vertically.

"A spotting 'plane," Dawlish said. "If Hamblin's got the sense to write a message in the snow, we're near the end of this show."

"He won't have time," Felicity said.

The machine was coming towards them again, as if prepared to make yet another flight round the village. Its engines brought a welcome note, confirmation that they were not completely forgotten. Dawlish had little doubt that the aircraft had come to Hurn in the hope of finding a message marked out in the snow—thank heavens the police *knew* that Hurn had once been the home of Hortelan.

"I think—" began Felicity.

She stopped as a rattle of machine-gun fire sounded, shrill above the deep note of the engine. Tracer bullets, looking like little flashes of silver, streaked towards the belly of the aircraft. The pilot took quick evasive action and began to climb. The machine-gun continued to pour its bullets upwards, but the target was soon out of range.

"Well, well!" said Dawlish, in a strained voice. "Hortelan's big mistake, my sweet!"

"You mean the pilot—"

"Won't be long in radioing *that* story," said Dawlish, and his eyes were glistening. "Hallo, it's coming lower again." He saw the aircraft make a gradual descent towards the village, still out of range. Suddenly two objects dropped from it, dark, cylindrical shapes. Parachutes opened; and as they began to fall, the aircraft made height again and flew straight towards the south. As if in defiance, the machine-gunner loosed off another few rounds.

"Look!" exclaimed Felicity.

Hurrying across the ground from a field behind the cottage were two men, and their voices travelled back to the house— angry, authoritative voices. They reached the machine-gun post. The man at the machine straightened up, and then went down as the first of the newcomers struck him a vicious blow on the face.

Dawlish laughed grimly.

"Hortelan knows it was a mistake," he said. "I wouldn't like to be that gunner for the next hour, my sweet! Well—it certainly can't be long now."

"It might make Hortelan attack here," said Felicity.

"Why look on the dark side?" asked Dawlish. He heard Gordon hurrying from the bathroom, wrapped in his dressing-gown. "It's all right, Sol!" He told the fat man what had happened, and Gordon's face took on a new expression, a curious mixture of delight and anxiety.

"Well, well! It means that the crisis will not be long delayed, now. Hortelan will probably try to fight his way out, hoping that the snow will be hard enough to make it possible. We must be more than usually careful, Patrick!"

"Tell us how," invited Dawlish, ironically.

He went downstairs, meeting Carter in the hall. The men had been woken up by the aeroplane, and had watched from their window, unable to see exactly what had happened. They had noticed the smoke, but seen nothing of the attack on the machine-gunner. Carter looked thoughtful when he heard about it.

"We can expect action, then."

"We seem to be agreed about that," said Dawlish, dryly. "And we can also expect a message from Hortelan before long, I think."

Carter looked towards the drive.

"I look for such things to happen almost as soon as you voice them," he said, but there was a smile in his eyes, and for the first time Dawlish felt really sure of the man. "Much depends on whether he knows that we are here."

"Yes," said Dawlish. "I—"

"It is *incredible!*" Carter broke in. "Look, there is a man coming!"

He stepped to the side of the room, with his men, to make sure that they could not be seen from the windows. The new-comer, the man who had brought the terms of the first ultimatum, was striding up the drive, quite confident that there was no danger.

Dawlish met him on the porch.

He had the same supercilious air, the same confidence and assurance. He had no letter this time, but said brusquely:

"You are to go to the garage at once, Dawlish, taking your wife and Gordon with you."

"Won't it be—" began Dawlish.

"There is no time for argument or refusal," said the man sharply. "If you go to the garage you will be safe, if you stay here your lives will be in danger. Señor Hortelan is generous to allow you the opportunity. There is a fire in the garage," he added. "You must be there within half an hour. Do you understand?"

"Yes," said Dawlish, heavily.

"Then obey," said the other, and turned and stalked away.

Dawlish, Felicity and Gordon, huddled up in all the clothes they could find, and carrying blankets as well as supplies of tinned food, walked from the kitchen door towards the garage. There was no indication that Hortelan knew that Carter and his men were in the house, and Carter had not hesitated to say that he would stay behind. They had not speculated on the reason for the order, but at the back of Dawlish's mind there was an uneasy feeling that Hortelan might now put his earlier threat into effect, and destroy *Timbers*.

"How I do dislike electric fires," said Gordon, as he stepped into the garage. "How I do dislike the smell of oil and the fact that we are again forced to do nothing."

"We've done a little," Felicity said, mildly.

"Yes, yes, but of what importance? All the time we have been here, we have no idea what is happening. We do know that there must be an underground room—no, rooms—of some size, because of all the men whom Hortelan has hidden away. We do not know what has been happening there—we just do not know. I am frightened, Patrick, frightened in case it is something of such great importance that it would be disastrous." He looked woefully solemn as he stood in front of the bench, putting down tins of food from a large basket. "I am, of course, an old rogue. You know that, the police also know that. I confess I have been a lucky man to escape without a prison sentence in the course of my long life, and yet—I am English, Patrick. You admit that, don't you?"

"Now what's worrying you?" demanded Dawlish.

"Oh my, oh my!" cried Gordon, raising his hands towards the roof. "What is worrying me, is that all you can say? Listen, Patrick! I deal in stolen jewels, I have made a fortune with them, I am not a poor man. True, I have done a little good here and there, I have not kept all my money to myself, and there are people in London who love old Sol Gordon. In the big air-raids, was I not there among them, helping where I could? Was I not a man who informed against looters, because I would not allow such crimes? I tell you all this, my friends, because I have never talked about it before, and because perhaps you may think that I am only interested in what money I can make, no matter how I make it. But I also tell you this: I would give every penny I possess, yes, and I would make a full confession of all my crimes to the police, if only I could know what Hortelan is doing here. I am first an Englishman, and then a rogue. Do you believe me?"

"Of course," said Dawlish, and he was wary now. "It is what we had only guessed about you before."

"You are kind, Patrick, very kind," said Gordon. "And you, Felicity. Good people, both of you. Now, I have made a will. I have left most of my money to the London hospitals, they did such wonderful work during the air-raids, and it will not matter if the money *they* receive was not honestly come by. See that there is no trickery with my will, Patrick."

"What do you mean?" demanded Felicity, sending Dawlish a puzzled glance. "What makes you talk like this, now?"

Gordon said: "Because I am going to find out what is under the ground here. Yes, Patrick, I am going. You are not, because you have a pretty wife, a lovely wife, and I am an old man. If I die trying to do this, then no one will be much the loser, but if you die—well, my boy, there is no need to talk more. I have made up my mind. I am going into that shed, Patrick, to find out how to get underground, if I can. I expect they will take me prisoner, but they *might* let me see what is there, and I *might* escape. It is a slim chance, but just a chance." He shrugged his shoulders. "I am glad that you do not argue with me, because I will not listen to arguments."

"You won't have a chance in a thousand," said Dawlish.

"I know, my boy, I know. But there it is. I have been thinking of this, wondering how I could best help to end this thing, and perhaps, who knows? a way may be opened for me. I want you to promise one thing: that you will not follow me."

Dawlish said: "You're wrong to go."

"No, please! You, who have dared so much in your life, you should know better than to say such a thing. Well, I go!"

"You're staying here," said Dawlish.

"Patrick, I insist—"

"Right here, Sol," said Dawlish, gently. "You're a rogue and a scoundrel, and yet's there's something about you that I like so much that I'm not going to let you go." There was a new note in his voice, something which Felicity recognized and which made Gordon look at him narrow-eyed. To Felicity it seemed the kind of talk in which Dawlish would indulge when he was trying desperately to gain time. The words gave no clue to it, but the struggle between these men had been born in the last few seconds, and was not trivial.

"Now, Patrick, *please*," said Gordon. "If I wish to throw my life away, that is my business."

"Ours," said Dawlish.

"Patrick—"

"*Ours*," repeated Dawlish, heavily.

"My dear boy, I am sorry you take it like this," said Gordon,

"I tell you there is a chance. I am a rich man, Hortelan might be persuaded—"

Dawlish laughed, but there was a harsh note in his voice, and his eyes were hard.

"No, Sol. We'll stick together."

Gordon shrugged his shoulders.

"It is a great pity, Patrick. I did not wish that we should quarrel, but—" he dropped the basket he was holding, making Dawlish and Felicity dodge away from the tins which fell from it, and with his other hand he snatched an automatic from his pocket. "I am *really* sorry, Patrick, but I must go."

There was not a sound in the garage but their breathing.

The gun in Gordon's hand was quite steady, pointing towards Dawlish's chest. Felicity was by Dawlish's side, her clenched hands raised in front of her. She looked incredulous, as if some sudden storm had swept her from head to foot and left her limp and weak. The struggle was between Dawlish and Sol Gordon, that funny little fat man, still bundled up in coats and blankets; and it was deeper than the last few minutes explained. She realized that there had been suspicion of Gordon in Dawlish's mind for some time, suspicion which now seemed crystallized into certainty.

Gordon broke the silence.

"It will distress me to hurt you, Patrick, but I must go, and I will not hesitate to shoot if you try to stop me. I have business to do. I came here to do business with Hortelan, you see. I knew what was happening some time ago. *I* arranged for the Alexis jewels to be smuggled into this country. There were two sets, the genuine ones and the fakes, which you have seen. Yes, I was responsible for that, I sold the real ones to Barney. *He* stole the fakes from me."

Dawlish said: "Go on."

"I tell you this so that you should know how determined I am to see Hortelan," said Gordon. "He does not know who I am—he does not know that I have helped him a great deal in many ways. There is much money in this, and I love money. Oh, I give much away, as you know, but I still love it, *and I am going to bargain with Hortelan.* You see, there must be a safe way out of this place, and Hortelan is probably the only man who knows it. I need freedom and money. I forgot to tell you, Patrick, that before I left London there was a warrant out for my arrest. It concerned the Alexis collection. Somehow the police learned that I had handled them, somehow they learned of their importance to Hortelan. I cannot explain more," he added, softly, "I must go."

"Aren't you forgetting something?" Dawlish asked.

"What, my boy?" Not once had Gordon's tone altered; he spoke now as he had done throughout their stay at *Timbers,* like a benevolent, likeable old man.

"The paper I took from the fake diamond," said Dawlish.

Gordon smiled.

"Oh, no! Before I woke you up last night and told you of the tapping I took it from your pocket. It was a good opportunity. I will tell you this—I will swear it on oath, if you like. I will *try* to make sure that Hortelan is caught before he leaves the country. I do not know what he is planning, but I will prevent him from succeeding, if I can. But I must have my chance to get away, Patrick. You see, if the police from London get here, I will be arrested, and I should not like to end my days in gaol. You do understand, don't you?"

"I understand a lot of things," said Dawlish. "You are telling only half the truth now. Hortelan knows you, and that is why we have been left unmolested most of the time."

Gordon shrugged his shoulders.

"Perhaps he has a suspicion, my boy, that is all—just a suspicion. Well, I am going. Don't jump at me, I beg of you. I should hate to shoot you. I shall insist on you remaining free and unhurt. I like you very much, both of you. Now—"

He swept his arm round, sent a dozen tins flying off the bench at Dawlish's feet, lunged forward and pushed Felicity against Dawlish. Then he rushed out of the garage, slamming the door behind him. In trying to save Felicity, Dawlish stumbled over a tin and fell heavily against the bench. Felicity kept her balance, and they clung to each other for a few seconds, until Felicity broke away and Dawlish pulled open the door.

Gordon was disappearing into the shed, a blanket flying from his shoulders. He had got up the steep, slippery path without trouble and remarkably quickly. Dawlish took two steps in his wake.

The *crack!* of a rifle-shot made him stop; the bullet struck the wall of the garage two feet away from him. He saw the sharp-shooter near the shed; the man had not fired to kill, and did not shoot again when Dawlish stopped.

"Warning," he said. He leaned against the door and looked at Felicity with a one-sided smile. "I suppose that's the truth about Sol Gordon. I've been afraid that he knew more than he professed, and yet—I wasn't altogether convinced, were you?"

"It seemed out of character," Felicity said, and added hastily: "I mean, he's been such a dear old boy, and even now he's gone off without harming us, as if what he said at first is right, and he wants to try to find out the truth without bringing any further harm to us."

"I think he's sincere about that," said Dawlish. "In his way he's fond of us. I don't know how much of the rest is true, but they did let him go up to the shed, and they stopped us."

There seemed no point in talking about it. It was impossible to guess how much of Gordon's story was true and how much invention. He had left a curious atmosphere behind him, by a feeling that he could have said much more, and they did not know his real motive. Dawlish lit a cigarette. The electric fire had been on when they arrived and the room was warm. It had been tidied even since they had last been there, but when he examined the bench closely he found more traces of iron or steel filings.

"You know," he said, "we've taken a lot for granted, my sweet. We haven't asked ourselves how Hortelan came to have a piece of artillery up here, for one thing, nor how long he's been established here, nor any one of a dozen different questions which ought to have given us a lot to think about—"

"Everything does that," said Felicity. She stared at him for a moment, and then laughed. "It's crazy, but I feel almost as if the worst is over, a kind of wild exhilaration. Nothing matters any more! You're here with me, Gordon's got the paper which might have caused serious trouble, we're in no man's land with Hortelan's promise of safety, and there's no reason why he shouldn't keep it."

"And three men were murdered in *Timbers*," said Dawlish.

"How can we possibly do any more? Carter's the official representative of the police. Hamblin is alive to the danger. The pilot of the aeroplane will surely bring relief before long. Pat, it *is* over, for us."

"I've never heard a worse case of wishful thinking," said Dawlish. "If we get a chance of doing anything more you'll take it as quickly as I shall."

"I don't think there'll be an opportunity," said Felicity. "Darling, sit down on that tyre and light a cigarette for me, and try to stop worrying."

"Yes, ma'am," murmured Dawlish.

"I'd like someone to paint you now," said Felicity. "Your hair's more unruly than I can remember seeing it, you've just that look of the devil in your eyes which makes you attractive, and you're half inclined to smile at my feminine folly, but at the same time trying to make yourself think severely of Sol Gordon as well as reminding yourself of your duty to your country! No, don't get up! Let me see if I can catch the expression." She took a pencil from her handbag and a small note-book, and sketched quickly.

"And so on, *ad absurdum*," he said. "Finished?" She nodded, and he stretched out his hand.

She handed it to him; and just then a shadow passed the window.

He took the sketch without looking at it, jumped to his feet and looked out. One of Hortelan's men had just passed. He could not see where he had gone, so he opened the door, the sketch fluttering in the light wind. The bright sunlight on the snow hurt his eyes, but he stared towards the top of the garden, and saw several men walk out of the shed. Hortelan was among them, and by his side, talking swiftly and gesticulating wildly, was Sol Gordon. Hortelan seemed unimpressed by what he was saying, and one of the other men stretched out a hand and slapped him on the side of the face. Gordon took no notice, and went on talking. They walked slowly up the path, towards the hill which was surely impassable a little further on.

They went behind a beech hedge; snow had been knocked off part of it, and they could see the dusty brown of the winter leaves. Their heads and shoulders were clearly visible, their legs and feet hidden. Just behind the hedge they stopped.

"There's a doorway," Felicity said, in a hushed voice.

The side of the hill seemed to open; they saw a black shape, like a doorway. The men disappeared one after the other,

Gordon among the last to go. Two or three men were in the grounds, out of reach of revolver shooting, and all of them carried rifles. Dawlish took three steps towards the shed, and another warning shot made him stop.

"What's Carter doing?" Felicity asked, helplessly.

"Hortelan probably knew they were there," said Dawlish, with a shrug. "If not, Gordon's probably told him by now. In any case, there isn't much that Carter can do."

The words were hardly out of his mouth when there was a rifle shot—and one of the men watching the garage staggered, and fell slowly forward. The rifle slipped from his grasp, and he lay still on the frozen snow. The shot brought a volley of machine-gun and rifle fire, directed towards *Timbers*. More shooting came from the house. Obviously Carter had seen something and was trying to make a sortie. He did not have a chance in a thousand.

Suddenly Hortelan appeared by the hillside. His supercilious envoy was with him, and another man, with mufflers about his neck, a cloth cap pulled low over his eyes, and wearing an ulster which nearly touched the ground. He walked more slowly than the others, and two armed men followed him.

The shooting near the house grew more violent. The little party, as if unperturbed, walked down the slippery path towards the garage. For some time Hortelan and his companion hid the stranger, but suddenly Dawlish caught a glimpse of him, and Felicity tightened her grip on his arm.

"Is it—" she began.

"Yes," said Dawlish, in a wondering voice. "That's *Barney*."

CHAPTER XIX

BARNEY DAY

Hortelan and his companions knew that Dawlish was armed, yet showed no weapons themselves as they walked steadily towards the garage. Now and again Barney was hidden from view, but Felicity and Dawlish were in no doubt as to his identity.

One thing was certain: it was not the Barney of the cottage, not the man who had been taken to the village. This was the real Barney, tall, healthy-looking, keeping his balance easily. He looked sombre, but he did not look ill.

Now that he saw him, Dawlish was appalled by his own credulity. He had not questioned the identity of the man he had first seen. The difference between his appearance and that of this man walking towards them was marked, yet the very fact that it was so marked had helped to aid the illusion. Jane had played a part—perhaps the most important part—in maintaining the deception, yet she herself could surely not have been deceived.

As they approached, the shooting grew fiercer near the house. Several men, standing fifty yards or so from the sitting-room window, and protected by mounds of snow, were shooting with an unruffled calm which characterized most of the things Hortelan and his men did.

"Go inside, Dawlish, please," said Hortelan.

Dawlish obeyed. There was nothing else to do. Felicity followed him, and in a few seconds the others were standing in the garage, and one of the men closed the door.

Barney looked stonily at Dawlish.

Dawlish, conscious of Hortelan's steady gaze, looked at the older man and then quickly away. He had the impression that Barney was trying to convey something to him, something he was desperately anxious that Hortelan should not learn. Yet not a muscle of his face moved. He held himself erect; he had a supercilious appearance not unlike Hortelan's envoy. When he pushed his cap back Dawlish saw that his white hair was cut short.

"I have one question to ask you, Dawlish," said Hortelan, "and on the truth of your answer depends your life and that of your wife. Do you know this man?"

He touched Barney's arm.

Dawlish drew his brows together in a puzzled frown, calculated to make Hortelan uncertain of himself and to gain time. He stared at Barney's impassive face, more than ever sure that this was the *real* Barney Day; yet the other had shown no sign of recognition, that must surely indicate what he wanted Dawlish to do.

"I am not sure," said Dawlish, at last.

"The answer is not good enough," said Hortelan, harshly. He thrust Barney forward, making him stand beneath the light, and switched it on. "Look well. Do you know this man?"

Dawlish said: "He is remarkably like Barney Day used to be."

Barney stood stiff and unbending—but Dawlish thought that there was a gleam of approval in his eyes. Hortelan snapped his fingers in annoyance, and barked:

"*Is he Barney Day?*"

"Surely Day is in the village?"

"Never mind that! Is this man Day?"

Dawlish hesitated, and then turned to Felicity. She was staring at the fence, frowning, seeing what he wanted, wondering how best to make sure that Hortelan was deceived.

"What do you think?" Dawlish asked her.

She shook her head.

"It's not Barney," she said, "he's too hard, his eyes are not the same shade—"

"Do you expect me to believe you remember the shade of a man's eyes?" snapped Hortelan. He swung round on Felicity and put a hand on her shoulder. "Mrs. Dawlish, I have warned your husband that your lives depend on the truth of what you tell me. If you have studied the face of the real Day well, tell me, without lying, whether this man is he."

"I've told you," said Felicity, and went a step nearer, looking at Barney with great intentness. "I am quite sure he is not," she said. "The bone structure beneath the eyes and at the temples is different." She sounded professional, then gave a little puzzled laugh. "He is more like the Barney we know so well than the real Barney, because of the ravages of illness, but he isn't Barney."

"She's right," said Dawlish slowly.

Barney said to Hortelan: "I have told you the truth, these people bear me out. I have masqueraded as Day for some time, and I have helped you." He shrugged his shoulders. "If you are not satisfied, I cannot help it."

The *timbre* of his voice was exactly like Barney's, and yet he spoke with a clipped harshness which sounded foreign to him. The cold expression in his grey eyes did not alter, unless it was with another fleeting gleam of approval. There was a short silence, which seemed pregnant with menace, before Hortelan turned to the door.

"Very well, Dawlish, you and your wife must stay here and keep the door closed. I will promise you safety if you do that, but I cannot be responsible for what happens if you disobey. Do you understand me?"

"Fully," said Dawlish, dryly.

"Let us go," said Hortelan.

He turned towards the door; one of his men opened it. Barney followed him, and as he went Felicity saw something fall from below his long ulster. It was a tightly folded piece of paper. Neither of the men who followed Barney noticed it, because they were close behind him. Felicity waited until the door had closed and the party was on the way up the hill again, before she bent down for the paper. Dawlish watched her, made himself forget that odd interview.

"What is it?"

"Barney dropped it," she said.

The sheet of thin foolscap paper was filled on both sides with small pencilled writing—not unlike that on the paper which had come from the diamond. It was in Barney's hand, closely written, and they took it to the light, Dawlish's heart-beats quickening, Felicity with a sense of excitement which showed in the colour on her cheeks.

"Are we getting somewhere at last?" she asked.

"I think so," said Dawlish. His voice was low-pitched, and he glanced around carefully to make quite certain that they could not be watched or overheard. "Listen . . ."

"*If I succeed in getting this to any disinterested person* (Barney had written), *take this note to the police or to the military authorities at once. Inform them that in the hill behind* Timbers *there is a large underground workshop, which has been used in the past for secret experimental work by the Government, but which for some time*

*has been left vacant. A Spaniard, calling himself Hortelan, Horlan
or Telan, has taken control of it with the connivance of certain individuals in the village of Hurn, individuals whom I do not know by
name. Hortelan has also obtained, from stores of Home Guard equipment in the village, two small pieces of field artillery, several Lewis
guns, Mills bombs, hand-grenades and automatic rifles. He has also
obtained sufficient ammunition to cause considerable damage if he
should be forced to fight. He is an extremely dangerous man and he
will not hesitate to commit murder or massacre if it will help him to
escape from any threat of danger.*

*"Tell the police or the authorities that I am Richard Barney Day
of Line Street, Fulham. The police know me as a dealer in precious
stones and* objets d'art. *Some six months ago I was offered a set of
jewels known as the Alexis Collection. The purchase was to be made
in Spain, and the responsibility for payment of duty on the gems was
mine. Among the jewels which I bought were two fakes. One was
cracked—paste diamonds frequently crack in great heat—and I broke
it open. Inside I found a document, written in Spanish, which I was
able to translate.*

*"This document was part of a larger one. There was enough in it
for me to understand that Hortelan—the man from whom I bought
the jewels in the first place, and who I believed had every right to
negotiate their sale—was a party to a plot to take control of the
Spanish Government, if necessary by force of arms. I know that individuals in England are in some way involved, and that the success
or failure of the plot largely depends on the attitude of the British
Government. Through diplomatic channels, I believe, efforts are being
made to gain the approval of the Government for this* coup, *which is
to usurp the authority of whatever Government is in power in Spain,
irrespective of political influence. I also know that several of the individuals involved in the plot are Germans who have been in touch with
Hortelan while in Spain.*

"*Circumstances which I will explain if I live long enough, made it necessary for me to convince Hortelan that I am not, in fact, Barney Day, but a German agent acting for certain factions in the Reich. In this deception I was able to enlist the help of my first cousin, whose name is also Day, who is an older man but remarkably like me in general appearance. The deception was also aided by my housekeeper, Jane Meakin, and in the event of my death I wish to make sure that Jane Meakin is well provided for out of my estate, the balance of which is to be divided among charities in the poorer districts of London at the discretion of Mr. Patrick Dawlish my very good friend, and Superintendent William Trivett of New Scotland Yard. These provisions have already been made in my Will, which has been duly signed and attested, but may have been destroyed.*

"*I cannot impress upon the recipient of this note too strongly the fact that Hortelan is extremely dangerous, and that authorities must be advised as quickly as possible that he has possession of this workshop, a force of men at least twenty strong, arms and ammunition, and that he has frequently declared that he will not allow himself to be captured alive*

"*Richard Barney Day.*"

It was a long time after reading the letter before either Dawlish or Felicity spoke. They stood looking at each other, hearing the shooting outside yet hardly aware of it. Dawlish took out cigarettes and they lit up before he folded the letter up and slipped it into his wallet.

"Presumably the police know most of that, now," he said.

"Yes," said Felicity. "And Sol Gordon was right."

"About the politics—yes. A lot is explained."

"And we are back where we started," said Felicity, brushing back her hair. "Hortelan wasn't fooling when he told us to stay here."

"I doubt whether we would do much good if we were to break out," said Dawlish. He took out his loaded automatic and frowned. "It's an odd business." His voice was low-pitched and far away, as if he were thinking of something else. "Gordon gave me this gun. Gordon did a lot of things which aren't in keeping with what he told us. I wonder if he knew the truth about Barney, and was determined to get to see him."

"Why should he?" asked Felicity, helplessly.

"Mixed motives, perhaps," said Dawlish. He weighed the gun in his hand, and added thoughtfully: "According to Hortelan, they're getting out now. According to Carter, Hamblin is going to attack again to-night. If we could delay Hortelan by a few hours—" He broke off, and laughed humourlessly. "Now I'm doing the wishful thinking!"

He dropped his cigarette and trod it out. The shooting had lessened, but sporadic shots were still being fired. Dawlish looked out of the garage window towards *Timbers*, the back door of which was plainly visible.

As he stood watching, he saw the door open a little.

"Look!" he said, and gripped Felicity's arm.

The door opened wider. A man appeared, and Dawlish recognized Carter, bare-headed except for a bloodstained bandage round his head. He carried a small rifle. He edged from the door to the porch, and then went down on his stomach. The path made from the kitchen to the garage had thrown up a wall of snow, several feet high, and obviously Carter hoped to crawl to the garage without being seen. He started slowly. There was no shooting in his direction. He pushed the gun in front of him, crawled a little farther, pushed it again, and then came on. His movements were agonizingly slow.

"Open the door," said Felicity.

"Not yet," said Dawlish.

Carter was half-way between the kitchen and the garage when another burst of shooting, which seemed as if it were directed toward him, made Dawlish step towards the door and open it an inch or two Bullets spattered against the wall above the kitchen door. For the first time he saw one of Carter's men standing by it, probably just visible to whoever was shooting at him. Obviously he was there to draw the fire.

Carter did not raise his head, but came on doggedly. Not until he was within a yard of the door did Dawlish open it wide, and call him. Carter kept his head, and did not look up. Dawlish bent down and brought the rifle in. Carter followed, not straightening up until he was inside and the door was closed. There was no colour in his cheeks; he was wounded in the leg as well as in the head. He dragged himself to a tyre and sat on it, gasping for breath.

"We must—get to—the village," he said at last.

"It won't be easy," Dawlish said.

"We must—somehow. They're getting—away."

Dawlish said: "What about the snow?"

"They have managed to build a snow-plough. It's working on the other side of the hill. Once it reaches the road it will enable them to move fairly freely. We must stop them." Carter clenched his fists and stared at Dawlish. "We must—" He broke off, and there was a hopeless expression on his face, one of utter despair. "Oh, what a fool I am! We cannot stop them, we can't do anything. Anything!" His hands were trembling, and his body began to shake. "Two of my men are dead. We tried to get through, there wasn't a chance. Not a chance." He turned his haggard eyes towards the window. "Can't you *try,* Dawlish; can't you *try* to stop them somehow? If they get on the road and people in other villages try to stop them, there will be slaughter, you know what they're like."

"Pull yourself together," said Dawlish, roughly enough to make Felicity glance at him in surprise. "Either the country is impassable or it isn't. If Hortelan can fashion something with which to cut a path through to the main road and then along it, Hamblin can do so in the village."

Carter said: "They mustn't be allowed to get away!"

"They can't get away yet."

"They can!" cried Carter. "They can, they'll go by air." He had lied before, and they could guess the reason, but the truth was in him now and there was a passionate pleading in his voice. "They'll go by air, they've a helicopter almost assembled, they're clearing land on the other side of the hill for a take-off now. Hortelan will go with the leaders, the men will be left to fight their way out as best they can." When Dawlish did not answer, he shrieked: "I tell you it's true, I helped them to build it! I didn't know what they were planning before, but I was working with them. Now I know, I'd die to defeat them! You must prevent Hortelan from getting away. He has kidnapped two members of the Cabinet as hostages, he plans to take them abroad and then force some arrangement on the Government. I don't know what it is, but I know that's what he plans. *You must stop him from getting away.*"

CHAPTER XX

MEANS OF ESCAPE

The explanation, so simple and yet sufficient, made Dawlish aghast. He understood at once why the fact that the Cabinet Ministers had been cut off by the blizzard had been mentioned in the radio news, and also understood Hortelan's cold-blooded determination. His prize was worth all the effort he could make, as well as all the planning. Carter's share in the plot was unimportant by comparison, and the reason for Carter's change of heart was equally unimportant.

There was no fear that this was a trick; Hortelan need not adopt such tortuous methods if he wanted to kill him. In any case, the expression in Carter's eyes was evidence enough that he told the truth.

Dawlish said: "There are three of us here, and a dozen or more men outside. All the approaches to the house and the grounds are covered by men who know how to shoot. There isn't a chance in a thousand of getting to the ground which you say they're clearing; and even if we managed to get there, we would be able to do nothing."

"I thought *you* would find a way," said Carter.

"A touching faith! If you'd warned me what was afoot before, something might have been done."

"You mustn't give it up as hopeless," cried Carter, in a broken voice. "Don't you understand, Dawlish, two members of the Government, men vital to the country, will be taken away unless you can prevent it. It's no use talking about what I've done now. I'll take my punishment, I'm not asking for any remission because I've changed my mind, *but you must save those men!*"

"There isn't any way to do it," said Dawlish.

Was that true? He put the question to himself as he looked into Carter's bloodshot eyes. Probably it was only partly true. Alone he could do nothing, but Barney was still with Hortelan, and Sol Gordon was also there. Barney was reliable, beyond any doubt; Gordon might be playing a peculiar double deception, and planning to sabotage Hortelan's plans. Two men whose loyalty to the Spaniard was at least questionable were with him.

"You've thought of something," Carter said. "I can see from the expression in your eyes. Dawlish, listen to me. I'll take any risk you like to ask of me, if it will help—*any* risk."

"What arms have you got?" asked Dawlish.

"I've three hand-grenades with me, and some spare clips for my revolver, that's all. The rest is at the house, or else used up. I'll go back for more!"

"You aren't in a condition to go back," said Dawlish. He looked across at the house and saw that the glass of the window above the kitchen was shattered by a bullet. There the man covering Carter had been standing, but there was no sign of him now. The shooting had stopped completely.

Suddenly the silence was shattered by a deafening roar and a deep throbbing noise which made the garage shiver with the vibration—and in front of their eyes snow which had gathered on the window-ledges of the house tottered and dropped down.

The roar increased as they stood tense, and then it ceased as abruptly as it had begun.

"They've got the engine working," Carter said. "They won't be long now!"

Sounds like those of an engine which refused to start followed the roar. The noise was coming from beyond the hill in which the cellars were built, and they saw smoke rising above the snow—dark fumes from an exhaust pipe. Minutes passed before the engine fired again, lasted for a few moments, and then faded out.

"It's been frozen up," Dawlish said, absently. "It will be some time before they'll trust themselves in the air with that."

"They've plenty of time before dark, when Hamblin is to attack again," said Carter. "There isn't enough time to do what we have to do, you mustn't lose a moment."

"Very brave, aren't we?" said Dawlish. He stood looking at the kitchen window, debating the chances of getting there and back with more grenades and perhaps a few Mills bombs. Wild thoughts were going through his mind, which he rejected almost as soon as they occurred to him. Some kind of distraction was necessary if he were to have even the slightest chance.

The engine roared again, but for a shorter period. Voices travelling faintly from the hill carried on a steady wind which was blowing south. A few seconds later there was the shrill *peep* of a whistle. It was repeated thrice. None of them spoke. Dawlish was conscious of Felicity's gaze, and guessed what was passing through her mind, but he knew that she would do nothing to prevent him from making an effort if there appeared the remotest chance of success. He glanced at her, and beyond her saw three petrol tins on a shelf. Next to them were two five-gallon oil drums. He stepped towards the shelf, pressing Felicity's arm as he passed, and lifted the petrol tins. They were full.

"What are you doing?" demanded Carter.

"Thinking," said Dawlish. His face was set.

"I tell you there's no time to waste," said Carter. "This is the only chance. That whistle means they want all available men in the workshop, to work on the helicopter. There aren't many men outside now."

"Be quiet!" snapped Felicity, and the man fell silent. She looked at and through him, and then Dawlish saw her stiffen. She stepped to the window and peered out cautiously. There was a hint of excitement in her manner as she beckoned him. Carter stood up with an effort, and joined them at the window.

The men who had been stationed about the house were moving up the drive or towards the hill. Almost as Dawlish reached the window one of them passed. In five minutes eight men had passed the garage and disappeared behind the beech hedge. A ninth went into the small shed.

"Now you can go!" cried Carter.

"It looks as if you're right," said Dawlish. "Fel, give him what first aid you can, will you? I won't be gone long."

She raised no objection, but her face was also set.

He opened the door cautiously, then stepped out to make sure that all the men within sight had gone. Nothing happened. He walked across to the kitchen, looking right and left, but was not fired at. The scullery was freezing cold, and the fire in the kitchen had gone out. He was shivering as he hurried to the hall. The front door was wide open, and Carter's two men lay there, stiff and dead. By the wall at their side was a small box of grenades. He made sure that the men were beyond help, and hurried upstairs, to find the man who had been by the landing window, above the kitchen. He was alive but unconscious; there was a wound in his shoulder and another in his chest, and the bleeding had almost stopped. Felicity might be able to help him, the question was whether he should spend time in carrying him to the garage now; it would mean coming back for the grenades.

"Nonsense!" he said aloud.

He lifted the man and carried him to the kitchen, laying him on a table. Hanging on a hook behind the door was a laundry bag, shaped like a kit-bag. He loaded it with grenades and ammunition, slung it over his shoulder, and was about to lift the wounded man again when he heard a sound in the passage. He swung round, taking out his gun. He heard a sharp intake of breath, and thought he saw a man standing behind the door. If it were one man the danger was not acute, but if he were the forerunner of several more—

"*Patrick!*" came a cry, and the door opened wider. Wide-eyed, hands raised about his head to make sure that Dawlish did not loose a shot at him, was *Sol Gordon!* "Patrick," he cried again, "what a relief, what a relief to see you. I was afraid it was Carter!"

"Why afraid?" asked Dawlish, watching the fat man warily. "Don't come too close."

"Carter is dangerous, my boy, he works with Hortelan, I have managed to find that out from Barney. Patrick, our dear friend is a prisoner, the man in the village is his cousin, isn't that masterly on Barney's part? Isn't it? And don't look at me like that, my boy, I am for you, I have always been for you. You ask why I talked as I did in the garage—but come, my boy, this is no time for a lot of explanations. Believe me I was never your enemy, never! I thought we were overheard, I meant to talk to Hortelan somehow, to make sure that he trusted me, and I succeeded in part, I did really—otherwise, would I be alive?" When Dawlish did not answer immediately Gordon took a step forward and stretched out his hands, beseechingly. "Patrick, my boy, don't look at me like that, I am not untrustworthy. I did what I thought was best for all our sakes, and I have discovered how to get from the shed to the house! Come with me, and I will show you!"

"Or walk into my parlour," said Dawlish.

"You mustn't be sceptical. I did my best and it was a good best." Gordon's face was twisted in dismay. "Oh my, oh my, what can I do to convince you that I am a man of goodwill? Oh, what—Patrick? I know what I can do. Here, my boy, look at this—look at it!"

He put his hand to his pocket.

Dawlish kept him covered, but Gordon seemed unafraid of the gun. He drew out a sealed envelope which was filled with something bulky, and tore the flap open. Two diamonds glittered on the palm of his hand, and there was a folded scrap of paper, badly creased—the paper which he had taken from the broken gem.

"Here, look! The two gems which Hortelan took from the garage, I have them back, and also the paper which you found, my boy. Take them!" He put them on the table by the side of the wounded man and rubbed his hands. "*Now* will you believe that I mean well, Patrick? Listen to me! They are going to get away by air, they have a helicopter which will carry five men, the engine is already being warmed up, surely you heard it? And Patrick—they have two Cabinet Ministers, prisoners in their hands!"

"I know," said Dawlish.

Gordon gaped. "You *know?*"

"Carter told me," said Dawlish. "All right, Sol, I'll have to take your word for it. We'll get this fellow to the garage first—"

"No, we mustn't waste time. We can get to the shed and from there—who knows what we will be able to do? There are still men posted near the hedge, out of sight; if you go back to the garage you will be shot. What is the life of that man compared with what is at stake? Don't lose time, please don't make a mistake now."

He was right, of course.

Dawlish dropped his gun into his pocket and stepped towards him. The bag of grenades swung over his shoulder. Gordon turned and hurried along the kitchen passage, and then to the dining-room. Once he turned and beckoned, and there was something in his manner which told Dawlish that he was sincere, that he had worked in his own way to outwit Hortelan.

The dining-room door was open, so was a door built into one of the wooden panels.

"I will go first," said Gordon, "then you will lose any foolish ideas you may have. I am unarmed, too, they took my gun—that shows that I mean what I say." He squeezed his way into the passage, where there was only just room for him to walk along, and turned right. Dawlish followed. A single electric bulb was hanging from the ceiling, close to a narrow doorway. A flight of stone steps led downwards from there, and at the foot was another door. Gordon pushed it open cautiously.

"We are all right," he said. "They haven't missed me, that was the thing I feared. They put me in a small room and locked me up, Patrick. We have one thing in our favour, Barney is still trusted by them. Isn't it astonishing about Barney?"

"I've seen him," said Dawlish.

"You've *seen*—" Gordon looked over his shoulder and gave a comical grimace. "What don't you know, my boy?" He reached another door. "Hush, now, no talking."

Immediately beyond the door was a flight of steps like that down which they had come. Gordon's arms rubbed against the side as he made his way up them. A door at the head was closed. Gordon turned the handle and pushed gently—and then he stood quite still, and his shoulders drooped as if a great depression had fallen upon him.

"Oh, my!" he wailed in a low-pitched voice, "they have locked it, they have locked it!"

"Let me pass," said Dawlish.

Gone was all his suspicion of Gordon; gone were doubts as to their ability to stop Hortelan from getting away. He remembered how he had felt when Felicity had been kidnapped; how his thoughts had crystallized and doubts and fears and speculations had been thrust aside. He felt like that now as he took out his pen-knife, examined the lock, and smiled to himself as he began to work.

"Be careful," Gordon said, with a sob in his voice, "they are capable of any kind of trickery, the door might be mined."

"I'll be careful," said Dawlish.

The lock was not difficult, but the light was poor and he had not the proper tools. Gordon's warning had brought the sense of danger much nearer, too. The possibility that if he forced the lock the door would blow up was heavy on his mind. As he worked, conscious of Gordon's heavy breathing, he was thinking chiefly of Felicity. She would be frantic by now. He hoped that she would not be foolish enough to come to the house to find him.

The lock clicked back.

"Patrick," whispered Gordon. "Patrick, be careful now. There are explosives behind some doors which go off at a touch, I know that. There was one behind the door leading from the shed to the underground workshop. Barney managed to tell me. I made it go off. I said it was an accident, but it blocked the passage between the shed and the workshop, so since then they have had to go across the garden. Be careful, Patrick."

Dawlish pushed the door gently.

Gordon had a hand on his arm, and his fingers were

tightening. The door opened an inch, then another. Nothing happened. It was open six inches when Gordon said:

"Get your hand inside, Patrick, try to find out if there is anything fastened to the door, there's a good fellow."

"All right," said Dawlish.

He could get his arm through the gap, and he felt gingerly along the whole length of the door. He touched nothing but smooth wood. Satisfied, but with perspiration warm at his neck and forehead, he pushed the door another foot. It was wide enough now for him to get through, but not enough for Gordon. He stepped into a small room, and Gordon whispered:

"The switch is near the door."

"Have you a torch?" asked Dawlish.

"Yes, but the switch—"

"According to you, it might be a booby trap," said Dawlish.

"My, my!" breathed Gordon, and he handed Dawlish a torch. The bright light illuminated the room, which was bare and unfurnished. The unshaded electric bulb was hanging innocently enough from the cable in the centre of the ceiling. He turned the torch towards the door.

"Don't come in yet!" he ordered, sharply.

If he had pushed the door another six inches it would have touched a small box standing on the floor—and with Gordon's warning in mind, he was careful about that box. He moved it gently. It had no lid, and he could see the little cartons inside. He suspected that Gordon was right, and that if the cartons were jolted they would blow up. He put them in the corner out of danger, and then opened the door for Gordon, who stepped through, blinking in the brighter light.

"Well done, Patrick!"

"If you came through this way, you should know what's here," said Dawlish.

"There was nothing here when I came," Gordon assured him, "but there was some talk of making sure no one could get in, and I remembered the other door which blew up," and pushed forward towards the next door. "This leads into a dormitory, and that leads into the workshop itself. There are several doors to the field beyond."

"Thanks," said Dawlish.

Neither of them had spoken of what they were to do when they reached the workshop. Dawlish's hope was that he would be able to get near enough to toss hand grenades at the helicopter, damaging it enough to prevent it from taking off, but that was a last resort. Somewhere near at hand were two Cabinet Ministers, and Hortelan would probably murder them out of hand if he realized that his hopes of taking them away were dashed.

"Locked?" asked Gordon, when Dawlish tried the handle.

"Yes." Dawlish worked at the lock. It was the same make as that which he had already opened, and he managed it more quickly. He pushed the door back gently, going through the same precautionary process as before. This time he was helped because there was a light in the dormitory. He heard nothing, although the moment when he ran his hand down the length of the door was filled with suspense, for fear that one of Hortelan's men might be inside.

Nothing happened.

He squeezed through and glanced behind the door; there was nothing there. He pulled the door wider open to admit Gordon, and then for the first time he saw two men stretched out on single beds which were ranged against the wall. There were a dozen beds, but only the two were occupied. The men on them were either asleep or unconscious. As he stepped towards them he saw that their hands and feet were tied. They were dressed in lounge suits, both middle-aged men, judging from their grey hair. Their backs were turned towards him.

He reached them and looked down.

"Who are they?" breathed Gordon.

"Two honourable gentlemen," said Dawlish, in a low-pitched voice. "Our main prize, and the first thing is to get them away from here. Try the door to the workshop."

"It's open," Gordon said, a moment later.

"Is the key in the lock?"

"Yes, yes, here it is."

"Lock it, will you?" said Dawlish, and he took out his automatic and handed it to the fat man. "Then stand on guard, Sol, and if you have to shoot, don't shoot wide." He grinned at Gordon's expression, and then turned his attention to the helpless men. One was a short, wiry individual, whom he recognized as Sir Arnold Livesey, Secretary for Foreign Affairs; the other was a tall, plump man—Gordon McKay, Minister without Portfolio. Both looked ill, and there was a bruise on McKay's forehead. When Dawlish touched them they did not stir, and he had no doubt that they, too, had been dosed with morphia.

"Perhaps I could carry the little one," said Gordon. "Shall I try?"

"No," said Dawlish; "they would be able to catch up with us too easily." He hoisted McKay to his shoulders, fireman fashion, and the man's head lolled against his back. "I won't be long," he said, and walked across the dormitory.

With every step McKay seemed to grow heavier. The most difficult part of the journey was at the stairs, and by the time he reached the top of the flight leading to the dining-room passage he was gasping for breath. He carried the man through to the dining-room, lowered him into an easy chair, and stood looking at him while he recovered his breath. There was still danger from the grounds, and it might be wise to put him in a room which could be locked. He lifted him again, took him to the morning-room, and sat him against the wall. He went out, locking the door, still breathing hard.

He turned back—

"*Pat!*" came Felicity's voice. "Pat!"

She was standing in the doorway of the passage leading to the kitchen. He imagined what she had felt as she had heard him moving, and his eyes lighted up at the sight of the gun in her hand. In a moment he was by her side, and she talked swiftly. Carter was still conscious, but very weak from loss of blood. He was watching from the door of the garage, ready to shoot if anyone came from the garden. She had been watching the hall, in the hope that she would see Dawlish.

"Keep near the kitchen door and help Carter," said Dawlish. "We've a chance of foxing them—one of the great men is in the morning-room, sleeping off a dose of morphia. I'm going back for the other. If you should see Gordon," he added, "remember he's on our side."

Felicity asked no questions.

He left her walking towards the kitchen, and was back with Gordon within five minutes. The fat man was standing by the door, gun in hand, and he beamed broadly when he saw Dawlish.

"No trouble, my boy, no trouble in here, at all events. They are having great difficulty with the engine, they cannot get it to go at all now. Fate watches over us, you see, kind fate! What are we to do next?"

"I'd like to get Barney," Dawlish said.

"So would I, my boy. *And* Hortelan."

"I'll do without him," said Dawlish; "but when they discover that their prisoners have gone, they'll probably turn on Barney. Will you keep guard again?"

"Of course, my boy, of course!"

Dawlish lifted Livesey in his arms, finding the light-weight easy after the big Scotsman. He did not slacken pace as he went through the passages and into the house. McKay was still unconscious. He sat them both together, loosened their bonds, and put an automatic in front of McKay. Then he hurried back to join Gordon.

As he opened the dormitory door he was deafened by the roar of the engine, and Gordon clapped his hands to his ears. Men were obviously working at it inside the underground workshop, and the vibration shook the floor and the walls. They waited for it to stop, but this time it went on and on and they could hear the engine developing power as it warmed up.

"They will be nearly ready to start, perhaps," said Gordon, nervously. "What shall we do?"

"Take a look," said Dawlish laconically.

He unlocked the door and opened it cautiously. A bright light made him narrow his eyes, and the wind created by the whirling propeller of the helicopter caught his breath. The great propeller was turning near the roof of the large workshop, round the sides of which Hortelan's men had gathered. Hortelan himself was smiling, as if this were the final reward. The other men, most of them black with grease, seemed to be relaxed after a long period of tension.

Barney was near Hortelan.

Hortelan spoke to him, and then turned round and raised his voice. He seemed to be staring straight into Dawlish's eyes, but did not appear to see him. His words were drowned by the engine, but those nearest him heard them, for several of them turned and moved towards the dormitory.

CHAPTER XXI

FIGHT FOR SAFETY

"Here they come," Dawlish whispered.

The nearest man was twenty yards away from him, and, like all of them, had narrowed his eyes against the wind from the propeller; that was probably why Hortelan had noticed nothing. Dawlish closed the door and backed to the wall, putting a hand on Gordon's arm and pushing him behind the door. They stood waiting tensely, and it seemed a long time before the handle turned.

They covered the door with their guns.

The beds on which the two prisoners had lain were not in the line of vision of anyone who entered, and there was no immediate exclamation. Four men came through—and then Dawlish pushed the door to with his foot. The men swung round. The surprise was so complete that none of them moved or tried to speak, until suddenly one, quicker-witted than the others, dived for the door.

Dawlish fired at him.

The noise of the shot was drowned by the roaring engine. The man, hit in the thigh, lost his footing and fell forward. He struck the door with his head, rolled over, and lay unconscious.

The others backed away.

Dawlish said: "Turn round."

Two looked blank; the other spoke swiftly in Spanish. There was no hesitation, and they turned their backs on him.

"Have you ever used the rabbit punch, Sol?" asked Dawlish, in a voice high-pitched with the reaction.

"Have I, my boy! Just you watch, just watch!"

Gordon advanced slowly, with his eyes glistening, and turned his gun in his hand. He stood behind the first man with the gun raised, butt foremost, and brought it down sharply on the back of his victim's neck. Before the fellow had fallen, he repeated it on the others; his speed and thoroughness was such that Dawlish had to repress a laugh.

"Well, *have* I?" demanded Gordon, beaming.

"You'll do," said Dawlish. "Do you know how many men Hortelan has altogether?"

"At least another dozen, my boy."

"I suppose so. Open the door an inch, will you?" Dawlish reached Gordon's side as the fat man obeyed. Peering through the gap he saw Hortelan scowling towards the door. He shouted something which Dawlish could not hear because of that constant roaring. Two more men moved towards the door, and then Hortelan followed, with Barney at his side.

"Quick!" said Dawlish. "Put one of these men on the bed!"

He lifted one of the unconscious men and carried him to the bed on which McKay had been lying. Gordon came up, staggering under the weight of a second man. Dawlish had time to haul the others behind the door, completing the deception, and to stand there with Gordon, before the door was opened wider and Hortelan came through first. The roar was so loud that Dawlish could hear no other sound, and the beds were shaking on the cement floor.

Barney and two others came through.

"Your turn, Barney," said Dawlish.

On his words, Hortelan swung round and the other two men dropped their hands to their guns, but Barney, quick to grasp what had happened, pushed them against each other. They staggered and fell. Only one got his gun out, and Barney kicked it from his hand. Gordon slammed the door and turned the key, while Hortelan, recovering his balance, backed towards the beds and stared incredulously at the gun in Dawlish's hand.

"Too bad, isn't it?" said Dawlish. "You thought we were still in the garage, but you never can tell." He grinned inanely, and for the moment felt an exhilaration which made him look and sound foolish. "The best laid schemes of mice and men, you know. How are you, Barney?"

"Incredulous!" said Barney, his eyes shining; "but we haven't much time to spare."

"Never much time," said Dawlish. "I wish—"

For the first time a sound louder than the turning engine hit against his ears. It was an explosion outside the door, the wooden panels of which splintered and caved inwards. A sheet of flame licked along the floor as far as one of the beds, and the bedding caught alight. Smoke billowed into the room, and then the door crashed open and several men appeared, half-hidden by the smoke.

The speed of their reaction nearly brought about disaster. Dawlish emptied his gun towards them, and one man fell forward through the smoke and lay huddled up. Two others jumped through, unhurt. Dawlish tossed a hand grenade towards the door and shouted at the same moment. Barney, Hortelan and Gordon dropped on their faces, and Dawlish fell sideways as the explosion came.

When it had died away, the doorway was a shambles.

Hortelan was crawling towards it, Barney was trying to get up, with blood pouring from a cut in his cheek. Gordon bounded to his feet, unhurt. Dawlish was untouched, but breathless. He had another grenade in his hand as he backed towards the door leading to the house.

The grenade-throwing appeared to have made the Spaniards think twice about a frontal attack, but Dawlish was thinking less of the immediate danger here than of the possibility of an attack on the house from the garden. He gave up all hope of taking Hortelan a prisoner. The man was on his feet now, shouting through the smoke. The engine had stopped outside, and two more men appeared as Dawlish lobbed a grenade over their heads into the workshop.

Barney plucked at his sleeve.

"Follow Sol," said Dawlish.

The men who had arrived seemed in two minds. They were armed—and then Dawlish realized that they were looking for their leader, and afraid of shooting recklessly. He tossed two more grenades before one of them fired at him through the smoke. He had time to move aside. Gordon called out to him in a lull which followed the third explosion. Undoubtedly there was great destruction in the workshop, and he felt a deep satisfaction at the knowledge that the helicopter would certainly not be used that day.

"Hurry, Patrick, hurry!" screamed Gordon.

Dawlish tossed another grenade into the blasted doorway. Hortelan flung himself down in the act of firing. Then Dawlish turned and ran into the small outer room. Gordon was just ahead of him; Barney was already in the passage.

Dawlish slammed the door.

Gordon ran across the little room. Dawlish saw the box of

explosives in the doorway and wondered if there were time to utilize them. Footsteps by the door of the dormitory warned him that there was not, until he heard Hortelan say:

"Wait for others!"

He picked up the small box and carried it into the passage, put it where the men would fall over it when they came on, and then scurried in Gordon's wake. The fat man was standing at the foot of the first flight of steps, imploring him to hurry. Barney was near the foot of the second flight, dabbing his cheek.

There was no sound of pursuit.

"It'll come," said Dawlish. "Sol, don't go into the dining-room yet." He followed the others until they reached the passage alongside the dining-room—and as they got there, an explosion, a long, muffled booming sound, deafened them. The walls shook, and their breath was forced from their lungs. Gasping they fell against the wall; minutes passed before they were able to move again.

"What—what was that?" gasped Gordon.

"Their booby trap," said Dawlish. "Others might still get through, Sol, so take half a dozen grenades and wait here, will you? If you see anyone, toss a grenade at him and duck behind the corner. In ten minutes, come to the garage."

"All right, all right," said Gordon. "You hurry."

Dawlish joined Barney, who was stepping into the dining-room. It was surprising how quiet it was there, how far away the fighting seemed. Barney was smiling constrainedly, but Dawlish grinned and led him to the door, saying: "They'll send some men through the garden, that's our big danger now. Felicity's in the kitchen, and the Cabinet Ministers in the morning-room. Distinguished guests, Barney!"

Barney smiled. "Must you joke now?"

"Meaning there's a time and a place for all things," said

Dawlish. He stood in the passage, listening intently, trying to decide on the best course of action. They would not be safe in the house, for there were too many doors and windows, and Hortelan's men would not act mildly now. The garage was probably the safest place, but it had one big disadvantage. It could be surrounded and blown to pieces if Hortelan's men had enough explosives with them. A few shots from the piece of field artillery would be all that was required.

He said: "Can you carry Livesey?"

"Yes."

"We'll go to the garage," said Dawlish.

By the time he had McKay over his shoulder and Barney had the smaller man, they heard shooting from the grounds, and then an answering shot from the kitchen or the garage. Soon he saw Felicity standing against the kitchen door, obviously keeping under cover but showing herself for long enough to shoot at the men who were coming cautiously down the slippery path. The fact that it was slippery was the most important thing in Dawlish's favour. He reached Felicity, shifted McKay's weight from one shoulder to another, and then peered round the doorway.

Only two men were in sight, and they were at the top of the path, near the tool shed. The others had not yet appeared. Dawlish took a grenade from his pocket and lobbed it towards the shed. It was too far away for accuracy, but the men saw it coming and ducked. He tossed two more, and the roar of the explosions shattered the quiet. Smoke and flame burst out, then the flame disappeared and only smoke remained, a thick cloud hiding the shed and the two men.

"Now's our chance," said Dawlish.

He led the way across the snow. Felicity followed, Barney was close on her heels. As they staggered into the garage, where Carter was on his knees with a gun in his hand, Gordon appeared at the kitchen door. Soon all of them were together in the garage, and still there was no sign of a major attack from outside.

"They're either preparing big things," said Dawlish, "or else they've had trouble getting out of the workshop. That piece of artillery worries me."

"It needn't," said Barney, while Felicity strapped his cheek. "It's still down by the river, and they've only left two men— they'll never be able to turn it to bear on us."

"Reassuring fellow," said Dawlish. He brushed his hand over his hair, looked at McKay and Livesey, who were still unconscious, and then back at Barney. "That reminds me, Barney— how are you?"

Barney laughed. "You haven't changed."

"My, my!" cried Gordon. "Here we are, standing on the threshold of eternity, and that is the way you talk! I cannot understand you, I really cannot understand you! They may come at any moment, and they also will have grenades."

"I thought you were on guard," said Dawlish. He grinned at the fat man, who shrugged his shoulders in despair, and then peered out of the door. The smoke was thinning, and he could see men standing near the shed, one wall of which was caved in. He did not see Hortelan.

"They're waiting for instructions," Dawlish said.

"While we are wasting time!" howled Gordon.

"What do you think we should do?" asked Dawlish.

"Get away from this place, my boy, what else can we do? It is not safe, if we allow them to surround the garage we shall all be finished; that would be a fine thing after all we have gone through. You must find a way of getting out, Patrick!"

Dawlish said: "Always up to me!" He laughed and ruffled

Gordon's curly hair. "Sorry, Sol. You're right, of course, and an idea has just dawned on me. Have you any chains for the car wheels, Barney?"

"Yes, they're on this shelf." Barney stepped across the garage, leaving Felicity and Gordon to keep watch from the door, and the next moment there was the rattle of tyre-chains. "Let's get them fixed," said Dawlish. "We can put our two prize specimens inside, with Carter, Felicity and Gordon—"

"And Barney," said Gordon, "and Barney. I am more able to fight than he is just now."

Barney was already fitting the chains. Felicity called a warning: the men had split up and were moving in different directions. Dawlish lifted the politicians, one after the other, and carried them to the car. He went back for Carter, who could only walk with assistance. He crowded in the back with the two unconscious men.

"Let Felicity take the wheel," said Dawlish. He called to her, and she hurried across the garage. Gordon was fidgeting by the door, poking his head out every few seconds and calling plaintive warnings. The silence was eerie; obviously Hortelan was trying to make sure they were completely surrounded, and the man would be possessed by a hatred which would show itself in utter ruthlessness.

"Patrick!" cried Gordon, "there is a man at the side of the house, they are coming round that way!"

"Shoot him," said Dawlish.

"Oh, my boy!" cried Gordon. As he fired, Felicity climbed into the car and Barney got in next to her. "Come on, Sol," called Dawlish, "you're due for a ride on the running-board." He was still feeling a sense of exhilaration as if they could not fail now that they had got this far.

"He dodged back and I missed," Gordon said, sadly. He

skipped across the garage, and then saw Dawlish lifting one of the petrol tins from the shelf. "Patrick, what now, man, what foolishness now?"

"Get a tin," said Dawlish.

They put the tins into the car, on Barney's lap, and Felicity pulled at the self-starter. The garage had been so warm that the engine started at the first pull. Dawlish stood on the running-board by the rear windows, and Gordon clung on the other side.

Felicity eased off the brakes.

For the first time Dawlish really looked at the nature of the run ahead of them. The drive, as steep as one in three in some places, had snow piled on either side, but there was just room for the car to pass between the white walls. If Felicity could keep it on a straight path they would reach the drive gates. They might even be able to drive along the road as far as the broken bridge.

The men who had been waiting by the front of the house for the signal to attack, realized what was happening. Shooting started. More shots came over the garage, for they were visible now from the shed at the top. None of the bullets scored a hit, but the movement of the car was agonizingly slow, and Felicity dared not increase the speed. They bumped and rattled on the chains, swaying a little from side to side. Once Dawlish's legs were pressed against the frozen snow, and he felt it graze his knees. Then the car eased off to the other side, and Gordon cried out in alarm.

They were half-way down the drive. The shooting was quickening, but they were past the side of *Timbers* and the danger was less acute. Men came downwards, across the snow, but it made them flounder and they could not make swift progress. The car edged forward and drew level with the gates.

Dawlish held his breath.

The path made by Carter's men and afterwards by Hortelan's,

was no wider as it turned into the gates than it was on the straight. The odds against keeping going were considerable, but not once did Felicity put on the brakes. Gently she eased the car round the corner into the road. Gordon cried out again.

"My legs, mind my legs."

Dawlish stared back at the men coming down the garden and at others coming down the steep path. They were slipping and sliding in their haste, and what shots they fired went hopelessly wide. The great danger now was from the two men who were guarding the river.

The car turned into the straight again.

"*Very* well done," breathed Dawlish.

"Don't forget the bridge is down," called Gordon from the other side of the car. "Don't forget that, Patrick!"

"We won't forget," said Dawlish. "Sol, keep looking ahead for the men by the river." He lowered his voice. "Give me one of the petrol cans, Barney, and unscrew it, first. Barney did so, and Dawlish took the tin in one hand, handing Barney two grenades which he was still carrying. He turned the tin upside down, and the suffocating smell of petrol filled the car. The petrol poured out, and he swung the can to and fro, so that the stuff covered as large an area as possible. It trickled along the frozen surface in places, in others it began to sink into the snow.

The car went on, a little more swiftly. Inside, Carter had lost consciousness, and looked ghastly. At a distance of ten yards from the petrol, Dawlish tossed a grenade.

"I hope it works," he said.

The explosion was followed by a sheet of flame which stretched from one side of the road to the other. It ran to and fro, an inferno reaching a height of five or six feet. Barney looked up at Dawlish with a grin of appreciation. The car lurched to one side after the explosion, but settled down again.

The bridge was only a few yards ahead.

"Anything in front, Sol?" Dawlish called.

"I can see no one, my boy, no one at all," said Gordon. "I think perhaps—'

As he spoke a shot rang out from a field on one side. It hit the roof of the car and ricochetted off. Gordon fired in return, while Felicity put the front wheels on to the frozen water where the river had overflowed its banks. In spite of the chains the car slithered dangerously from side to side.

Dawlish was thinking: "We shall be all right if they haven't a Lewis gun."

CHAPTER XXII

RIVER CROSSING

Another rifle shot rang out, echoing loudly, but the bullet missed. The car edged further forward. They were within a few feet of the broken bridge; one post stuck several feet above the ice.

"How deep is the river, Barney?" asked Dawlish.

"Three feet or so, normally—four now, probably."

"I doubt if the ice will hold us," said Dawlish. "We'd better not chance it. Can you pull up, Fel?"

She eased the brakes on slowly. Two more shots from the hidden sniper rang out, and one struck the car and made a resonant *boom*. It went off into the hedge. Then more shooting started, and Barney peered ahead while Dawlish's heart almost turned over.

Barney said in a strained voice:

"It's from the other side."

"At us?" snapped Dawlish.

"No, at the sharpshooter. Look!"

As the car pulled up, Dawlish stepped gingerly on to the ice. He slipped, and kept his balance only by grabbing the door handle. Felicity opened her door, while Dawlish and Barney watched a man who was standing near the opposite bank. He was gesticulating wildly, and then pointing towards the left—to the side of the road from which the sniping was coming. He was calling out, too. The engine drowned his words at first, but Felicity switched off, and they heard him clearly.

"*Machine-gun! Machine-gun!*"

"Touch and go," said Dawlish, levelly. "Get the others across the river somehow," he added. "Drag 'em over, if needs be. Sol, can you hear?"

"Yes, but—"

"Lend them a hand," said Dawlish.

He guessed that the machine-gunner was having difficulty in turning his gun towards the car. Probably it was because of the rampart with which it had been protected. He stepped back along the ice, slipping all the time, but he reached the snow safely. There was still no machine-gun fire. He plunged knee-deep in snow near the hedge, which showed dark streaks against the whiteness. The man on the other side of the river had been joined by two more, and they were coming forward to help Felicity, Barney and Gordon. Another man, further up the hill, was firing towards the Lewis gun.

Dawlish peered over the hedge.

The gun was only fifty feet away from him, and he could see the head and shoulders of the fellow manning it. He was hacking at the frozen snow rampart with a rifle, and the snow was flying in all directions. He stopped as Dawlish took aim, and dodged beneath what remained of the wall. Suddenly Dawlish saw the ugly muzzle of the Lewis gun pointing towards him. He ducked. The gun turned slowly until it was trained on the party by the river.

Dawlish fired, and the bullet buried itself in the snow. The machine-gunner did not seem to know that there was a threat from the side, and pressed the trigger. A burst of fire followed. Dawlish turned his head and saw the bullets kicking up little clouds of ice from the river, ten yards away from Felicity.

Steadying himself, he took out a grenade.

If he failed with this, the damage might be done. He seemed to be an unconscionable time taking aim, but when he tossed the grenade it curved towards the Lewis gun and he knew, even before it exploded, that he had managed to get the range. Another burst of shooting came—and then the grenade landed and exploded.

"The luck's changed," said Dawlish aloud.

The gun and ramparts disappeared, and when the smoke cleared away he saw only an untidy heap on the ground, and the figure of a man lying some feet away from the wreckage. He looked towards the river. Felicity was on the far bank, with one of the unconscious men. Men from the village were hauling the others across, and Gordon, half-way across, suddenly slipped and sat down. Dawlish chuckled; it was easy to chuckle now. This was surely the end, there could be no more danger, that odds against chance had come off, and Hortelan—

Suddenly he heard an explosion on the road within twenty yards of him. He stared towards the smoke still rising from the burning petrol. The flames had nearly died down, and advancing on either side of the road, taking advantage of the cover behind the hedge were five men, Hortelan among them. As he watched, Dawlish saw them lobbing grenades towards the bridge. They were falling short, but Hortelan's men could move more quickly than those who were crossing the ice.

Had they seen him?

He had the answer a moment later when a grenade burst uncomfortably near. It fell deep into the snow before exploding, and caused no harm, but if the aim got truer he would have no more chance than the man who had manned the Lewis gun. He could not see where the grenade came from, but suddenly a second appeared, curving through the air towards him.

He flung himself down.

The explosion was near enough to shift the snow in which he was lying, and to move him several inches. By some freak of blast it took the breath from his body, and he lay helpless, covering his head with his hands, waiting for a third explosion.

It did not come.

His ears were filled with a droning sound, and he could not see properly through the wet snow which filled his eyes. He wiped it away as best he could. He was feeling numb with cold, now; in the excitement of the journey he had not noticed it, but now he had difficulty in moving his arms at all and he could not get a grenade from his pocket. Cautiously he peered over the rim of the hole he had made in the snow.

A man was climbing over the hedge. Obviously he thought he had scored a hit. Dawlish waited until he was only twenty yards away, and then, with a great effort, managed to toss a grenade before he dropped back into the hole. He caught a glimpse of a startled face, a look of sheer terror—and then the explosion came.

It was not the last.

Other grenades were bursting near the river. The main party of Hortelan's men were now in front of Dawlish, between him and the bridge. He saw that only two men were on the ice. Others were hiding behind hastily erected heaps of snow. He saw Felicity's dark, ruffled hair; she had lost her hat.

Then, as he was starting to move to a position from which he could do most damage, a machine-gun on the opposite side of the river opened up. Two of Hortelan's men fell at the first burst.

The others dropped into the snow. Dawlish stood watching, aching all over with cold now, but filled with that sense of exaltation which made him indifferent to discomfort. The last man from the car—Carter—was safely on the other side. Now that the defences were in action there was no chance of Hortelan following the party, and even if he succeeded in manning the field-piece, Barney would see that no time was lost in getting out of range.

"So it's over," Dawlish thought, and he realized that he was speaking aloud. "Over, over." He stood upright, but suddenly was seized with a violent fit of shivering. His legs were so numbed that he could not move them without great effort. For the first time he realized that the light was failing; he could not see the other bank so clearly. He could just make out Hortelan and his men as they crawled towards the hedge, to take cover from the machine-gun, which was now silent.

Were they planning to stay there and to make sure that no one got across?

Dawlish watched closely. Hortelan was less than fifty yards away from him, yet it seemed an immeasurable distance. The far bank was a little more than a hundred yards away—and it seemed on another continent. He knew that if he could climb the hedge and get into the middle of the road, he would be able to whip his flagging strength to stumble down to the river and to cross; but he could not fight any more. The cold had got him, was chilling him, was making him helpless. He looked at his ungloved hands; they were nearly as white as the snow. Frost-bite? If not, something very near it. His cheeks seemed frozen, and when he tried, he could not open his mouth. The snow he had fallen into had melted at first, and then coated his face with ice.

Pain began to prick at his eyes; it was trivial at first, but soon began to burn. He could not see clearly, and that was not only because of the gathering darkness. He rested against the hedge, knowing that he could do nothing more.

He grew conscious of a new sound.

It reminded him of the roaring of the engine inside the workshop, but it sounded much further away.

Much further? Was it? Or was it getting nearer?

He stirred his flagging senses into attention; even that was difficult. In a matter of minutes he had become numbed in body and lulled in mind, yet one thing did piece his consciousness. There were engines roaring, not far away, and many more than one.

Many more than one—

Suddenly the sky seemed filled with their roaring, and looking up, he caught sight of the dark shapes of aircraft sweeping across the sky, some flying low, some at a fair height. He watched in fascination. They passed over him, and then, when he judged them to be immediately over the village, dark objects fell from them. Cannisters or men, he wondered.

Parachutes opened—

Parachutes opened, too, further away although he did not see them. They were drifting towards *Timbers* and the cottage, while Hortelan and those few of his men who remained were trying to get back to the cottage to make a last stand.

The authorities had spared no effort.

Fifty parachute troops landed on Hurn, and another fifty within a short radius of *Timbers*. When they landed, Felicity and the others were in the village High Street, and a man fell almost at their feet. He was up in a trice. Another fell just in front of them, and in the half light Felicity saw the crown on his shoulder.

He was a youthful, crisp-mannered man, who saluted Felicity promptly, and said:

"I hope we're in time."

"It's nearly over," Barney said.

"Nearly," said Felicity, and there was a catch in her breath. "My husband," she added with an effort, "is on the other side of the river, and he may be hurt."

"Can I have a guide?" asked the Major.

It was pitch dark.

Dawlish was hardly conscious of cold or light or dark. He lay in the snow, without moving. When his mind did work he tried to get up, realizing that it would be fatal if he failed to get the blood working through his veins. It was no use, he could not get to his feet, he could not even find the strength to move his arms across his chest. Odd, the effect of snow. It would not be so bad if it were daylight, but this damnable darkness made it almost unbearable. He shifted his position a little. At least he had the comfort of knowing that Felicity was all right. Hortelan would not have a chance of getting away, either. A pity the troops had not arrived an hour sooner, there would have been nothing like so much trouble.

At least Hortelan's plot was smashed.

It would be ironic if he did not live to hear the whole truth. The mystery of Barney's behaviour, for instance; and of Sol Gordon's; why *had* the little fat man conceived such an idea, and not said a word to him about it? The explanation that he was afraid of being overheard did not hold water, for he had had plenty of opportunity for talking before they reached the garage. Then there was Carter and his sudden change of heart. At least he knew how it was that Hortelan's men had been so well armed. A bad business, allowing the local Home Guard weapons to remain in the district so long after collection had been ordered. Very odd. Carter, presumably, was responsible—

"No!" exclaimed Dawlish, aloud. "No, no!" It was not Carter, surely the local commander would have the last word, Carter was responsible to Hamblin. What a fool he was not to have realized that before—*only Hamblin could have let Hortelan have those arms!*

The police might never find out. Carter might be loyal to Hamblin, or he might die from his wounds. He had been unconscious in the car, and might not come round. Hamblin *must* be guilty of complicity, but he might get away.

Suddenly he saw a light.

He thought it was an illusion. It seemed brilliant, almost as if a star had come close to earth and he could stretch out a hand and put it in the circle of its radiance. Absurd! He could not move his hand. It was surprising how physically comfortable he felt now. No pain, not even in his eyes. He even felt snug and warm. Another illusion—

A man said: "Here's something, sir."

It was an earthly light then; men were talking; men were bending over him. He did not recognize them, but then he could not see them clearly.

"It might be one of Hortelan's fellows," said the Major. "Be careful with him."

The military had taken complete control of Hurn. Food and medical supplies had been dropped with the troops, as well as two doctors and male nurses. The school had been turned into an emergency hospital. It was crowded with wounded men who had suffered in the first fruitless attack by Hamblin's men. Hortelan's men were brought in from across the river, too, for a small bridge had been built, and passage to and fro was now fairly easy.

The Major was with Hamblin.

"To say that it's a bad business is something of an understatement, I'm afraid," said Hamblin. "Still, it would have been much worse if you hadn't arrived."

"Not so much worse for our side, sir," said the Major, properly respectful to the local Home Guard's late commander. "The people who got away from *Timbers* did a fine job of work. We wouldn't have got Dawlish back, of course. Astonishing fellow, that."

"Remarkable," said Hamblin. "Will he come round?"

"Oh, yes; he wasn't exposed for long enough to be killed," said the Major.

"Does his wife know?"

"She's at Carter's farm with him," said the Major, "and I don't think she is worried now."

"Carter's farm," said Hamblin, slowly. "I wish the report on Carter were as good as that on Dawlish. He won't come round, I'm afraid. Exposure on the ice was too much for him after that loss of blood. Hortelan has a lot to answer for. Did you capture him alive?"

"Yes," said the Major.

"Has he talked?"

"He hasn't been interrogated yet," said the Major; "he is to wait until special authority arrives."

"I see. What *is* it all about?" demanded Hamblin.

"I really don't know," said the Major, politely.

Hamblin left him and went to a small house in the village where his daughter was staying. Because it was dark he did not know that he was followed, and that armed men stood on guard outside the house. That was because Dawlish, already conscious, had urged the Major to take no chances with him, and because one of the doctors who had examined Carter had discovered in his arm a hypodermic needle puncture, recently made, and possibly a contributory factor in his death—for Carter died before midnight while a passenger aircraft was approaching from London with 'special authority' on board.

CHAPTER XXIII

RETIRED LIST

Among the passengers on board the aircraft were several Government dignitaries and Superintendent William Trivett of New Scotland Yard. The members of the Government repaired at once to the cottage where McKay and Livesey were recovering from their ordeal under morphia; neither of them was in any danger. Trivett went to Carter's farm, to the room where Dawlish was lying, with blankets piled on him and hot-water bottles to make him even warmer. Felicity, bright-eyed with fatigue but with no sign of strain, was sitting by his side. Barney and Gordon were in saddle-back chairs on either side of the fireplace. Half-a-dozen candles added to the light of the blazing log fire.

Trivett, a tall, dark-haired, well-dressed man of forty, turned his handsome face towards the bed and spoke urbanely.

"Did you ever hear the adage—set a crook to catch a crook?" he inquired.

"That's not even funny," said Dawlish in a hoarse voice. "There are no dishonest men here, William!"

"Don't say you're all on the retired list," said Trivett, with a lift of his eyebrows. "I heard that Barney proposed to retire, but I can't believe that Gordon has given up his evil ways."

"Just listen to him," squeaked Gordon. "Here we are, having nearly sacrificed our lives to catch his man for him, and he deals in old, old jokes—and very poor ones, too. I ask you, Trivett, if you think I am a criminal, why have you let me stay unmolested for so long? And also Barney. As for Patrick Dawlish—oh my, oh my! What peculiar notions policemen do get in their heads!"

"Do they?" asked Trivett. He settled back in his chair and smiled at Felicity. "Now listen carefully," he said, and waited for them to settle down comfortably. "Listen very carefully," he added. "We know that the Alexis jewels were smuggled into this country, but we have lost trace of them. We also learned of the fake gems, and knew something of their contents. Just at the moment I am only interested in the fakes."

There was a noticeable easing of tension in Barney's manner as Trivett looked at him.

"You bought the fakes, Barney, didn't you?"

"They were very fine copies," said Barney, "and I was proud to have them." Sol Gordon's eyes nearly popped out of his head. "It wasn't until I had had them for a few weeks that I heard by telephone from Hortelan, who sold them to me. He said he had made a mistake and sold me the wrong set. By then, I had discovered that the fakes contained written matter, to do with a Spanish plot which involved some highly-placed English people. Then Hortelan stole the paper, my only evidence, and there was nothing conclusive, nothing which the police could use as evidence."

"I see," said Trivett, rather heavily.

"At that time my cousin was visiting me," said Barney, "and Hortelan mistook him for me. We are not unlike. He actually saw Hortelan. I, naturally, wanted to find out more about the plot. I knew that there were Germans involved, from the paper

I had seen, and I managed to convince Hortelan, when I went to visit him afterwards, that I was a German masquerading as Barney."

"Well, well!" said Trivett.

"Now, Trivett, no sarcasm," interpolated Gordon. "This is the gospel truth you are hearing, Barney told me about it some time ago."

"Hortelan was deceived," went on Barney. "I saw an opportunity of working my way into his confidence and finding out more about the plot. I came down to *Timbers*—which I had bought some time before—and continued with my preparations to start the gallery in Shaftesbury while I waited for Hortelan. He discovered through someone down here, the man Carter, I believe, that there was a large underground workshop at the back of *Timbers,* one of the many experimental places which were used during the war and afterwards abandoned. He took it over. I had no idea that with Carter's help he was storing arms and ammunition. In the workshop his men were busy making something which I was unable to identify—I learned only two days ago that it was a helicopter."

"Go on," said Trivett, lighting a cigarette.

"A few days before," said Barney, "I discovered that Hortelan had been drugging my cousin. I was suddenly ordered to take up residence in the cottage, which Hortelan had bought. My cousin came to *Timbers* with my maid who had stayed with him to aid the deception. I was unhappy about the whole business, but knew that my own as well as my cousin's life was in danger if Hortelan discovered the deception. I asked a number of friends to come to *Timbers,* thinking that they would be able to deal with Hortelan when I told them the trust through my cousin. The snow spoiled that little game."

"The snow spoiled a lot of things," said Trivett, dryly. "Why was Hortelan so interested in your cousin—whom he thought to be you?"

"Surely that's obvious," said Barney. "He still wanted the other faked gems that contained the rest of the documents outlining the plot. Only my cousin and I knew where they were. I felt quite sure that nothing would happen until he got them back, and thought that with Dawlish and Gordon here I could make sure he didn't get them. I underestimated the effect of the drug on my cousin, who was forced to disclose the secret hiding-place. Meanwhile, Hortelan had become suspicious of me, and I had no opportunity of getting away even for an hour. I had to put my hopes on Dawlish and Gordon—"

"Who both knew what was afoot," said Trivett, heavily.

"Gordon had an idea, Dawlish none at all," said Barney. "Gordon was also interested in the Alexis jewels, which we knew were on the market, and before Hortelan made me come down here I told Gordon what little I knew."

"And I," broke in Gordon, shrill-voiced, "tried to make the police understand that there was some roguery on foot. I actually sent *four* anonymous letters to the police!"

"Why anonymous?" demanded Trivett.

"Oh, my dear Superintendent, we know each other! I am an honest man, yes; all the world except Scotland Yard knows that, but you have never thought so. I did not wish to do anything which would attract your attention. Tell me, did you work on the strength of those letters?"

"Yes," said Trivett. He drew on his cigarette, and added: "The Foreign Office knew that trouble was brewing in Spain and that some of our reactionaries were financing a *coup*. We didn't know who. The Foreign Office was actually approached through diplomatic channels to give its blessing to a new régime. That made us realize that it wasn't a thing to take lightly, and we got busy. I was brought in because I know you two so well, and you were involved. You know, Sol," he added, putting his head on one side, "it's a lucky thing for you those anonymous letters weren't scurrilous. We traced them to you."

"You mean you *thought* you did," said Gordon. "My dear boy, would you have left us alone if you had been able to prove it?"

"We did. We had you very well watched," said Trivett; "and we first got on to Hurn because you were heading here."

"My, *my*!" squeaked Gordon.

"We also knew that McKay and Livesey were in this part of the world," said Trivett. "They were kidnapped before they reached their destination. Hortelan's men—they were known to us in London, but we had no evidence against them—did that, of course. Then the snow—" He broke off, and shrugged his shoulders. "Well, where are the fakes now, Barney?"

"I hope you'll find them on Hortelan," said Barney. "And there is another thing you must be told. I asked Dawlish to come because I knew he was lately in the Intelligence service, and I thought he would be able to advise me better even than the police. Had I been at home when he arrived—"

"I would have sent for every agent in England!" said Dawlish.

"And one or two policemen, I hope," said Trivett.

Dawlish did not know whether Trivett was convinced; he himself was fully satisfied, however, that he knew why Barney had invited him.

Not long afterwards Trivett was called out; and while he was gone, Felicity leaned forward and looked hard at Gordon and Barney, both of whom coloured a little.

"Why did you really start after Hortelan?" she demanded.

"*Hush!*" said Dawlish, closing a hand over hers. "They wanted the real Alexis stones. Hortelan sold you the fakes in mistake for the real ones, didn't he, Barney?"

Barney laughed. "Yes, and I was fool enough for once to have them sent to me instead of collecting myself. It was to be my last deal. I shall have to retire on a pittance instead of a fortune."

"And me, too," said Gordon, mournfully. "I had a half-share in that purchase—oh, we were very clever, I don't think! But Patrick—Felicity! Believe this, please—we were only interested in finding what Hortelan was really doing. If we had found the jewels as well we would have liked it, of course, but there it is." He rubbed his fat hands together with a sliding noise. "Everything that happened was done to try to make sure that Hortelan failed in his plot. I did not want to confide in you, Patrick. I did all I could to help you while reserving the right to change sides—*oh-oh-oh!*

"What a shock that was to you! I was not wanted by the police, of course, that was to give colour to my story. By then you had begun to suspect me, hadn't you? I wanted you to. If Hortelan questioned you, I doubted whether you would say you suspected *me* unless you *did*. And then in the garage, Patrick, I was alarmed in case we really lost, and so I determined to be so brave—but you would not let me. Hortelan, you see, had already spoken to me through the walls, and I had let him believe that money would serve to buy my allegiance!" He laughed again, rubbing his stomach with the joy of it. "Off I went to the shed, of which you had told me, and Hortelan treated me only fairly well—one of his men actually struck me! But I found Barney, and they left me in a room on my own and I was able to find my way out—you must admit that I got results."

Dawlish laughed. "Gladly!"

"I always liked Patrick Dawlish," said Gordon, beaming. "An honest fellow, I said to myself. If you think I am worthy of a little reward for my services persuade your beautiful wife that I am worthy of her friendship."

"I don't need persuading," said Felicity.

"So!" Gordon jumped up. "A thousand thanks, my dear

Felicity!" He trotted to her sioe and pressed her hands. "For that I shall make a large payment to charity, I will indeed."

"I thought you were a poor man now," croaked Dawlish from the bedclothes.

"Oh, yes, I am," said Gordon, "but for a special thing—well, I can find enough, I think!" He patted Felicity's hand again. "One other matter—Trivett is very good, I am glad he came himself. No questions asked, he knows many things, or rather he suspects them, but he is big enough to admit that Hortelan is the man who matters. I *like* Trivett, he—"

"How touching," said Trivett. He opened the door, and Gordon jumped round in alarm. "It's all right," Trivett went on, "that's all I heard." He was not smiling, and his voice had lost something of its urbanity. "I've just come from Hamblin," he said. "You were right, Pat. He was in it with Carter. He says that he did not know what Hortelan wanted, tells some story of thinking he was drilling for oil. Anyhow, we've got him."

"And the faked jewels?" asked Felicity, eagerly.

"Those Hortelan had, yes. We've been on the radio to London, and they've discovered more information there, too— the *coup* in Spain is planned for to-morrow. The kidnapping was a desperate effort to get British support. Curious mentality these Fascists have, haven't they?"

"Fascists?" echoed Felicity.

"Oh, yes, the same breed. German inspired, too—another incubating chamber for the next war is out of action. We've the full details of the plot in those jewels, and I brought a man who knows Spanish—we shall be able to radio Madrid with full details before the *coup* gets under way. Oh, another thing— McKay and Livesey have come round. They want to know if they can come and express their thanks in person."

"Now?" asked Dawlish, surprised.

"Yes. A strip has been prepared for taking off, and they're leaving soon for London."

Gordon gaped. "Two Cabinet Ministers want to thank *me*!"

"Remarkable, isn't it," said Trivett.

The august gentlemen were very generous in their thanks. They stayed for half an hour, and went off, still murmuring. Trivett went with them. When they had gone, Gordon stared at the door, and then stood up and shrugged his shoulders, and said:

"Now I will *have* to retire!"

Dawlish laughed. "Trivett will see to that! Now that he's gone, let me into the final secret, will you? Where *are* the Alexis jewels?"

Gordon beamed. "How shrewd, Patrick! Of course, I managed to get the real ones. Hortelan, the foolish fellow, brought them to England and tried to bargain with them for the fakes. And of course Barney didn't buy blind—he wanted to learn the secret of the fakes. The real gems have been paid for, my boy! They are in my banker's safe. I have an American buyer; Barney and I won't do so badly after all. Now, now, Felicity, do not start changing your mind about me!" He beamed across at Barney. "Barney, we have an occasion to celebrate, I never expected you and I would be thanked by such gentlemen as Cabinet Ministers. Shall we celebrate by making a partnership? Let me have a share in your Gallery, with your cousin as the third partner—oh, my!" broke off Gordon, raising his hands. "I forgot to inquire after him, will he recover?"

"With care, yes," said Barney.

"I *am* glad, my boy, I really am! Now, let us leave Felicity and Patrick together, they are dying to be alone, I can see that." He waved to them, pattered to the door, and then turned round and raised a hand. "Patrick, one thing I must make clear. I am out of the business. If you wish to sell stones of dubious origin, do not, I beg you, come to me."

He winked broadly, and led Barney out of the room.

When Dawlish and Felicity were back in London they received a call from Tim Jeremy and several other young men, all extremely reproachful. They would not believe that Dawlish had started for Shaftesbury with no knowledge of what was likely to happen. They were, they said, cheated, and they felt sore about it. Also, they did not think that Dawlish should associate with people like Barney Day and Sol Gordon; but, of course, if Dawlish cared to tell them the whole story, with no half-truths as they had doubtless told Trivett, they might forgive him for his shabby treatment of them.

Dawlish began to talk. . . .

ABOUT THE AUTHOR

John Creasey, born in 1908, was a paramount English crime and science fiction writer who used myriad pseudonyms for more than six hundred novels. He founded the UK Crime Writers' Association in 1953. In 1962, his book *Gideon's Fire* received the Edgar Award for Best Novel from the Mystery Writers of America. Many of the characters featured in Creasey's titles became popular, including George Gideon of Scotland Yard, who was the basis for a subsequent television series and film. Creasey died in Salisbury, UK, in 1973.

THE PATRICK DAWLISH MYSTERIES

FROM OPEN ROAD MEDIA

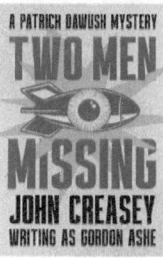

OPEN ROAD

INTEGRATED MEDIA

INTEGRATED MEDIA

Find a full list of our authors and
titles at www.openroadmedia.com

FOLLOW US
@OpenRoadMedia